She knew Zack was lying.

He had no intention of sharing information with her. At least, not willingly. But thanks to the global positioning device, she would track his every movement. If he got a lead on her sister's location, Sabrina would head there as soon as he made his move.

And in the meantime, maybe *she'd* find the location first. Zack was wasting his time going to Sacramento. If there had been any clues at Shelby's house, Sabrina would have found them already.

They needed to focus on the kidnapper, not her sister. And so Sabrina would study the files using her training and instincts to get inside the kidnapper's head. Then she'd take her father's bag of tricks—and her gun—and go hunting.

Dear Reader,

You're about to read a Silhouette Bombshell novel, one of the most engaging, exciting and riveting books on the shelves today. We're pleased to bring you fast-paced, compelling reads featuring strong, admirable women who will speak to the Bombshell in you!

In *Sophie's Last Stand* by Nancy Bartholomew, Sophie Mazaratti's trying to start over after her marriage ends *very* badly—but it seems her slimy ex has left her in a sticky situation involving the mob, the Feds and one darned attractive detective....

Get ready for a thrilling twenty-four hours as military author Cindy Dees continues the powerful Athena Force continuity series with *Target*, featuring an army intelligence agent on a mission to save the President-elect from being assassinated. To gain his trust, she'll give the villain someone new to chase—herself....

It's a jungle out there when a determined virologist races into the Amazon to stop a deadly outbreak—a danger that authorities seem determined to cover up, even at the cost of Dr. Jane Miller's life. Don't miss *The Amazon Strain* by Katherine Garbera!

And a protected witness must come out of hiding after her sister mysteriously disappears, in Kate Donovan's adventure *Parallel Lies*. It's up to Sabrina Sullivan to determine which of two charismatic men is lying—or if they both are—to save her sister's life.

The stakes are high and the pressure is on! Please send me your comments c/o Silhouette Books, 233 Broadway, Suite 1001, New York, NY 10279

Sincerely,

Natashya Wilson

Natashya Wilson
Associate Senior Editor, Silhouette Bombshell

Please address questions and book requests to:
Silhouette Reader Service
U.S.: 3010 Walden Ave., P.O. Box 1325, Buffalo, NY 14269
Canadian: P.O. Box 609, Fort Erie, Ont. L2A 5X3

KATE DONOVAN

PARALLEL LIES

Published by Silhouette Books

America's Publisher of Contemporary Romance

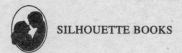 SILHOUETTE BOOKS

ISBN 0-373-51358-5

PARALLEL LIES

Copyright © 2005 by Kate Donovan

www.SilhouetteBombshell.com

Printed in U.S.A.

Books by Kate Donovan

Silhouette Bombshell

Identity Crisis #20
Parallel Lies #44

KATE DONOVAN

is the author of more than a dozen novels and novellas, ranging from time travel and paranormal to historical romance, suspense and romantic comedy. An attorney, she draws on her criminal law background to create challenges worthy of her heroines, who crack safes, battle wizards and always get their man. As for Kate, she *definitely* got her man and is living happily ever after with him and their two children in Elk Grove, California.

This book is dedicated to my parents
for their loving encouragement.
Thanks, Mom and Dad!

Prologue

When the cell phone on her nightstand began to ring, twenty-year-old Sabrina Sullivan went from soundly sleeping to fully alert in an instant. The fact that it was 2:00 a.m. only heightened her instinctive response. After all, this particular phone had one purpose and one purpose only—for her father to contact her in case of an emergency. And given "Sully" Sullivan's dangerous lifestyle, an emergency seemed to lurk around every intrigue-laden corner.

Flipping open the phone, Sabrina said simply, "Dad?"

"Sweetheart, this is Uncle Theo. I'm standing outside the door to your apartment. I didn't want to knock and scare you, but I need to talk to you."

The daughter's heart began to pound. "Is he hurt bad? Is he even alive? Uncle Theo—"

"Come to the door, Breezie."

"Right." She jumped to her feet and sprinted from her

small bedroom into the study area of the dorm suite she shared with her sister Michelle. Then she yanked open the door, ready to demand a million details.

But the expression on Theo Howell's face told her everything she needed to know, and it did so with the force of a well-aimed kick to her solar plexus. "Oh, no…"

"Breezie." He pulled her into a bear hug. "I'm so sorry."

Tears stung her eyes. "He was here just last week for a visit. He looked so h-healthy. What happened?"

"He was murdered, hon. By Adonis Zenner."

Sabrina pulled free, shocked by the announcement, and perversely grateful for the rush of white-hot hatred that chased her tears away.

"Zenner?" She practically hissed the name. "How did *he* get into the country?"

"We don't know. We don't know anything yet."

"This is the thanks Dad gets for tracking that psycho's father down? We *knew* Adonis might try to get revenge for Pluto. Didn't we take precautions?"

"Come and sit with me," Theo advised, adding over his shoulder, "you men secure the premises."

Sabrina winced as two middle-aged men dressed in black pants and black shirts strode past her. She hadn't even noticed the burly pair of strangers. Her father would be so disappointed in her.

Except her father was dead.

"Is this the only window?" one man was asking. "What about in there?"

"My sister's in there. Sleeping. And of course there's no window," she added, insulted at the implication that she'd let Michelle sleep alone in a room with exterior access. Then she bit her lip, realizing for the first time that this nightmare was about to invade her younger sister's world, as well.

"I should wake her up," she told her uncle. "Zenner's trail is getting colder by the second."

"There's a decision to be made, Brie. Your father would want *you* to make it. You're the oldest."

"A decision?" She felt her temper flare. "You mean, like funeral stuff? Who cares! We have to go after Adonis before he gets out of the country."

Theo's gaze was steady and direct. "We think he'll come after you and Michelle next."

"*What?*"

"When your father killed Pluto, he wiped out Adonis's whole family. He might want to return the favor."

Sabrina turned to stare at the closed door to Michelle's room. Then she sank down onto the sofa next to Theo. "We need to get her to someplace safe. Immediately."

"We need to get you both someplace safe," he corrected her. "There are two choices. My home in Monterey. Or a safe house here in Boston, which would be a stopover on your way into a protection program."

"A protection program?"

"The government offered us two spots in RAP. That's a relocation assistance program for compromised agents and their families, similar to witness protection."

"Are you talking about new identities? Isn't that a little drastic? Just take Shellie to your house while I go after Adonis."

"Is that what your father would have wanted?"

Sabrina's eyes stung with the return of her tears, but she wiped them with miserable determination. There would be plenty of time—the rest of her life, in fact—to cry. Right now, she had to concentrate on protecting her sister and avenging her father.

In that order.

Because she knew exactly what her father would want her to do. She could almost hear his voice instructing her, the same way he'd done just one week earlier at the end of his visit.

Take care of your sister. I'm entrusting her safety to you. I know you won't let me down.

He had charged her with this responsibility since early in their childhood, and she had always taken it as a compliment. Now she knew it for what it was—a curse.

"What's going on?" a sleepy voice demanded from across the room, and eighteen-year-old Michelle stepped into view, her feet stuffed into fuzzy pink slippers, her lightweight robe belted haphazardly and her arms cradling their new kitten, a black-and-white fur ball known as Zorro. "Uncle Theo? Is everything okay?"

Theo crossed to her, clearly intending to hug her with the same unrestrained affection and sympathy he had bestowed on Sabrina. But Michelle sidestepped him and walked over to her big sister.

"Brie?"

"It's Dad, Shell. Adonis Zenner killed him."

The girl's blue eyes widened. "With a gun? Or a bomb?"

It was another blow to Sabrina's equilibrium, and she grabbed her sister into an embrace while demanding over her head, "Uncle Theo? It wasn't a bomb, was it?"

When his gaze fell, she wailed in disbelief. "I'll strangle him with my bare hands!"

"Me, too," Michelle insisted, but her voice was hushed and broken by sobs.

"Shh…" Sabrina patted her sister's blond curls. "There'll be time to cry later, Shell. We have to get moving. Uncle Theo thinks Zenner might come here next."

"Bring it on," Michelle retorted, raising her tear-filled

eyes to stare straight into Sabrina's. "I *want* him to come here. Then we can kill him for Dad."

"No. We're going away. Someplace safe. The CIA will go after Zenner. That's what Dad would have wanted."

Michelle took a step backward, then folded her arms across her chest. "I'm not going anywhere but after Zenner. I can't believe you want to run away."

"Listen to your sister," Theo murmured. "The CIA will catch Zenner. And in the meantime, you're in danger. He's a ruthless assassin. You're no match for him. I know, I know, your father trained you to shoot and fight and take care of yourselves. But not against men like Zenner. If you don't cooperate with our efforts to protect you—to give you a new life where you can be safe—one or both of you could die. Is that what you want?"

"Brie?"

Sabrina banished her own misgivings and said in as authoritative a voice as she could manage, "We're going into some kind of witness protection program. Once they catch Zenner, we can be ourselves again. Go and pack."

"No packing," Theo corrected her. "Just put on jeans and a sweatshirt. Leave everything else behind. We'll supply what you need at the safe house. But we have to move now."

Michelle seemed about to argue, then she leaned down and scooped up the kitten instead. "Come on, Zorro. Let's get dressed."

"The cat can't come," Theo began, but Sabrina waved her hand at him in cool dismissal.

"The cat was a gift from Dad. He comes with us. That's not negotiable. We'll leave everything else behind though."

Theo hesitated, then nodded. "We can bend the rules a little."

"What about you, Uncle Theo?" Michelle demanded. "Aren't you worried Zenner will come after you, too?"

"Your father killed Pluto as part of a CIA operation. It wasn't directly related to his job at Perimeter. In fact, as you know, I disapproved of— Well, none of that matters now." He touched Michelle's cheek, then turned to Sabrina. "I won't see you again after tonight. I hope you'll always remember that I loved you like daughters."

"We'll see you soon," Sabrina reminded him. "As soon as Dad's crew and the CIA catch Adonis."

"Right." His red-rimmed gaze faltered, but he recovered and agreed more heartily, "Shouldn't take them too long. Then you'll come to live with me in Monterey."

"And we'll work for Perimeter, just like Dad promised we could," Michelle said. Then her hands flew to her face and she began to cry again. "He can't be gone. He was just *here*."

Sabrina and Theo hurried to her, murmuring words of comfort mixed with gentle reminders that they had to get moving. Quickly. Before Adonis Zenner had a chance to kill another Sullivan.

Chapter 1

Five years later

"Can I help you, miss?"

Sabrina hesitated, knowing that the next words she uttered would change the course of her life. But she had carefully weighed every alternative before making this decision and, absent new information, wasn't about to second-guess herself.

Her father had trained her better than that.

Smiling at the young man guarding the entrance to Theo Howell's Monterey estate, she announced, "I'm Briana York. A friend of Mr. Howell's. I don't have an appointment, but I can guarantee you he'll want to see me."

"I'm sure he will," the guard said, returning the smile as he scanned her bare legs. She had dressed in shorts and a tank top for the long, hot drive, not really caring how she looked.

Well at least he can see you're not armed, she told herself ruefully.

"Just give me a second, Miss York." Stepping back into his booth, the guard punched a button and an intercom began sputtering static.

Then a female voice from Sabrina's childhood demanded, "Fred? Is the repairman here?"

"It's someone to see Theo. Her name's Briana York. She doesn't have an appointment."

"Briana York?"

Until now Sabrina had been so focused on the danger in visiting Theo's house after all these years, she had failed to anticipate how wonderful it would be to see the place— and its inhabitants—again. Thoroughly charmed, and no longer hesitant about revealing herself, she waved her hand to catch the guard's attention. "Is that Marietta? The cook? Tell her it's Sabrina Sullivan. She'll know who I am."

"Sullivan?" The guard's eyes widened. "As in *Sully* Sullivan?"

"Just tell her."

The guard nodded, then cleared his throat. "Marietta, the guest says her name is Sabrina Sullivan."

A delighted squeal emanated from the intercom, then the cook instructed Fred to admit the guest right away.

"Go on up to the house, Miss Sullivan. Stay to the right—"

"I've been here before. Thanks." Sabrina edged her car up to the gate and sped through as soon as it had opened.

He didn't even ask you for identification, she told herself in amused disbelief. *If Dad were here, he'd give that poor guy such a lecture!*

It didn't bode well for the state of affairs at Perimeter Security Incorporated, she decided. Apparently discipline had fallen apart after her father's death. Hopefully they still knew how to run a background check, which was all she needed from them.

And security aside, she was relieved to see that the estate was as stunning as she remembered it, with the sound of waves crashing in the distance while the wind whistled through the twisted limbs of hauntingly beautiful Monterey cypresses.

The house that Perimeter built, she reminded herself, proud that her father had been part of Theo Howell's phenomenal success. The story was a classic. Howell had come from modest wealth, eventually inheriting the family business—a burglar alarm company. In a stroke of brilliance, he had invested every dime—including a few borrowed ones—and had transformed the company into a full-scale security provider called Perimeter, utilizing sophisticated computers, state-of-the-art monitoring and highly trained bodyguards. Almost immediately, Perimeter gained global prominence, and in the years that followed, became the preeminent provider of security to corporations, dignitaries, movie stars and other assorted clients.

But not without some growing pains. Despite all the successes, Theo Howell and Perimeter had had three pivotal failures. The first—a bomb smuggled into a peace summit—had been a mixed blessing, leading Howell to recruit the brash young CIA agent who had disarmed the device just seconds before the timer reached zero. That agent, Sully Sullivan, thereafter revamped the company's procedures, trained its staff and basically took it to even higher heights.

Perimeter's second disaster, more than twenty years later, had resulted in the assassination of a client in the Ca-

nary Islands. Desperate to salvage the company's reputation, Sully had rejoined forces with the CIA to bring the
assassin—Pluto Zenner—to justice. Pluto had been killed
resisting arrest, leading to the third and most tragic fail-
ure of all—the revenge taken by Pluto's son, Adonis,
against Sully.

For Sabrina, that was where the Perimeter story ended.
She had no idea what had happened over the past five years.
All she knew for sure was that Adonis Zenner had never
been apprehended or punished for her father's murder.

Coupled with the lax behavior of the guard at the gate,
Adonis's continued existence didn't speak well for the cal-
iber of Perimeter's current staff, she decided grimly. But
it was too late to turn back. Sabrina still believed she'd
made the right choice in coming here, so she parked her
red convertible alongside a black one at the curb of the cir-
cular driveway in front of the Howell mansion. Then she
took the steps two at a time, reaching the front door just as
Marietta opened it wide.

"Miss Sabrina!" The servant gave her a hearty hug. "I
thought we'd never see you again."

Sabrina returned the embrace. "It's so great to see you.
Are you in charge of the place these days?"

The dark-haired woman shook her head. "It's just me
and my husband now. Money's tight for Mr. Howell. But
we're really all he needs. Sebastian does the gardening
and driving. And I still do *all* the cooking, so don't worry.
I'll put some meat on those skinny bones of yours in no
time." She studied the guest fondly, then asked, "Is it okay
to call you Sabrina?"

"Absolutely."

"What about Miss Michelle? Is she coming, too?"

"She's on vacation." Sabrina sighed. "We can visit in a

little while, but for now, I'd better go see Uncle Theo. Was he shocked to hear I was back?"

"I didn't tell him." Marietta gave her a wide smile. "I can't wait to see the look on his face."

Sabrina laughed. "Let's hope he's not annoyed. You and that guard really shouldn't have let me come up without permission."

"He'll be too happy to complain. Come on." The cook headed down the hall toward Theo's study.

Sabrina surveyed the entrance hall with wistful thoroughness. Nothing had changed. The same sweeping brass and oak staircase, oak flooring and vibrant red carpets. No furniture except for a brass table holding a vase filled with red roses.

She smiled, remembering how many times her sister Shelby—or Michelle, as she'd been called in those days— had knocked that table over as she'd raced down the stairs and around the corner toward the kitchen. They had spent hundreds of hours visiting and playing in this gorgeous home. Then suddenly it had become off limits, a part of a past that could never be revisited.

Until now.

"Miss Sabrina," Marietta said, hissing slightly and motioning for her coconspirator to join her at the closed double doors at the end of the hall.

When Sabrina had complied, the cook opened one door and poked her head into the study. "Sorry to interrupt, but there's someone here who needs to speak to you, Mr. Theo." Without waiting for a response, she stepped aside and swept her hand back in Sabrina's direction. "A ghost from the past. And more beautiful than ever. Come give your niece a hug."

Sabrina stepped into the room and had to smile at the

stupefied look on Theo Howell's face. Striding over to him, she opened her arms, murmuring, "Hi, Uncle Theo. Long time no see."

"My God," he whispered, yanking her into a bear hug. "Sabrina! After all these years. Is something wrong?"

"No. Not really." She stepped back and gave an apologetic smile, noting that he was a little grayer around the temples than she remembered—and ten or fifteen pounds heavier. And he had switched from tortoiseshell eyeglass frames to wire rims. But otherwise, he hadn't changed a bit. "I was probably crazy to come here, but Shelby and I met a guy recently, and I want to run a background check on him, just to be on the safe side. Since I don't have the kind of connections Perimeter has, I decided to come here for help."

"A background check?" came an accusatory growl from the shadows. "You've got to be kidding."

Sabrina turned toward the unfamiliar voice. "Pardon?"

The speaker—a dark-haired man in his early thirties— shook his head in apparent disgust. "For five full years we don't hear a word. Then you just show up? Asking us to run an *errand* for you? After you practically drove the company into the ground?"

"Zack," Theo murmured. "Don't."

"No. Let him talk," Sabrina countered, her gaze fixed on the stranger. "How did I hurt Perimeter?"

The young man glared. "You left us with no money. No manpower. No soul. *We* couldn't contact *you,* even when we really needed to. But you can waltz in whenever you please, asking to use our connections? Like we're your goddamned errand boys?"

Sabrina turned back to Theo and demanded, "Who is this clown?"

Theo gave a nervous chuckle. "Sabrina Sullivan, meet Zack Lansing. Zack took your father's place at Perimeter."

"What?" She took a step back, physically repulsed by the suggestion that this unpleasant upstart could ever take Sully Sullivan's place. It was ridiculous. Her father had been the world's most positive, inspiring man. This guy was like a dark cloud!

And it wasn't just the attitude. It was everything. Her father had been a big man—six and a half feet tall—with shoulders a mile wide. This lean young man was barely six feet in height, with scruffy black hair and a five o'clock shadow—in the middle of the afternoon.

And the biggest indictment of all—the truest contrast with Sabrina's father—was that fact that it had only taken Sully eleven months to track and apprehend Pluto Zenner, arguably the most brilliant assassin ever inflicted upon the world.

Now under this new "leadership," Perimeter had had five full years to catch Pluto's son Adonis—by all accounts a less talented man than the elder Zenner. But Adonis was still free. Sabrina knew that for sure, because she had combed the newspaper every morning for those five years, hungry for some mention of the assassin's arrest or death. And she had checked the FBI's Web site daily, too, anxious for the day she and her sister could be Sullivans again. The day they could regain their old lives. The day Sabrina could stop hiding and start living, hopefully as an agent of the CIA—her dream since the first moment she'd learned the agency existed.

"Sabrina?" Theo said softly.

"This silence is her way of saying I'm not worthy," Zack muttered. "Right?"

Sabrina shrugged. "I don't know you. But so far, I'm unimpressed. Would you mind waiting outside so I can speak to my uncle in private?"

"I'm the errand boy who'll be running the background check for you, so I need to hear the details. But if this is about some guy who said he'd call you after the first date, then never did, I can probably explain it to you. He ran screaming for the hills."

"Zack!" Theo glared. "Sabrina's right. You should wait outside."

"No," she murmured, holding up her hand to stop him. "He's got a point. If he's the best Perimeter's got—and that's a scary thought by the way—he needs to hear this."

Zack walked over to Theo's desk and sat on the edge. "Okay, let's have it."

Sabrina studied him, again trying to figure out what had impressed her uncle enough to give this guy her father's job. Zack was dressed in faded jeans and a navy-blue polo shirt, barely disguising a good, lean build. His forearms in particular were pure muscle, all of which would make him a good bodyguard, she conceded. But head of Perimeter operations? No way.

It was discouraging, but she reminded herself all she really needed was background information, not "Sully level" skills. So she gave him a perfunctory smile and said, "The guy's name is Johnny Miller. He's an attorney. Supposedly with a tax firm. He's been dating Shelby, aka Michelle, for a couple of weeks. They took off on a trip and I haven't heard from her in almost four days. We've never been out of contact for that long."

"She didn't say where they were going?"

"Some sort of tropical island. He wanted to surprise her." Sabrina bit her lip. "It all happened pretty quickly. And it seemed innocent. It probably is. I hope I'm overreacting, but, like I said, we keep in touch. Always. No exceptions. Four days for us is like a lifetime."

Theo cleared his throat. "It sounds like she's in love."

"Head over heels," Sabrina confirmed. "But even so, she'd keep in touch. She even told me she would. Listen." Rummaging in her purse, she pulled out a recorder disguised as a pen. "She left two messages on my answering machine. I rerecorded them on this."

"Wait!" Theo arched an eyebrow. "That's Perimeter-issue. Where'd you get it?"

"It was a gift from my father."

"You weren't supposed to take anything with you to RAP that night. Clean slate, remember?"

"Dad trained me better than that," she said with a shrug. "I took the things I needed to protect Shell. We couldn't know for sure whether Adonis Zenner would come after us next. I had to be ready."

Theo was clearly struggling not to smile. "I escorted you personally. All you had were the clothes on your back."

"And the kitten," she reminded him, biting back a smile of her own. "The pet carrier had a false bottom. Big enough to hide a few tools. And my gun, of course."

"Are you armed now?" Zack interrupted, eyeing her purse.

"None of your business."

"Actually, protecting me *is* part of Zack's business," Theo told her gently. "I don't allow guests to carry weapons in my home."

"It's outside. In the trunk of my car. Frisk me if you don't believe me," she added in Zack's direction.

"That's not necessary." Theo stepped between his two visitors. "You were going to play a recording for us, weren't you?"

"Right. There are two messages, both from Shell."

Sabrina pushed the switch, and Shelby's recorded voice said, "Hey, Brie. Pick up if you're there. I was hoping we'd get to say goodbye. Johnny's whisking me away for a week of lust on some top-secret tropical island. We'll be incommunicado, but I'll call you as soon as I get home. Take care. We love you!"

The first call disconnected, then a second message began.

"Breezie?" Shelby's voice was hushed. "I've only got a sec. Johnny was in the room before, and he's really hot on this incommunicado thing, so I've been pretending to go along. But obviously I'm going to call you. And I'll have my cell with me, so leave me messages, okay? I know I'll miss you. Plus, I've been getting a funny feeling lately— like in the Dad days. I'll be worried if I don't hear from you. Watch your back, okay?

"But don't worry about me," Shelby's voice continued, "because I'll be with Johnny, so I'll be safe. And happy. Sooo happy. Can you believe how great he is? And before you roll your eyes, I'm not just talking about the sex. He's so different from other guys. Doesn't just go to sleep when he's done, you know? We stay up for hours afterward, talking about everything under the sun. It's so—oops, I hear him coming. Gotta go. Love ya!"

Sabrina switched off the recorder, trying to keep a cool head. But the sound of Shelby's sweet, trusting voice had brought a lump to the older sister's throat again, just as it had every time she'd listened to the messages.

"How long ago did you say she left?" Zack prodded.

"It was Saturday morning."

Something flickered in his green eyes and she knew that even a jerk like Zack Lansing thought four days without a call was too long.

But she wanted him to be wrong, so she insisted, "Shelby doesn't have her cell phone with her. I know that because yesterday I finally began to panic, so I went to her house. Her phone was lying right on the kitchen table. The innocent explanation is that Johnny took it out of her purse when she wasn't looking. Because he wanted her all to himself. She didn't realize it was missing until they were already in the middle of nowhere and now she can't call even if she wants to. Or something. But…"

"Take it easy," Zack advised. "We'll check the guy out. We've probably got information on him already."

"Really?"

"Sure. We don't stalk you or anything, but we've always kept tabs." Turning to Theo, he asked, "Where's last week's report?"

"We don't get weekly reports on the girls anymore," Theo told him with a wince. "Just monthly ones. The next one isn't due for a few days."

"Monthly? I never authorized that."

"I know," Theo replied. "I did."

Zack's eyes flashed and Sabrina thought he was going to lose his temper again. Then he shifted direction, literally and figuratively, and pushed a series of buttons on the phone on Theo's desk.

After three rings, a recorded voice said over the speaker, "You've reached Connor Boyle's message service. Leave your name and number and I'll get back to you."

"Connor, it's Zack. Where the hell are you? I'm at Theo's and we need to talk right away. Call back on his home number, and make it quick."

Breaking the connection with a flourish, Zack gave Theo a scowl. "That guy never answers his phone. What the hell are we paying him for?" Without waiting for a response, he asked Sabrina, "Where did Shelby meet this Miller guy?"

"At my house."

"Huh?"

She shrugged her shoulders. "It's a nice story, actually. Like she said in her message, he's a sweet guy. And he's probably harmless. But I had to know for sure. So I came here."

Theo gave her an encouraging smile. "We're glad you did. Aren't we, Zack?"

"Yeah. Thrilled. Let's hear the sweet story."

Sabrina settled into a gray-velvet wing chair. "A few weeks ago, my cat disappeared. He does that a lot, so I didn't take it too seriously. But after a week passed with no sign of him, I started posting notices around the neighborhood. The next day, Johnny came to my door with Zorro. That's the cat's name. Anyway, he had a cast on his leg. Zorro, not Johnny," she clarified sheepishly. "Johnny explained that he had found him a week earlier, lying by the side of the road, hurt. So he took him to the vet."

"Miller lives in your neighborhood?"

"No. He was just visiting his sister in Sacramento. He's from Seattle. Apparently he was out jogging when he found Zorro. Anyway, I was grateful to him. Obviously."

"Obviously," Zack drawled. "Go on."

Sabrina wasn't sure what he was implying, but she was sure she didn't like it. Turning away from him, she addressed her uncle. "I invited him in. He stayed for dinner and we had a lot of fun. He seemed like such a nice guy."

"He probably is," Theo told her. "Your father raised you to be a good judge of character."

She smiled in genuine relief. "Thanks, Uncle Theo. I hope you're right. Even now, looking back, I can't imagine a nicer guy than Johnny. We had so much in common. We talked and talked, long into the night. I was coming down with the flu as it turned out. Otherwise—" She flushed but admitted, "Who knows what might have happened? But as it turns out, I was too sick to be even remotely attractive. So we just talked. About a million different things. Then the next day, when Shelby heard how sick I was, she came over to take care of me. Johnny came back to check on me, and they hit it off. Like an inferno."

Sabrina stared down at her hands, suddenly embarrassed. "Just listening to myself, I can imagine how I sound. Jealous, right? But I'm not. I guess I'm just overprotective. The truth is, she found someone. Someone terrific. And he wants to spend some time alone with her. Sounds like a victimless crime, right?"

"I have a question for you," Zack said.

She looked up, surprised. "Sure. Ask me anything."

"What specifically did you and Miller talk about?"

"Hmm?"

"You said you talked long into the night. About what?"

"Well, about everything. All kinds of things."

"Everything under the sun?" he asked, arching an eyebrow.

"What?"

He reached over and took the recorder from her hand, then worked the controls until he had rewound the tape a bit. Then he played back the part that said, "…doesn't just go to sleep when he's done, you know? We stay up for hours after, talking about everything under the sun…."

Sabrina licked her lips, confused.

"Give me a topic. Something you two talked about. Current events? Your favorite movies? Capital punishment? Smoking in bars?"

She struggled with her memory. Or rather, the lack of it. And despite all the training she had received from her father, she began to slowly, quietly, panic. "I don't remember. Uncle Theo? What does it mean? *I don't remember!*"

"Settle down," Zack murmured. "It might not mean anything. Just take a deep breath."

For the first time, and only in the slightest of ways, he reminded her of her father, and she responded by breathing deeply, in and out, until her nerves had steadied. Then she forced herself to look straight into his green eyes. "What does it mean?"

Zack cleared his throat. "Did your father ever talk to you about DT3?"

The panic bubbled back up her spinal cord and into her brain. Not because she had heard of DT3—she hadn't. But it sounded so ominous. "It doesn't ring a bell. What is it?"

"A drug. An experimental one that was being developed here at Perimeter— *Damn it.*" He turned toward the phone, which had begun to ring. "Give me a minute."

Punching the speaker button, he demanded, "Who is it?"

"Zack? Hey, man. It's me. Connor. Did you want something?"

"Where the hell were you? Don't you work for a living?"

"Lighten up," Connor advised with a laugh. "I'm here now. What's up?"

Zack glanced toward Sabrina, then murmured, "I need some information about one of Sully's daughters."

"Which one? The warrior? Or the con artist?"

Zack winced. "The younger one. Shelby. I heard she's got a new boyfriend."

"She gets a new boyfriend every week," Connor told him, laughing again. "She's got a big heart, if you know what I mean."

"I'm on the speaker phone. The other daughter's here with me."

"Shit." Connor cleared his throat audibly. "Sorry, Miss Sullivan."

"Don't worry about it," she told him. "I just need to know where my sister is."

"Huh?"

Zack took over, suggesting tersely, "Tell us about the new boyfriend."

"I haven't read the report yet. It's not due until Friday," Connor explained. "I've had my most reliable guy checking her place a couple of times a week. He mentioned the new boyfriend. Said he looked pretty solid. Hold on. Let me grab the file and see if we've got a photo. It's here somewhere and—oh, *shit*."

Zack leaned toward the machine. "What's wrong?"

"You're not gonna believe this, Zack. It's John Derringer! I'm looking right at him. A picture of him, I mean. Shit, shit, shit. I can't believe it. What does he want with Sully's kid?"

"Shut up," Zack instructed. "Just fax me what you have and stop causing a panic."

"I'll go over to her house right away."

"It's too late for that now. Just fax me what you have and stand by for further instructions."

"I'm sorry, Zack—"

"Just answer the goddamned phone when I call back."

"Right. Jeez, what could Derringer want with—"

The rest of the sentence was cut off and Sabrina knew Zack had terminated the call. He wasn't looking at her. He was looking at Theo, and both men seemed stunned.

She wanted to ask who John Derringer was, but it didn't seem to matter. All that mattered were those three little words. *It's too late...*

"Oh, God," she whispered, her heart and soul flashing back to the moment, five long years ago, when she'd heard about her father's death at the hands of Adonis Zenner. "This can't be happening. Not again."

"Don't worry," Zack told her. "We'll get her back."

"You just said it's too late!"

"That's not what I meant." He flushed. "It's too late for Connor to go and protect her. That's all. And I don't want him messing up the scene. I'll have my crew meet me there later, to look for clues."

When Sabrina exhaled sharply, he added, "She's fine. I'm almost sure of it. John would never hurt a woman. Especially not someone Sully cared about. He and your dad were close once. A million years ago, but it counts for something. I'm sure."

Sabrina crossed to him and grabbed his hands in her own. "I need information. I'm dying here."

"Yeah, I get that," he murmured. "Just breathe, okay? I'll tell you everything I know."

Reassured and a little embarrassed, she pulled free and backed a few steps away. "Who is this John Derringer?"

Theo stepped up to her and slipped his arm around her shoulders. "He used to work for us, honey. Years ago. Your father recruited him. Trained him. Just like Zack. Except Derringer was nothing like Zack. Nothing like Sully. We learned that the hard way."

She shifted so that she could gaze up at Theo. "What does he want with my sister?"

"Hard to say—"

"He wants information," Zack interrupted. "If all he wanted was to hurt her, he wouldn't have gone to all the trouble of pretending to save your cat."

"Pretending to save…?" Sabrina's stomach knotted. "You think he planned all that? You think he *broke* Zorro's leg? Oh, God…" She covered her face with her hands, struggling against a new wave of despair.

"He wants something from her," Zack repeated. "Let's

figure out what it is, okay? That's the fastest way to get her back. Safe and sound."

"Zack's right," Theo said with reassuring vehemence. "If he was after revenge, he would have killed her right away. There's something else going on."

"Revenge?" She forced herself to focus. "Are you saying Dad did something bad to him?"

"It's not revenge," Zack protested. "He used DT3 on her. That means he wanted information."

"Or he wanted to plant a suggestion," Theo countered. "Don't forget that."

"Okay, stop." Sabrina held up her hand. "DT3? You said it was a drug. What does it do?"

"It makes most people susceptible to hypnosis. But it makes some people sick to their stomachs. That's what happened when he tried it on you."

"My flu symptoms?"

"Right." Zack motioned toward the wing chair. "Sit for a minute. This is a lot to take in, and I need you to concentrate."

She nodded and sat down. "He used the drug on me, but it made me sick."

"Right. But it worked enough to allow him to plant a basic suggestion in your mind. The suggestion that you and he stayed up all night talking about everything under the sun, or some such crap."

"Right."

"And he may have planted other suggestions, as well. So I need to ask you something. It's going to make you mad, but just try to understand. Okay?"

She nodded.

"Is your weapon really outside in the car?"

"Yes. Why?"

"Do you have any feelings of animosity toward Theo? Feelings you can't explain?"

"No. I have some toward you," she added with a half-hearted smile. "But I can explain those."

Zack laughed. "Fair enough."

The light moment vanished quickly for Sabrina. "You think he might try to use me and Shelby to hurt Perimeter? That's sort of far-fetched, don't you think?"

"Yes. Just be aware. If you have feelings you don't understand—urges that seem uncharacteristic—report them to me immediately."

"I will. I promise."

"And you should probably get some tests done. Tonight or tomorrow." He grimaced, then explained, "For diseases. Pregnancy. Whatever."

"I didn't sleep with him, thanks to the vomiting. It was a definite mood killer."

"Just the same..."

"I didn't sleep with him," she repeated, annoyed at the stubborn suggestion. Then her shoulders slumped. "Obviously, Shell did. But I'm sure she used protection."

"Good."

"It's kidnapping, right? I mean, he drugged her and made her believe she's in love with him. That's the only reason she went away with him, so it wasn't really consensual."

"It's kidnapping," Zack agreed.

"And now he's out there somewhere, playing with her head. Trying to get information. Or torturing her as revenge for something Dad did to him. That's what you're saying, right?"

"He's not torturing her. It's not his style. But otherwise, yeah. He's messing with her head."

Sabrina turned away, her heart pounding with confusion. "This is so much worse than anything I ever imagined. I thought I was overreacting. I thought you'd say he was just a romantic fool. Or at worst, a gigolo or something, trying to get at the trust fund."

Spinning to face Theo, she insisted, "We hardly spent any of the money. We saved it for the day we could come back. So we could buy back Dad's share of the company. We didn't know you needed it. Please take it back—"

"Hey!" Theo silenced her with a hug. "Look around. Does it seem like I'm hurting? We had a cash flow problem for a year or so, but that's behind us. Thanks to Zack. He got us on our feet. Found us a client who's richer than Midas. We're fine. I promise."

With a wink he added, "Everyone knows I make my real money in real estate anyway. Perimeter's just a hobby. So give me a smile and let's not talk about money any more."

Sabrina squeezed his arm, then resumed her questioning. "Tell me about John Derringer. What did Dad do to him that was so terrible?"

Zack gave her a curious look. "How much do you know about the Zenner mess?"

"The Zenner mess? Do you mean, my father's murder? I'd like to think I know everything about it."

"Let's hear it, then."

Sabrina shrugged. "Pluto Zenner assassinated a Perimeter client during some meeting in the Canary Islands. To salvage the company's reputation, Dad helped the CIA track him down, and Pluto was killed resisting arrest. Then Pluto's son Adonis came after Dad and blew him up."

"Right." Zack's eyes clouded. "What you probably don't know is that John Derringer was responsible for the breach in security that led to the assassination in the Canary Islands. It was John's first big assignment for Perimeter, and he blew it. His ego took a serious beating."

Sabrina was beginning to understand. "Dad fired him?"

"No. Sully wanted to give him another chance. But John's pride got in the way. He quit in a huff. Disappeared for a few months, then surfaced as a petty criminal, using the knowledge he got from Sully's training to penetrate various security systems and pull some creative heists. His way of saying he was just as good as us, I guess."

"A disgruntled employee from five—no, six—years ago?" Sabrina shook her head. "It doesn't make sense. Why would he wait so long to come after us?"

"That's the question," Zack agreed.

She covered her face with her hands again, but this time the gesture wasn't one of despair. Instead she needed to blot out Zack and Theo for the moment. To return to her training. Her roots. Her legacy of strength from her father.

Fear doesn't hurt people, Brie. Panic does. It's an agent's worst enemy. Learn to control it.

"Okay," she said finally. "DT3. You said it's got something to do with hypnosis, right?"

"It's got everything to do with hypnosis," Zack confirmed. "You've probably heard that a person can't be hypnotized without their consent, right? And that you can't make them do anything under hypnosis that goes against their grain? Well, DT3 changes all that."

He pulled a chair over and sat directly in front of Sabrina. "It's what they call a hypnotropic drug. It gives the hypnotist tremendous power. With it, he can put the subject into such a deep trance, even without their consent, that they're virtually his slave. He can extract information from their memory or he can conceal it there. He can password-protect it so that he's the only one who can ever retrieve it.

He can plant powerful post-trance suggestions, like the one Derringer gave you." Leaning closer, he muttered, "It's a goddamned menace."

"I can't believe I've never heard of it."

"Perimeter developed it. But after a few tests, your father and Theo were so alarmed by its potential, they abandoned the project."

"But Derringer has it?"

Zack nodded. "We were both trained to use it. But the formula stayed with Sully. I guess John took a supply with him when he left. We're probably lucky he hasn't sold it to some foreign agency by now."

Sabrina looked over toward Theo. "You think he's planting ugly suggestions in her mind? Making her do creepy things?"

"That's unlikely," Zack protested. "My guess is he wants information. Something he thinks you girls learned during all those years with Sully. Maybe even some secret information Sully hid in your minds—"

"My father would never hide things in our minds!"

Zack flushed. "Take it easy. I'm just brainstorming here. If you can't take it, you should go lie down or something." He stood and turned to Theo, as though dismissing Sabrina. "Can you get Marietta to make copies of all Connor's faxes for me? And all the reports from his crew for the last three months. Derringer probably surveilled the girls for weeks before he made his move. Maybe there's something in the early reports we can use."

"Wait!" Sabrina jumped up and confronted him. "Let me help."

"You can help by staying out of the way. We do this for a living, you know. Go upstairs and rest for a while. If there's anything to report, you'll be the first to know."

Sabrina wanted to reach down his arrogant throat and pull out his tonsils, but counseled herself to stay calm. He saw her as a civilian. Fine. She could use that to her advantage. Wasn't that what her father would want her to do?

"I *am* a little beat," she said with an apologetic smile. "Give me a few minutes to splash some water on my face, okay? But after that, I really want to help." Heading for the double doors, she added over her shoulder, "I'll be back in five minutes. Don't make any decisions until I get back, okay?"

"Right," Zack drawled.

Theo corrected him with a warm, loving, "Take your time. We're just going to look at the files. And, Sabrina?"

"Yes?"

"You made the right decision, coming here. We're going to get little Shellie back. I promise you that."

Sabrina beamed, then turned and strolled into the hall as though completely reassured. But as soon as she was out of their field of vision, she sprinted toward the grand staircase, then took the steps two at a time, anxious to get to the music room that was located directly above Theo's study.

She only hoped things hadn't changed since the day, almost twenty years earlier, when two little girls—who were tired of being sent out of "Uncle Theo's" study every time he and their father had something important to discuss— had transformed the music room into their own personal, clandestine listening post.

Chapter 2

Hurrying past the baby grand piano that dominated the music room, Sabrina opened a set of louvered closet doors on the far wall. A brass chest filled with sheet music was sitting right in front of her, just as it had been during her childhood. Inching the chest aside, she knelt and ran her fingertip along the rim of a large black knot in the oak flooring. Years of wax had sealed the knot firmly into place, but she was able to loosen it with the blade from her pocketknife.

Prying the lump of wood free, she pressed her ear against the floor and heard voices, courtesy of the tiny tunnels she and her sister had poked through the various layers of insulation and Sheetrock that separated the music room floor from the ceiling of the study.

Zack's tone was predictably strident. "I get the point, boss. I was rude. I'll apologize to her as soon as I get the chance. But in the meantime, I need to start looking for the other one. Assuming the lecture is officially over."

"As long as we're clear," Theo replied. "I want you to treat her with kid gloves from now on."

"Done. But spare me the concerned-uncle act. You aren't worried about Sully's kid. You're just worried she'll share secrets with Derringer that might hurt the company—"

"That's not true! I love those girls. Their father was my best friend. And they—all three of them—were the only family I ever really had."

"Sully was family to me, too," Zack reminded him.

"Like a father," Theo agreed. "And Derringer was like a brother, right up till the time he betrayed your trust. If anyone's motives here are suspect, I'd say *yours* are."

There was a moment of silence, then Theo spoke again, this time in a conciliatory tone. "I have complete confidence in your ability to find Michelle, Zack. How do you plan to go about it?"

"My crew can check the airports, et cetera. See if there are any reservations in her name or activity on her passport. I'll head up to Sac tonight to check out her place. Maybe I can find something to show where they headed."

"Sounds good."

"Before I go, I want to hypnotize Sabrina—"

"That's out of the question."

"Huh? Why? It's our best source of information. If she can remember what John was trying to dig out of her memory—"

"That girl is already miserable. I'm not going to let you go on a fishing expedition in her brain. That's final."

"If she agrees—"

"I said it's final," Theo retorted. "Find Michelle some other way. Not at the expense of Breezie's sanity. Period."

Sabrina could easily imagine the angry expression on Zack's face at that moment. And while she was grateful to her uncle for trying to protect her, she agreed that her memory was the best clue available to them. Zack had to use it.

But Zack was obviously a zealot—*and* a hothead—so she was also glad Theo would be there during the hypnosis to protect her from his employee's excesses.

When the zealot finally spoke, his words were clipped and measured. "When this is over, you and I are gonna have a long talk. Either I'm running Perimeter or I'm not."

"You're running it. But it's *my* company. And I want Sabrina treated with kid gloves. Marietta can feed her and pamper her and I'll reminisce with her about Sully."

"You should show her the funeral video," Zack murmured. "I always thought it was a shame his kids missed that eulogy you gave him." Clearing his throat, he added more briskly, "We can postpone the London job for a few weeks, right? I need my full crew here if I'm going to find Michelle before Derringer's done with her."

"Of course. I'll make sure the client understands," Theo promised. "That leaves the birthday party in Dallas on Friday night, which can *not* be postponed. You know as well as I do that that particular client will *never* understand."

"We'll find the little sister before then. Or I'll send Connor to Dallas—"

"No way," Theo interrupted. "Our reputation stands or falls with our ability to please King Dominik. I need you there. That's not negotiable."

"It's not an issue," Zack said, his tone sharp with exasperation. "Just keep Sabrina out of my hair. I get the feeling she wants to play with the big boys, and ordinarily, it would be fun to watch her try. But I don't have time for games."

"She's not exactly a civilian," Theo reminded him.

"Sully started training her before she could walk. I'll never forget some of the crazy exercises he put her through."

"Kid stuff. She never went out on a job, did she? And she's been a million miles away from Sully's world— teaching school kids how to tie their shoes—for the last five years."

"She's no ordinary schoolteacher. Read the reports. She never misses a Saturday at the pistol range. And she runs three miles every morning."

"She's in great shape," Zack admitted. "The legs alone are gold standard. But this job's too dangerous for an amateur. Aren't you the one who said she needs to be pampered?"

"Sabrina will stay here," Theo agreed. "You'll take the lead on finding Michelle. But if you haven't succeeded by Friday, we turn the assignment over to Connor so you can go to Dallas. No arguments."

Zack's laugh was gently mocking. "So much for the concerned-uncle routine."

"Forgive me if I don't want to see the company go down the tubes again, like it did when Sully died."

"You mean, like it did when the daughters ran off with half the money and all of the cachet?" Zack chuckled again. "You're a hypocrite, Theo. Making it seem like I'm the bad guy, when you resent them as much as I do. Probably more."

"This conversation is over. Just review the faxes until Breezie gets back. Where is she, anyway?"

Grimacing, Sabrina plugged the knot back into its hole, then jumped to her feet and slid the brass chest into place, taking care not to make any noise. After making a quick stop in the bathroom, she rejoined the men in the study.

"There's my girl! Feeling any better?"

"I'm fine, thanks. Are those the faxes?" She shuffled through a handful of grainy images, mostly of Johnny arriving at or departing from Shelby's house, day in and day out for almost two weeks straight. "Unbelievable."

"Tell me about it," Zack drawled. "This guy comes and goes at will, and Connor's crew just sits there and takes pictures."

"It's no one's fault," Theo interrupted. "Let's just deal with the situation as it stands now, shall we?"

"Speaking of which, I was thinking…" Sabrina pursed her lips, feigning casual inspiration. "Maybe you should try to hypnotize me."

Zack's green eyes widened with surprise. Then he turned to Theo. "Interesting idea, don't you think?"

Theo scowled. "Hypnosis is serious business, Breezie. You're too upset right now to be a proper candidate. Maybe later—"

"I insist, Uncle Theo. It's the quickest way to find out what Johnny wants from us. Once we know that, we'll be in a better position to guess where he took Shelby." When Theo hesitated, she repeated firmly, "I insist. If you refuse, I'll pay a psychologist to do it."

"It's settled then." Zack's smile was triumphant. "We'll go easy on you, I promise. Just a quick in and out. Two, three questions tops."

Sabrina shook her head. "Take your time. Like I said, this is our best resource, so don't be afraid to use it."

Theo seemed unconvinced. "We don't need to do it right away, do we? I want you to relax and eat some lunch first."

Sabrina laughed. "What's the point? I'll just vomit it up. Remember?"

"Whoa!" Zack shook his head. "We aren't using DT3 on you. Just conventional hypnosis."

"But—"

"Do you have to argue about everything?" he asked,

adding more reasonably, "DT3 is designed for an unwilling subject. You're submitting to the process willingly, so we don't need it."

"But—"

"Zack's right, Sabrina," Theo interrupted. "We don't need it. And given the intensity of your allergic reaction last time, another dose could send you into shock."

She grimaced. "Really?"

"It's settled," Zack said, pulling out his cell phone. "You two have some lunch—and a nice visit—while I make some calls. I want to check for activity at the airports, particularly on Shelby's passport."

Sabrina remembered the men's conversation about the videotape of her father's funeral. She really wanted to hear that eulogy Zack had raved about, so she decided to jog her uncle's memory. "Do you have any pictures of Dad? I'd love to reminisce a little."

"Of course!" Theo exclaimed. "And I want to show you the funeral video, too. I'm glad you reminded me."

Zack's attention instantly refocused on Sabrina, his eyes narrowing, and she knew she had made a strategic mistake.

Then his gaze shifted—from her face up toward the ceiling, then back again—and she knew he was on to her. Confirming the suspicion, he spun around and stalked out of the study.

"What set *him* off?" Theo demanded.

Sabrina gave an innocent shrug. "He's a hothead, remember?"

"I'm sorry he talked to you the way he did, Breezie. In his defense, he was a die-hard fan of your father's."

"You said Dad recruited him? And also Johnny?"

"Yes. Connor, too, actually. They were all friends at

one time. The future of Perimeter, according to Sully. Strange, isn't it?"

Sabrina nodded, but her attention was focused on the room above her head. There was no noise. No sound of a brass trunk being pushed aside. Maybe Zack hadn't figured it out after all.

Then he strode back into the room, as quickly as he had left, and tossed the knot of oak into her hands. "Here's a souvenir. Sebastian's getting his saw as we speak, so your eavesdropping days are over."

Sabrina struggled not to smile as Theo asked his employee, "What are you talking about?"

"Believe me, boss, you'd rather not know." Zack arched a teasing eyebrow in Sabrina's direction. "How old were you when it started?"

"Seven. But Shell was only five. She's the one who did the drilling."

He laughed. "Derringer better watch his step."

"Believe it."

Theo glared at them. "Did I miss something?"

"I'll tell you later." Sabrina patted his arm. "Meanwhile, I'm anxious to get started on the hypnosis. Do you mind if we do it before lunch?"

"Works for me," Zack agreed. "The sooner I hit the road, the sooner I can search your sister's place and pick up Derringer's trail."

"I'm coming with you," Sabrina told him.

"No way. You're safest here."

"I don't want to be safe. I want to find my sister. I can do it with you. Or I can do it alone."

"If Derringer can't get what he wants from Michelle, he'll come after you. You're safest here."

"With *your* crackerjack security? Give me a break." She

shook her head. "There's nothing in Sacramento anyway. I searched Shell's house from top to bottom. If we're going to find a clue, it's through Derringer." She turned to Theo. "I need to see everything you have on him. He worked for Perimeter, right? That means there are employment files. Background checks. References. Every shred of information." To Zack she added cheerfully, "I bet I find him before you do."

"You already had him, remember? Standing right in your living room."

"Because *your* staff let him walk right up to my front porch."

"But *you* let him in. What happened to your so-called training? You fell for the oldest trick in the book—a lost cat. So lose the attitude, would you? We're just trying to help."

Sabrina turned away, stung by the truth. It *was* the oldest trick in the book.

Johnny had stood there on the porch, with that radiant smile and hunky broad shoulders, and all her training had flown out the window. That was the part she hadn't shared with Theo and Zack, although Zack had clearly picked up on it. She had been instantly attracted to Johnny, for reasons that had nothing to do with Zorro's leg. Her lonely body had reacted to the handsome stranger like a child reacts to Christmas.

"Hey." Zack came up behind her. "I was out of line. Again. Sorry."

"You were right," she countered, turning to grace him with a cool smile. "I thought he was the world's greatest guy. Apparently you did, too. Best friends—almost like brothers, right? Dad liked him enough to hire him. Uncle Theo trusted him enough to send him to the Canary Islands to guard our most valuable client.

"We were all conned by him," she finished with a flourish. "So let's just move on. Hypnotize me now and get it over with. Then you can hit the road."

"Maybe you should just leave now, Zack." Theo gave his employee a withering look as he patted Sabrina's arm. "I can hypnotize Sabrina myself. If we learn anything of value, we'll call you."

Zack spoke between clenched jaw muscles. "I have the most training. And we both know you'll go too easy on her. What's the point?"

Theo shrugged. "To be successful, she has to be relaxed. And she has to trust the hypnotist. I don't see that happening with you here."

"I want Zack to do it, Uncle Theo." Sabrina touched her host's cheek to soften the interruption. "He's right. You *would* be too careful. We have to be thorough, for Shell's sake."

Theo shrugged again. "I want to okay the list of questions then—"

"No way," Zack said with a growl.

"I agree," Sabrina murmured. "He needs to follow his instincts. That's what Dad would say if he were here, right?" Turning to Zack, she insisted cheerfully, "Let's do it."

"One hundred, ninety-nine, ninety-eight, ninety-seven… ninety-two… three…" Sabrina yawned, losing interest in the numbers as she succumbed to an uncharacteristic feeling of peace and tranquility.

"Sabrina Sullivan?"

"Yes?"

"How do you feel?"

"I feel good."

"Good." Zack cleared his throat. "I'm going to ask you a few questions. Just do your best, okay?"

"Okay."

"If you start feeling uncomfortable—for any reason—just let me know and I'll wake you up. Okay?"

"Okay."

"Good. Now tell me about John Derringer."

"Johnny?"

"Right."

She sighed. "I liked him. A lot. Now I hate him."

"He has that effect on everyone," Zack assured her. "Do you remember talking to Johnny the way you're talking to me now? In this kind of a mood? Calm like this?"

"I don't know." She squirmed in her chair. "I don't remember."

"Johnny gave you some instructions. Do you remember that?"

"I don't know."

"He told you to forget about your little chat with him. And you forgot it, just like he told you to do. That was good, Sabrina. But now I want you to try and remember what he said. Just a few words. Can you do that for me?"

She shook her head. "I don't *remember* any words."

"Okay, shh. It's fine. Let's talk about your sister for a few minutes instead. Is that okay?"

"Yes."

"Do you want me to call her Michelle? Or Shelby?"

"Her name is Shelby now."

"Okay, that's fine. When Shelby talked to you about Johnny, did she mention what they talked about?"

"Everything."

"Right. Everything. But did she mention anything specifically? Do you think he asked about your father?"

"Dad?"

"Right. Did Johnny talk to Shelby about him?"

"I don't know."

"Did Johnny ever ask *you* about him?"

"I don't remember! I don't want to talk about Johnny."

"That's fine. We won't talk about him anymore. Let's talk about your father instead. Would you like that?"

"Yes."

"Did *he* ever talk to you the way I'm talking to you now?" Sabrina nodded. "Yes."

"Okay, good. Do you remember what he talked to you about?"

"We talked about Shell," Sabrina murmured.

"What did he say about your sister?"

"He told me to protect her, because I'm the oldest. It's my mission," she added proudly.

Zack laughed. "How old are you right now?"

"I'm nine."

"Did your father tell you anything else? Maybe when you were older? Did he share secrets with you when he talked to you this way?"

"No. He just told me to protect Shell. But I didn't," she admitted unhappily. "I let a bad man take her away."

"Sabrina, listen to me. I don't want you to think about that right now. Do you understand? I want you to think about Theo Howell."

She felt the sense of calm return. "Uncle Theo?"

"Right. How do you feel about him?"

"I love him."

"Do you have any other feelings? Feelings you can't explain? Any desire to hurt him that confuses you?"

"Hurt him?" She shook her head. "No. Never."

"And what about Perimeter? Do you want to destroy it?"

"No."

"Do you want to hurt anyone?"

"Yes."

"Who do you want to hurt?"

"I want to hurt Adonis Zenner. I want to *kill* him."

"Okay, shh. That's fine. What about Johnny? Do you want to kill him?"

"I don't know."

"You told me you hate him. But you don't want to hurt him?"

"I want to find him," she explained carefully. "And I want to pay him back for taking my sister. But I don't want to kill him unless he makes me do it."

"Okay, I understand," Zack said, his tone soothing. "You hate him and you want to find him."

"Yes."

"Do you trust him?"

"I don't trust anyone but myself. And Shelby."

"You don't trust me?"

"No."

"You let me hypnotize you. That means you trust me a little, doesn't it?"

"I don't know."

"You trust Uncle Theo, don't you?"

"Sometimes."

"Okay, Sabrina." Zack's voice was steady and inspiring. "You did great. I'm going to wake you up now. Okay?"

"Yes."

"I'll count to five, and when you hear me say 'five,' you'll wake up. Is that clear?"

"Yes."

"When you wake up, you'll remember everything we've said. But it won't upset you. You'll feel refreshed. Rested. Is that clear?"

"Yes."

"Good. I'm going to count now. On five, you'll wake up. One, two, three, four, five."

Sabrina stirred and opened her eyes, then smiled sheepishly. "Hi."

"Hi." Zack's green eyes were twinkling. "You did great."

"I didn't remember anything Johnny said."

"He made you forget the session. But it seems like that's all he managed to accomplish. Your subconscious must have really resisted him."

Sabrina sighed. "You were right about Dad. He really did hypnotize me when I was a kid. I don't know why that bothers me, but it does."

"Seems pretty harmless. He just wanted you to look out for your baby sister." Zack's smile widened. "You must've been a cute kid. Calling it your mission."

"That's how it was with Dad. He made everything so much fun and dramatic. Life and death. But still just a game. I loved it. Then everything changed."

"When Adonis killed him."

She nodded. "And now Shelby's in danger because of her connection to Dad's past. It's *so* creepy to think of Johnny alone with her, hypnotizing her at will. Making her do things. Reveal things. Forget things." She cocked her head to the side. "If you could use DT3 on me, could you make me remember what Johnny was searching for in my head?"

"Theoretically," Zack admitted. "He gave you a posttrance suggestion to forget the whole session. With DT3, I could counteract that, unless he password-protected it. Then it would take more time and some serious hacking."

Sabrina winced at the harsh term, even though she realized he only meant it in the computer sense. "So if Dad did that—hid information in our heads and protected it with a password—Johnny could be trying to hack into that? That would explain why it's taking him so long, right?"

"It's a possibility," Zack confirmed. "But it doesn't seem like Sully did anything like that to you. And since you're the oldest, it's logical he would have hidden it in your head, not Shelby's."

"That makes sense."

Zack nodded. "My guess is, John's after a simple memory. But it's taking time—not because it's password-protected, but because he's fishing for it. Maybe he doesn't know exactly when the event happened, for example. So he's regressing her, probing, that sort of thing. Zeroing in on it, but it's taking some time."

"I like that better than the hacking scenario," Sabrina admitted. "Do you think he'll let her go once he gets what he wants?"

Zack hesitated. "I guess that depends on his ultimate agenda. And what shape she's in by then, mentally and otherwise. I just hope she still believes it's a romantic getaway. If she figures out what's going on, or if he stops pretending to care about her, she'll be scared."

"If she figures out what's going on, she'll try to escape," Sabrina countered. When Zack gave a skeptical shrug, she smiled. "I hope Derringer underestimates her the same way you do. That gives her a strategic advantage."

"The only strategic advantage we have is time. He doesn't know about the second message she left you, so he thinks he has three more days before you get suspicious. We need to use every minute, so I'm outta here." He handed Sabrina the stack of reports from Connor. "Find me the picture that looks the most like Shelby. I want to circulate it to my crew."

"I brought a great photo of her with me, just in case. It's in the trunk of my car."

"Good. You two girls change hair color so often, it's tough to keep track."

She bristled at the implied criticism. "We went brunette at RAP's suggestion. But over the years, we gradually phased back to blond." Fingering a lock of her own hair, she explained, "This is our natural color. Shelby's is the same, only longer, and with some added highlights, so it's a little blonder."

He pulled out a notebook and pen. "Height? Weight? You're taller, right?"

"Yes. She's five-five. Probably one hundred twenty pounds. She packed for a tropical island, which means lots of pink sundresses and strappy sandals. If any witnesses saw her, they'll remember her." She swallowed a lump of affection and concern. "I'll get that photo. Wait here."

She was glad for an excuse to head outside for a gulp of fresh air. All this talk about Shelby was getting to her. *Too* much talk, not enough action. And all the while, Johnny was invading Shelby's mind. Endangering her sanity. All for some nefarious, unfathomable purpose.

If only you hadn't been allergic, she accused herself as she fumbled for her car keys. *He would have taken you, and Shell would be safe.*

Popping the trunk of her convertible, she quickly located the glossy photograph of her sister, and as she looked at it, the tightness returned to her throat. Shelby was so innocent. So trusting. But if she figured out what was going on—well, she was a Sullivan. Trained from the cradle to protect herself.

Could Shelby really escape from a seasoned criminal like Derringer? Sabrina wondered. Neither of them had ever really been put to the test. But she had to believe their father's hard work hadn't been in vain.

If only Dad were here. He'd know what to do, she told herself. As competent as Zack was beginning to seem, Sabrina still had no illusions about him. He was too young. Too temperamental. Too driven by passion. He'd do his best because of his devotion to Sully Sullivan and his hatred for Derringer. He might even be able to find Shelby in time. But would he be able to outwit Derringer once he got there?

No. That's where Sabrina would be invaluable. She had her father's instincts. His cool head. She *had* to be there when Zack made his move against Derringer. But she knew he'd try to exclude her, either to protect her or because he thought she'd get in the way.

"Which is where this little baby comes in handy," she said out loud, pulling a black-leather shaving kit from her suitcase. Inside the kit—affectionately known as Sully Sullivan's "bag of tricks"—was the collection of gadgets she had smuggled into RAP via Zorro's cat carrier.

Locating a handheld computer, she dislodged the backing and retrieved a sheet of minuscule sensors. With one of these, she could easily track Zack's movements, using the computer's gridded screen and global positioning capabilities.

One of the tiny sensors was already missing from the sheet, having been affixed by Sabrina to the inside hood of Shelby's car the day it was purchased. If only Johnny had used that vehicle to kidnap her sister, they could have found her in an instant.

Now she was tempted to do the same with Zack's shiny black convertible, but if he switched to air travel, she'd lose him. She needed to attach it to something he'd carry with him at all times.

On impulse, she unhooked the gold chain she wore around her neck, then popped open the attached locket to reveal tiny photos of her mother and father. Pulling up the edge of Sully Sullivan's smiling face, she slipped a sensor underneath, then covered it with the picture.

Just as she was double-checking her handiwork, she heard a door slam. Looking up, she saw Zack coming down the steps of the Howell mansion with an overstuffed briefcase in his hand, so she closed the trunk, then smiled and offered him the photo of Shelby. "Here it is."

"Great." He cleared his throat. "Before I go, I'd like to apologize. I was a jerk when you first got here, and I'm sorry."

"Find my sister and all is forgiven. And if you see her before I do, give her this." She held out the necklace.

Accepting it, he looked inside the locket. "Your mom? I never saw a picture of her before. You girls look a lot like her. A lot like Sully, too."

"Take good care of it, okay?" Sabrina asked softly. "When Shelby sees it, she'll know she can trust you."

"Good idea." He nodded his approval. "She might not believe she needs to be rescued, right? She'll trust John, and be suspicious of me."

"Right. And even if she realizes she's been kidnapped, she'll be suspicious of everyone. Except me. Which is why I need to be there." She touched his arm. "Call me as soon as you get a lead, please?"

"Sure. You'll be the first to know." He flashed a confident smile. "I'll check in tomorrow. In the meantime, if you think of anything else I should know, call me. Here's my number."

She accepted his business card, then thanked him and waved goodbye until he had roared away in his sports car.

She knew he was lying, of course. He had no intention of sharing information with her. At least, not willingly. But thanks to the global positioning device, she would track his every movement. If he got a lead on Shelby's location, Sabrina would head there as soon as he made his move.

And in the meantime, maybe she'd find the location first.

Chapter 3

"Shelby? Baby, wake up."

Shelby York, aka Michelle Sullivan, snuggled under a lightweight blanket, craving another few minutes of sleep but unable to resist the sexy voice that called to her. Opening one eye, she murmured, "Johnny? Did I fall asleep again?"

"You're hopeless," he confirmed. "We were supposed to go for a walk, remember?"

She struggled to a sitting position on the overstuffed couch, then glared playfully. "You're the one who keeps wearing me out with the swing-from-the-rafters sex."

He laughed. "I'd offer to wear you out a little more, but I've gotta get started on dinner. You're already looking like you've lost some weight. I don't want that Banshee sister of yours mad at me when we get home."

"Hey!" Shelby stuck her finger to within centimeters of

his face. "Watch what you say about Briana. She likes you a lot, you know. Even though you make her sick to her stomach."

She was tempted to ask him again to let her call her big sister, just to let her know everything was fine. But every time she mentioned making contact with the outside world, it seemed to hurt Johnny's feelings. He was *such* a romantic. And so unbelievably devoted to her, it humbled her. He had designed this getaway so that they could shut out the rest of the world—no phones, no e-mail, not even any newspapers.

And she had pretended to agree to his terms, all the while planning to check in with Sabrina every day. But he had foiled that plan by sneaking her phone out of her purse when she wasn't looking. And because he was so darling and romantic about it, she hadn't had the guts to confess to him that she had left a second message for her sister, promising to call.

Instead she had assumed she could sweet-talk him into letting her use his phone—the one he'd brought "strictly for emergencies"—to eventually call Sabrina. But Johnny had been resistant to her charms on that one issue, making up for it by slavishly indulging her every other wish.

As much as Shelby wanted to just let it go, she knew Sabrina well enough to guess that she was about to come unglued with worry. And since Plan A had failed—as had Plan B, which involved secretly mailing a letter to her sister—she had no choice but to turn to Plan C.

Looping her arms around Johnny's neck, she murmured, "You know what would really hit the spot?"

"Depends on the spot," he replied with a wink.

Shelby pretended to be shocked. "Get your mind out of the gutter. I'm talking about dinner. I'd kill for a pizza. I've been craving one all day."

"Pizza?" He frowned. "I'm not sure I've got the ingredients. For the crust, sure. And I brought cheddar cheese, so I could probably rig something up—"

"Johnny?"

"Yeah?"

"I want the kind that comes to the door in a cardboard box. There must be places in Truckee that deliver, right?" She jumped to her feet and scurried into the kitchen, where she began rummaging through drawers. "I'm sure there's a phone book around here."

"I thought you loved my cooking."

"Cravings can't be ignored," she told him. "We'll have to pay the guy extra to drive all the way up the hill, but it'll be worth it. Do you like pepperoni?"

"What happened to our deal?" he protested. "Just you and me. Alone in the woods. I don't remember anything about a threesome with a pizza delivery guy."

Shelby laughed. "You're so funny. I promise I'll get rid of him quickly, and then I'll make it up to you for the rest of the night. Just give me your phone—"

"Sheesh, baby, our whole romantic getaway is falling apart." He wrapped his arms around her waist. "We said no phones for a week, remember?"

"No phones for *me*," she retorted. "But *you* got to bring *yours.*"

"Because I can be trusted, and you can't." He flashed a seductive grin. "You'd be gabbing to your sister or your students all day long if I let you. But I want you all to myself." Lowering his mouth to her neck, he began to nuzzle expertly.

As always, Shelby weakened. He was *so* sexy! But she had to stick to the plan, so she insisted, "If you really loved me, you'd respect my cravings. What if you and I get married and pregnant some day, and I want pickles in the middle of the night? Are you going to deny me that, too?"

"Married and pregnant, huh? That sounds pretty good." He gave her a gentle kiss. "Tell you what. And this is a one-time-only deal. We'll drive into town and order a pizza. Then we'll bring it back here to eat it."

"That's *more* contact with the outside world, not less."

"Yeah, but it'll give me a chance to get some gas for the trip home. Take it or leave it."

Shelby pursed her lips. "I'll take it. On one condition. You go alone. It'll give me some time to fix myself up for you."

"You're already so beautiful it hurts," he murmured.

She loved it when he said those corny things, and had to resist an urge to melt into his arms. "There's certain maintenance a girl would rather do when she's all alone in the house. You see the glamour prep—the shampoo and lotion. But there's another, scuzzier side—the shaving, the plucking, the callus removal. *Please?* I promise you'll love the results."

"Let me guess," he drawled. "You want me to leave my phone with you?"

Shelby pretended to be wounded by the remark. "You're the one who'll be driving that dark, twisty road. I wouldn't let you leave here without a phone."

He winced in apology. "Okay, it's a deal. Pepperoni? Anything else?"

"Just hurry back," she told him, missing him already. "But first, give me a kiss goodbye."

He obliged her with a kiss so warm and loving, she ached with guilt. She would definitely have to find a way to make this up to him.

"'Bye, Johnny. I love you." She waved from the porch until his truck was out of sight, then she sprang into action.

She had to find a phone, and probably had less than forty-five minutes to do so.

There has to be one here somewhere, she told herself, grabbing a set of keys off a hook by the door and heading for a storage shed near the garage. *There are outlets in every room. Either Johnny hid the phones himself, or the owners put them away for safekeeping.*

She had already looked through the various cabinets and closets in the house over the past four days, taking advantage of every trip Johnny made to the bathroom. But she hadn't dared check the storage shed with him around. And there was a locked closet on the second floor that was clearly marked Private—Keep Out. Those were the likely spots.

Running along the path in her bare feet, she scolded herself for taking this clandestine approach, rather than just being straight with her boyfriend. Hadn't he earned her honesty? Look how great he was—going for pizza just to please her! And this was how she repaid him?

It's like Dad always said. You turn everything into a spy mission, she told herself, then she laughed out loud. It was true. This was so much fun. She'd find the phone, make the call, douse herself in perfume and seduce the heck out of Johnny when he got back. And someday, on their golden anniversary, she'd tell him how she had outwitted him.

Reaching the shed, she tried each key until she found the right one, then she swung open the door. "Ick," she muttered, scanning the garden tools and sacks of manure. "That handyman should put some sort of air freshener in here."

She had seen the worker on the premises once or twice, trimming trees and gathering fallen limbs. He never came close enough to the cabin for her to meet him. And Johnny had explained to her that the man was "a little slow" and that she shouldn't try to talk to him, even though he was reportedly harmless.

Still, the handyman figured prominently in Plan B, which she had never had a chance to execute. Frustrated by Johnny's rules, she had written her sister a letter—just a short one, explaining that she was safe, happy, in love and truly incommunicado. She had hoped to sneak it to the gardener to mail for her, but he never seemed to come close enough to the cabin for her to succeed. And in the meantime, she had worried that he might tell Johnny.

Plan C—finding a phone among the belongings of the cabin owner—was much, much better.

The shed was a dead end, so she sprinted back to the cabin and up the stairs to the owner's private closet where again she tried the keys, but none fit. Undeterred, she retrieved a bobby pin from her overnight bag then returned to the closet and skillfully picked the lock. Opening the door, she was pleased to see several stacks of boxes.

She searched one container after another, being careful not to leave any sign of her invasion of the owner's privacy. By the time she was on the last box, she was getting a little annoyed.

"There has to be a phone here somewhere!" she insisted out loud. "There are outlets in every room! But this is taking much too long."

She realized too late that she should have just gone into town with Johnny, as he had suggested. She could have made an excuse, gone off to find a ladies' room and tracked down a pay phone.

"Think, Shelby. What would Breezie do? What would Dad want you to do?"

She winced, knowing that her father would probably just build himself a phone out of little twigs and berries or something. And Sabrina would have held a gun to Johnny's head long before this, demanding that he hand over the phone, the laptop and the keys to the truck.

The laptop...

Shelby felt a burst of hope and congratulated herself for all the hours of study she had dedicated to keeping her computer skills at cutting-edge sharpness. Even though Johnny hadn't brought a modem cable—she had checked his case for that the first day—she might be able to rig something up.

But she didn't have much more time, so she ran down the stairs as she brainstormed with herself. His laptop was sitting on the coffee table, where he had been using it to write in his journal. She knew from previous snooping that all the entries for the last three weeks were about her, and she loved him for that. Almost enough to respect his privacy, but at this point, her honor as a Sullivan was at stake, so she opened the lid of the computer and pushed the power button.

To her surprise, a screen asking for a password popped up. She hadn't seen that before, and only now remembered that the computer had always been turned on when she'd done prior invasions of Johnny's privacy. And the screen saver hadn't been password-protected.

Fine. You've gotta hack it, and fast. Luckily he's an open book. Guessing his password should be easy.

With a hopeful smile, she entered the letters S-H-E-L-B-Y on the screen, and was a little hurt when the word was rejected. With lightning-fast fingers she began feeding in other combinations—his birthday, his middle name, his sister's dog's name. Nothing worked.

You just need to bypass the main program completely, she counseled herself. *This is low-level software. It shouldn't be much of a challenge.* She worked diligently, trying every trick she had ever learned, but each effort was unsuccessful.

Which told her the software wasn't quite as "low level" as she had suspected. In fact, this whole setup was beginning to seem more sophisticated than it appeared.

"What exactly do you have in here, Johnny Miller?" she asked, turning off the machine, then flipping it over and unfastening the back panel. Again she was surprised, this time by the hardware, including a miniature modem unlike any she had ever seen.

Satellite? she asked herself, stunned to think Johnny had had the capacity to access his e-mail all this time. After his lectures on tuning the world out!

He wouldn't lie to you, she chastised herself. *Just because he has the technology doesn't mean he's been using it. His firm supplied it, right? And he's so clueless when it comes to this kind of stuff, he probably doesn't even know what he has.*

Fascinated, she slipped the satellite modem out of the casing, turning it over in her hands, examining it with admiration. If only she could get past that stupid, stupid password!

But the software was probably as sophisticated as the modem. Maybe even something developed at Perimeter, her father's old company. With time, she could hack it—and would enjoy every minute. But the sound of tires on gravel outside the window told her she had more immediate challenges.

You're busted, Shelby. Hook this thing back up and get ready to be adorable....

She had barely managed to replace the backing on the laptop and jump to her feet before Johnny strode in, a sexy smile on his face and an extra-large pizza box in his hand.

"Hey," he said, his eyes sweeping over her. "What happened to the makeover?"

"Hmm?" She kicked herself mentally for neglecting such an important detail. Now she really *was* busted, and had no choice but to either go on the offensive or throw herself on his mercy.

The solution came out of her mouth without any advance warning. "You had a satellite modem all this time? What other secrets have you been keeping from me?"

His eyes widened. "What?"

"You heard me. I'm really upset with you, Johnny. You lied to me. And worse, you made *me* lie to *you*."

He studied her for a long, drawn-out moment. Then he murmured, "How did I lie to you? I never said what kind of modem I had. It was irrelevant, because I had no intention of using it. It just came with the computer."

She forced herself not to back down. "Fine. You didn't lie to me. But you violated my trust when you took my cell phone out of my purse without telling me."

He tilted his head to the side, studying her again.

And again, Shelby struggled not to apologize. "I spent the whole time you were gone looking for a phone. The place is loaded with outlets, but not one damned phone anywhere! I even broke into the owner's closet. *That's* how crazy you're making me."

"You broke in?"

"That's right. All because you're a chauvinist. Your business is *so* important. Your emergencies are *so* vital. What about *my* emergencies? My sister is probably worried sick about me right now. *That's* an emergency. And if you don't let me use your phone right now to call her and tell her everything's okay," she warned, "then I'm going home tonight."

He licked his lips, but still didn't speak.

"There's something you don't know," she admitted unhappily. "I left Sabri—I mean, Briana—a message before we left. I promised to check in with her. And I specifically asked her to leave me messages on my cell. I know I shouldn't have done that. I'm sorry. But you just don't understand how close we are. She's probably worried sick by now. It's unnatural, asking us not to talk for a whole week. Even when we're not speaking to each other we talk every day. Or at least we send polite e-mails or something. You're being unreasonable. And it's making me do things that are a little unreasonable, too."

He hesitated, then a grin spread over his features. "I guess I really am in love with you."

"Pardon?"

"You lied to me. Pretended to crave pizza just to get rid of me. Broke into someone's private closet. And who knows what else? If that doesn't scare me away, I guess nothing will." His tone warmed. "You should have told me you left Briana that message. I don't want her to be worried. And I definitely don't want her blaming me. So let's give her a call."

"Really?" Shelby bit her lip, touched. "Thanks for understanding, Johnny."

"No problem." He set the pizza on the dining room table, but when she started to approach him, he held up a hand. "I want something in exchange. Something X-rated."

She laughed. "When have I denied you anything like that?"

"This is something else. A fantasy. And it's sort of time-sensitive, so it would be great if we could get to it before the call. I promise it'll only take a half hour or so."

"A time-sensitive fantasy?" she asked, intrigued.

His cheeks flushed to a gorgeous red. "When I was driving up here with the pizza, I started worrying about you. Thinking I shouldn't have left you alone. I thought to myself, what if some escaped prisoner breaks in and ties her up?"

"*This* is your fantasy? Me getting attacked by a maniac?"

"Actually, me rescuing you from a maniac. The idea is, I get here before he does anything but tie you up. Or maybe he just opened a couple of buttons on your blouse. Then I burst in, kick his ass, throw him out the door, and you're grateful."

She was warming to the idea. "I'd still be tied up."

"Yeah. Is that a problem?"

"Actually," she admitted, "it's my favorite part."

His tone grew hoarse. "Mine, too."

She felt a shiver of delight, knowing that he fantasized about saving her. She was glad he didn't know the truth—that she could kick the ass of any escaped convict who dared try to tie her to a chair. Someday she'd probably have to tell him about all that—about her father and her training—but for now, it was going to be fun to play damsel in distress.

"The pizza will get cold," she reminded him.

"We can warm it up later." His eyes twinkled. "Are you really okay with this?"

She nodded. "There's some rope in the drawer under the microwave. How do you want me? Like this?" She plopped herself down in a straight-backed chair and put her hands behind her.

"Yeah, just like that." He headed for the kitchen and was back quickly with the rope. First he tied her hands—not too tight, but enough to make it quite realistic. Then he tied her left ankle to one leg of the chair and her right to another.

"I'm already getting excited," she told him mischievously. "We should have tried this weeks ago."

He stood back and looked at her, his hands on his hips.

"Go outside. I'll start screaming, then you come in and untie me," she suggested. "Okay? Johnny?"

He was still looking at her, then to her surprise, he grabbed a second chair, placed it in front of her, then sat down. "We need to talk."

"Now? I'm all scared and distress-y. I need my big, strong man to rescue me."

He flushed. "Cut it out, Shelby. I'm serious. I need to tell you something. And you need to listen carefully. And try not to get upset. Okay?"

Little hairs on the back of her neck were standing straight up and she had to gulp before she could respond with a simple, muted, "I don't like this anymore. Untie me please."

"I will. After you've heard what I have to say."

"Untie me. *Now.* Or we're through. I mean it."

He rubbed his eyes with his palms, then gave her a half-hearted smile. "I know who you are, Michelle."

Oh, God...

"I'm not really an attorney," he continued. "I work for Theo Howell at Perimeter. I was sent to protect you, and that's what I've been doing. I'm sorry I lied to you about it, but it seemed like the best way to ensure your safety." He leaned forward and murmured, "I'm crazy about you—"

"Shut up!" She pulled back as fully as she could, given her predicament. "I don't know what you're talking about. I've never heard of anyone named Theo Howell. And if you're so hot to keep me safe, how come you're the one holding me prisoner?"

"I only tied you up because you threatened to leave. I'll untie you as soon as I'm done explaining things to you."

"Hurry up and finish then," she ordered. "But don't expect me to believe you."

"Shelby—"

"I can't believe I fell for this. For *you*. It makes me sick. *You* make me sick. And…" Her lip curled into a snarl. "If anything happens to my big sister—anything—I'll break your neck with my bare hands!"

"Sabrina is safe. So are you. But only because Theo and I took these drastic precautions."

"You must think I'm stupid."

"You're brilliant. And beautiful. The most amazing girl I've ever met. I knew you'd be special," he added reverently. "You're Sully's daughter after all—"

"I never heard of anyone named Sully."

"God, you're cute." He smiled, edging closer. "He'd be so proud if he could see you now. All tied up, but still defiant. Still trying to protect Sabrina. And Perimeter." His tone grew somber. "Three weeks ago the CIA intercepted a message meant for Adonis Zenner. It was garbled, but they got enough from it to know Zenner plans to kill you and your sister."

Her stomach knotted, but she managed to insist, "Those names mean nothing to me. Zenner? Sabrina? Are you mentally ill or something?"

"Theo sent me to Sabrina's house. To check on her. And to find a way to protect her. We knew it wouldn't be easy. Her first instinct would be to stay and fight. But even with all her training, she's no match for Zenner."

Shelby stared at him, her bravado crumbling rapidly. "You're talking about the day you came to her house? With the cat? Oh, my God! *You broke Zorro's leg?* You stupid jerk!" She struggled against her bonds. "We trusted you! We thought you were so sweet. But you broke his poor little leg—"

"His leg is fine. It always was. All we did was put a splint on it. So I'd have an excuse to visit her." He grabbed a tissue from a box on the credenza and wiped Shelby's damp face gently. "I swear, Shell. The cat's fine. And so is Sabrina."

"I want to see her. *Now.*"

"You can't. It's not safe."

"I don't understand."

"That's right. You don't understand. But once I explain, you'll see that everything we did—everything I did—I did to protect you and Sabrina. Just listen. Okay?"

"You have two minutes."

"Thanks." He gave her a rueful smile. "Theo sent me to Sabrina's house to find a way to protect her. Our best hope was that I could seduce her, using the cat as an entrée into her life. We knew she'd be tough. Suspicious. But I'm pretty good with women, so I decided to give it a shot. Unfortunately she was coming down with the flu, remember?"

Shelby rolled her eyes. "Otherwise you think you could have seduced her? Guess again. She's smarter than that. Smarter than me."

"It has nothing to do with brains. It's all about trust. Women trust me instinctively. It's a gift."

She wanted to protest, but knew it was true. Not just because she had fallen for him, but because Sabrina hadn't seen through his cat-hero act, either. Given her sister's suspicious nature, that was actually quite a coup on Johnny's part.

"Go on."

"She got sick. Then you came over, and when I met you…" His voice faltered. "I fell for you. I don't expect you to believe that right now—"

"Good, because I don't."

"I know you don't, but it's true. You really got to me.

So I called Theo and begged him to assign me to you instead of Sabrina. And he did. So I started hanging out with you. We thought that would keep you safe enough. Then we got word that Zenner was about to make his move, so I convinced you to run off with me."

"That's crazy. You just left Sabrina there? At Zenner's mercy?"

"No way. She's with another Perimeter employee. A friend of mine. His name's Zack Lansing, and he's the best. He won't let anything happen to her, believe me."

"Let me get this straight," she said, glaring in disbelief. "You're telling me some guy named Zack went to Sabrina's house and seduced her? Just like that? Give me a break. *I* may have been a pushover, but Breezie's a different story. She'd kill him and eat him."

"Don't be so sure. She's lonely as hell—"

"She is not!"

Johnny arched an eyebrow. "She almost fell for *me,* and I'm not even her type. I'm guessing she hasn't had a lover in a while, right? She's too suspicious of strangers to let a guy that close."

"Gee, I wonder why."

He smiled in acknowledgment of her point. "Anyway, we knew she'd get really suspicious if a second potential boyfriend showed up out of nowhere, so we decided Zack would just monitor her from a nearby house. Keep an eye out for Zenner. That's what he did until this weekend, when we heard Zenner was going to make his move. We really needed to get both of you out of town, to two separate locations. I took you first. Then, on Sunday, Zack took Sabrina."

"You're telling me my sister went into hiding? With some stranger?" Shelby gave a derisive snort. "Now I *know* you're lying. She'd never do that."

"You're right. She's so hung up on you—on keeping you safe—she resisted the idea. So Zack had to subdue her. For her own good. He didn't hurt her. Just drugged her enough to make her compliant."

"He drugged her? Oh, no, Johnny." Shelby's stomach knotted again. "Take me to her."

"Adonis is hunting the two of you. Our best strategy is to keep you separated. Theo won't take a chance on both of you getting killed."

"I have to talk to her. She must be worried sick."

Johnny hesitated, then admitted, "I can arrange for a very, very brief phone conversation."

"Really?" She bit her lip. "That's better than nothing, I guess."

"We need to go over a few things first, then we'll make the call. There's a lot you still don't know."

"It still doesn't make sense," she agreed. "Why didn't you and Uncle Theo just tell us the truth from the start?"

"You tell me," he replied.

She hesitated, then nodded slowly. There was a certain logic to just conning them. Even drugging them if necessary. She and Sabrina never would have agreed to being split up. She wasn't even sure they would have agreed to go into hiding at all, even if they were allowed to stay together. They had run away from Zenner once, and neither of them had ever really gotten over it. Would they have run again? Or would they have chosen to stand and fight?

"Do you see? Theo knows the two of you pretty well," Johnny said. "He predicted Sabrina would have to be restrained, but we were hoping—especially after you and I fell in love—"

"Wait!" She eyed him in disgust. "You're still calling it 'love'? I call it 'kidnapping.'"

His face fell. "I know you're upset—"

"I'm not upset. I'm pissed. And I'm losing patience with this stupid conversation. Get my sister on the phone. Now."

His eyes began to twinkle. "This is great. You're tied up—helpless—but still giving me orders."

"FYI, the charming-guy routine doesn't work anymore, so drop it."

He laughed. "Before you talk to Sabrina, you need to hear the rest of the story. I'll untie your hands though, as long as you promise not to do anything crazy. Adonis Zenner could show up at any minute."

"You think Zenner's nearby? But you left me alone for almost half an hour?" She arched an eyebrow. "Explain *that*."

"You weren't alone. Remember the gardener?"

"Ugh. Another lie. I suppose he isn't simpleminded?"

"Let's hope not. He protects us while we sleep. While we make love—"

"Stop that!" She tried to glare again, but had to admit her anger was fading. For all Johnny's lies, he apparently had been trying to keep her safe. That meant something, didn't it?

"Okay, untie me. And I'll listen to the rest of the story if you'll make it fast. But I need to talk to my sister soon."

Relief spread across his handsome face. "Great. We'll have pizza and some Chianti—"

"No alcohol."

"Okay. Iced tea then." He jumped up and headed for the kitchen, adding over his shoulder, "You won't believe what's been happening at Perimeter. The hunt for Zenner has almost bankrupted us. Theo had to sell his place in Monterey—"

"Oh, no! I loved that house!"

"Yeah." Johnny returned with two glasses of iced tea and some plates and napkins, all of which he set on the dining table. "It's been rough on the old guy. But then again, he never really got over your dad's death. None of us did, I guess."

Shelby sighed. "How well did you know him?"

"Sully? He recruited me when I was still in college. Trained me for five years. I loved the guy. Always will."

She bit her lip, touched by the obvious devotion in Johnny's tone. "That's sweet."

"I'm a very sweet guy," he reminded her mischievously. "I made you fall in love with me once, and I'll do it again. Only this time there won't be any secrets between us, so it'll be even better."

She knew it was true. She was already falling for him again. And assuming he kept his word and let her call Sabrina, what was the harm? He was obviously one of the good guys—her father's protégé, her uncle's trusted employee. A girl could do a lot worse.

"I'm going to untie you now. Behave," Johnny told her.

"Okay." She stretched her arms in relief as soon as they were free. "Five minutes, and then we call Sabrina. In the meantime, you talk, I'll eat. The pizza smells yummy."

"Right. Here…" He served her a huge slice, then set a glass of iced tea in front of her. "Enjoy."

She took a bite of her food, nodded in approval, then reached for the drink. "Did you put sugar in this?"

"Of course. I know how you like it."

Without warning, the hairs on the back of her neck started dancing again, and she pulled back her hand, then murmured, "Did you put sugar in yours?"

"I don't use it."

"I think I'll quit using it, too. As of right now." She reached across the table and took his glass, then arched an eyebrow in challenge. "Any problem with that?"

"No. I can get another one."

"Actually," she countered softly, "I'd like you to drink the one you served me."

She could see right away that she had hurt his feelings, and she almost told him to forget it. But God had installed that warning system on Sullivan necks for a reason, so she forced herself to be strong.

"After you've talked to Sabrina and Theo you'll trust me again," Johnny told her sadly. Then he lifted her glass and took a long, deep drink from it.

"Sorry, Johnny." She gave him a smile that she knew was tinged with love. Then she took a sip from the second glass.

She shuddered slightly, first from the bitter, sugarless taste, then from the sensation that spread through her lips and mouth, paralyzing them. Paralyzing her throat. Her chest. Her fingertips.

The glass slipped from her hand and crashed to the table, but she couldn't move out of the way and was barely conscious of the cold liquid splashing onto her arms.

She was only aware of the regret in Johnny's eyes, and the apology in his voice as he assured her, "I'm sorry, baby. You didn't leave me any choice. But don't worry. I'll make sure you don't remember a thing."

"Michelle Sullivan?"

"Yes?"

"Hey, baby. How do you feel?"

"I don't know." Shelby forced herself to focus on Johnny's voice, which seemed to be reaching out to her through a fog. She knew she should be upset. Perhaps even scared. But her mind was as numb and compliant as her body. All in all, not the worst feeling in the world. No feeling at all, in fact. "I'm fine, I guess."

"Good. I want to talk to you about something important. You need to concentrate. Can you do that for me?"

"Yes."

"Do you want me to call you Michelle? Or Shelby?"

"Shelby. That's my name now. And I like it better."

"I like it, too. So, Shelby, I want to talk to you about the message you left for your sister. The one you left when I was out of the room. While we were packing for this trip. Do you remember that?"

"Yes."

"Why didn't you tell me about it before today?"

"It was a secret."

"I don't want you to keep secrets from me. Is that clear?"

"Yes."

"Do you have any other secrets you haven't told me about?"

"Yes." She nodded slowly. "This isn't my natural hair color. I had it high-lighted."

His laugh was tinged with frustration. "I don't mean little secrets. I mean big ones. Important ones."

She squirmed. "About RAP, you mean?"

"I know all about that." He paused, then said gently, "Never mind. Let's get back to that message. Tell me what you said to Sabrina."

"I said I would call her even though I was supposed to be incommunicado."

"Did you say you'd call on a particular day?"

"No."

"Do you think she expected you to call every day?"

Shelby struggled for a perfect answer, settling for, "I think she expected me to *try* and call every day."

"Do you think she got worried when you didn't?"

"Sabrina is always worried about me. But I told her she should worry about herself, not me. Because I had a feeling something was wrong."

"You told her that?" he murmured.

"Yes."

"What else did you tell her?"

"I told her I was safe with you. That she was the one who should be careful. That she should call me and leave messages on my cell phone so I'd know she was okay."

"Damn." He cleared his throat. "What else did you tell her?"

"I told her you were great. Not like other guys."

"In what way?"

"That we didn't just have great sex. We had great talks, too, long into the night."

"That's good. So how long do you think she'd wait for you to call before she panics?"

"Sabrina never panics. Panic is an agent's worst enemy."

"Yeah, right. I forgot." He laughed again. "So? How long before she springs into action?"

"I don't know. Four days, I think. That's why I wanted to call her today for sure."

"Okay, good. Tell me what actions she'd take."

"She'd go to my house. To look for clues about where you and I went, so she could contact me."

"And she'd see the cell phone on the table. Would that reassure her or make her more worried?"

"I don't know," Shelby admitted. "Maybe she'd think it was romantic. But she's very suspicious. And protective. She likes you, but she knows I'd try to call her anyway, even without the cell phone."

"Okay. So what would she do next?"

"She'd try to find out about you. On the Internet. Or

through the bar association. Or she'd try to figure out which house your sister lived in."

"And if none of that worked? Would she go to Perimeter? Or to Theo Howell's house?"

"Uncle Theo sold his house."

"Right. Would she try to find him some other way?"

Shelby pursed her lips. "No. I don't think so."

"Why not?"

"I've wanted to call Uncle Theo a million times. When Sabrina had her tonsils out. When my car got broken into. Stuff like that. But she always said no. Even last year, when the principal of our school told the faculty about reports of a creepy guy approaching students on the way to school and trying to get them to do things—even then, Sabrina wouldn't go to Perimeter for help."

"Did they catch the guy?"

"We caught him ourselves."

Johnny whistled. "How'd you do that?"

"We knew one of the victims, so Sabrina got a great description. Then we called in sick and staked out the different routes until we spotted him. We followed him to his apartment, put a sack over his head so he couldn't see who we were, then we duct-taped him into a ball and locked him in the trunk of his car."

She took a deep breath, then continued. "I made a 9-1-1 call from a phone booth, pretending to be the frantic wife of a vigilante dad who had tracked the guy down. It was so much fun," she admitted. "The best day in the last five years. Until you showed up. Then every day was the best. Until today."

Johnny patted her arm. "Try not to think about that. Concentrate on Sabrina. You really think she won't ask Perimeter for help?"

"It's too dangerous. It might attract Adonis Zenner's attention. She'd just look for us herself."

"Even if she thinks you're in danger?"

Shelby considered the question carefully. "At worst, she'd think you were just after the money. We've got a lot of it in our trust fund, you know. She doesn't know you're the kind of guy who would tie me up, so she won't really think I'm in danger, physically."

"Okay, Shelby, listen to me. I want you to forget everything we've just said, okay? I want you to forget I ever tied you to the chair in the first place. When you think about this afternoon, I want you to remember that I woke you up from your nap and surprised you with a pizza. We made love, then you dozed off again. Is that clear?"

"Yes."

"I want you to forget you were worried about Sabrina. You weren't worried about her at all, because you and she had a long chat on Sunday."

Shelby winced. "We did?"

"Yes. I could see that you missed her, so I agreed that you could give her a quick call to tell her you didn't have your cell phone. Is that clear?"

"Yes."

"You two had a long talk, and you laughed a lot. She said she wasn't worried about you because she knew I'd take good care of you. Because she could see how much I love you. Is that clear?"

"Yes."

"Okay, let's see how well you've been paying attention. Tell me about the call you made to Sabrina on Sunday."

Shelby sighed, comforted by the memory of her lovely talk with her big sister. "We laughed a lot. And she said nice things about you."

"That's good, Shelby. Tell me what you did while I was getting the pizza."

"I slept."

"Did you touch my laptop?"

"No."

"Did you break into the owner's closet?"

"No. I was asleep."

"What happened when I got home?"

"We made love. Then I fell asleep again."

"That's right. You sleep a lot up here because of the altitude. And because I tire you out with all the lovemaking, right?"

"Yes."

"Good." He exhaled sharply. "I wasn't going to drug you any more today, but since I had to get in your head for this anyway, let's pick up where we left off. You were telling me about Uncle Theo's house. About the way you and Sabrina used to listen from the music room."

"Sabrina let me drill the holes."

"I'm sure you did a good job. And I'm sure you heard lots of secrets. That's what I want to talk to you about this evening," he added softly. "Uncle Theo's secrets."

Chapter 4

"Sabrina? Are you ready to take a break yet? You've been studying those files for two hours straight. Marietta and I were hoping for a chance to visit for a while."

Sabrina looked up from her files and gave Theo an absentminded smile. "I need to learn everything I can about John Derringer. I'm really glad you kept such good records of his exploits." She rocked back in the leather desk chair she had commandeered behind Theo's desk. "It's hard to reconcile this criminal with the sweet, innocent guy who saved my cat and seduced my sister."

"As Zack said, we were all fooled."

She nodded, remembering the details of John Derringer's heists. Two burglaries a year—always for a cool million dollars each. Not one had ever been solved. And in between jobs, he always disappeared completely. "He must be pretty smart. They've never gotten close to catching him."

Theo shrugged. "He's never really been a priority with the government. Notice who his victims are—mob bosses and drug dealers. That makes him clever, not smart. He picks victims that no one will shed a tear over. Never touches a decent citizen. And never dares to come near a Perimeter client. That's how he succeeds. By preying on other criminals."

"Sounds like a risky strategy," Sabrina countered. "Don't the mobsters go after him?"

"If he took more, maybe they would. But a million is usually small change for Derringer's victims. And as tough as they may be, they're amateurs. They provide their own security, making the heists a walk in the park for a trained professional."

"Trained by Sully Sullivan himself," she mused. "It must have upset Dad to know Johnny was using his tricks to commit crimes."

"Sully had a soft spot for John. For all the young men in that group of recruits. Speaking of which…" Theo tossed a new handful of folders onto the desk. "Since you're determined to read yourself into a coma, here's more material. I had these couriered over from the office in San Jose."

"Johnny's employment records? Great!" Sabrina grabbed the top one eagerly. "Hey…" She scrutinized the label in confusion. "This is Zack's."

Theo pulled up a chair and sat across the desk from her. "You would have asked for it eventually, believe me. There were six young men in that group. Your father was recruiting a new crew. John was a part of that, but you'll want to see how they all interrelated."

"Okay." She was secretly pleased that she'd be able to find out what was so special about Zack Lansing that he had caught her father's eyes, earning himself the honor of being trained by the best. Still, Johnny was the primary concern, so she set Zack's file aside and dug through the stack until she'd found the one marked Derringer, John.

Flipping it open, she almost groaned out loud at the photograph stapled to the inside cover. As innocent as he had seemed on her front porch at age thirty-two, Johnny had been even more adorable—more sincere and sweet and harmless in appearance—in college. A broad, confident smile with overtones of mischief; sparkling blue eyes that gazed directly into the camera as though daring it to resist him; and a square jaw to anchor the entire effect.

"You bastard," she murmured under her breath. "What do you want from us?"

"He wants revenge."

She was surprised by the certainty in Theo's tone. "For what? We never did anything to him. *He* hurt *us* by screwing up that job, right?"

Theo's gaze dipped for a moment, then he rallied and looked directly into Sabrina's eyes. "He blamed your father for sending him to the Canary Islands on a job he wasn't qualified to handle. Or at least, that's my best guess for what's going on here. Otherwise, why target us after all these years?"

"Zack thinks Shelby knows something valuable. Something Derringer needs for one of his criminal schemes."

"I hope that's true." Theo hesitated, then shrugged again. "Study the files, then decide for yourself. I've racked my brain about this. But there's nothing. Nothing you girls could possibly know. Sully kept you out of the business. Sure, he trained you, but he also sheltered you. Never shared specific details about our operations with you. That was his way of protecting you."

Sabrina nodded. "Except for you, and sometimes Paul Hanover, we didn't really have much contact with Perimeter personnel. It's odd, isn't it? Such a huge part of our lives for so long, yet in some ways, it was a million miles away. And these last five years, it's been even more distant."

"According to Connor's reports, you kept up with your skills."

"I tried. I always thought the phone would ring at any minute with news that Adonis had been arrested. And then…well, then we could come back. I wanted to be ready. So, yes, I kept up, mostly with the target shooting and judo. The other stuff—the habits, the awareness— probably suffered the most." She exhaled in self-disgust. "As your guy Zack would say, I fell for the oldest trick in the book. And I let a creep like Derringer seduce Shelby right under my nose. So much for instinct and observation."

Theo smiled. "As Zack would also say, we all fell for Derringer's act. And meanwhile, I can't believe twenty years of training in observation and deduction have gone to waste. Let's put it to a test, shall we? Close your eyes."

Sabrina hesitated, but only for a second before complying. "Okay. Now what?"

"You've spent some time in this room. There are at least three things different from the years when you used to visit. See if you can name one."

Sabrina bit her lip, touched at Theo's attempt to reenact one of her father's games. "You're so sweet. Okay, let's see. The fox-and-hounds painting over the fireplace used to be in the hall, right? And it smells different in here. Gardenias, maybe? Something like that."

"Sebastian planted them two years ago," Theo confirmed. "Anything else?"

She nodded. "Obviously the computer stuff is new. And

the sound and video systems, although they're in the same cabinet the old setup was in. I remember that the floor was carpeted back then—that's a huge change. I love the wood floors much better, by the way. And this chair is new, which is great because the old one used to squeak. And the French doors to the atrium were white, now they're stained, right? And the chessboard's gone. So is the cuckoo clock. But I love the new grandfather clock in the corner. And let's see...."

She pursed her lips. "The frames on your diplomas and degrees are different, right? They weren't matted before, and the frames were wood, not brass. And speaking of frames—" She opened one eye to tease him. "Don't get me started on that shelf filled with photographs. I didn't think there were that many pictures of Dad in the whole world."

Theo laughed. "It's safe to say you haven't lost your touch. I couldn't have come up with half as many, and I made the changes myself! Sully would be so proud."

"Remember the quizzes he used to give us? Right in the middle of a meal at a restaurant?" She smiled at the memory of her father's favorite game in which they could earn ice cream for dessert if they could close their eyes and describe someone or something. The man at the next table. Or the lobby. Or the type of lighting. Whatever captured his fancy.

"It was so much fun. And between Shell and me, we could always do it."

"That was the most interesting part of the training," Theo agreed. "He never pitted you girls against each other."

"We were naturally competitive to an extent, but you're right. He always tried to emphasize the team aspect. And as my hypnosis session pointed out, he always stressed my responsibility to look out for her. My mission," she added, trying not to think about how badly she had failed.

"As I recall, he also stressed *her* responsibility to do what you told her to do. I saw an example of that the night Sully died. She would have gone after Zenner if you hadn't instructed her to cooperate with RAP."

Sabrina leaned back in the chair and closed her eyes again. "Five years of hiding. Waiting. And now she's in danger anyway. I almost wish we had just gone after him that night after all." Leaning forward suddenly, she dared to insist, "I would have found him by now. He'd either be dead or in prison. Or I'd be dead."

"You would have found him by now," Theo agreed.

"So? What went wrong? Dad's crew—Paul Hanover especially—were well-trained. And even Zack seems pretty…well, focused. And dedicated to Dad. I understand he was only twenty-seven or so back then, but it's been five years! Why hasn't he found Zenner?"

"Probably because I wouldn't let him look."

Sabrina sat back, stunned. *"What?"*

Theo didn't reply right away. Instead he seemed to be giving her a chance to recover. Then he explained. "When word came that Adonis had killed Sully, Zack went crazy. He wanted to go after him with guns blazing, but I convinced him it would put you and Michelle into danger. I made him promise to wait until you were safely in RAP's care. That night, you became civilians. My hope was that Adonis would respect that status. And he has. It's been something of a truce. But I was concerned that if Perimeter kept the vendetta alive, Adonis might just decide to go after you girls anyway. So I decided not to dedicate any Perimeter resources to the search."

"I can't believe what I'm hearing. After all Dad did for this company…."

"I wanted Zenner punished as much as anyone," Theo

assured her. "But I knew Sully would want me to put your safety first."

"The only reason we went into RAP in the first place was so you could focus all your energy on catching Adonis!" She caught her temper again and murmured, "All this time. Wasted. I can't believe Paul Hanover and the rest of Dad's crew went along with it."

"They agreed with me. The only one who fought me was Zack. He was so furious—well, let's just say, his temper was much, much worse five years ago. He almost quit, but he's got a loyal streak. He agreed to stay on for a few months, to help get the company back on its feet. It was in shambles, not just financially, but emotionally. And our reputation had been dealt a huge blow with Sully's death. How could we protect our clients when we couldn't even protect our own personnel?"

Sabrina forced herself to see the situation from Theo's point of view. "It's hard to know what Dad would have wanted. But he loved this company—"

"He loved his daughters. Keeping you safe was his first priority, and it was mine, too. If there had been a way to go after Zenner without endangering you, I would have done it, even if it signed the company's death warrant." Removing his glasses for a moment, Theo rubbed his eyes wearily. "For what it's worth, the CIA did what they could. And we cooperated with them fully. But Adonis went underground. There were even rumors that he had retired. They couldn't afford to make him their top priority forever."

"So five years later, he's still out there." She pursed her lips. "How often does an assassin like him make a hit? Like, once a year?" Before Theo could answer, she murmured, "It's funny, isn't it? I heard about his father, and then Adonis, all the time I was growing up, but until the

Canary Islands incident, I never heard of them bothering our clients."

"Your father always suspected that Pluto planted the bomb at the peace summit the day he and I first met. But once Sully came to work for me, the Zenners never dared bother us again. Not until the Canaries. And to answer your other questions, it seems to me like they came out from under their rock about once every two years or so."

"It's strange they left us alone so much. I mean, I know Dad was the best, but doesn't that mean we also had the most attractive clients? The best guarding the best."

"We always kept our client list small," Theo explained. "That was your father's design. When we grew, it was in the research and development area. And troubleshooting for other security providers who used our products. That left plenty of non-Perimeter clients for the Zenners to hit. Your father's mystique kept Perimeter safe."

"And your refusal to go after Adonis keeps him safe," she added, still sick over the pass that had been given to her father's murderer. Then she straightened her shoulders. "As bad as Derringer sounds, I'm glad it's him, not Adonis, who has Shell."

Theo seemed about to respond, then just shrugged instead.

"You don't agree? You think Derringer's just as dangerous?" Sabrina eyed him intently. "Something's bothering you? Tell me what it is."

He cleared his throat. "There's something Zack doesn't know. I've kept it from him because it would send him into a rage. Maybe even make him do something crazy, and endanger you girls in the process. But you have a right to know it, if I can trust you with the information—"

"Uncle Theo!" She leaned toward him, impatient. "What is it?"

Her host sighed. "There's a possibility—slim, but nevertheless, a possibility—that Derringer was involved in your father's murder."

"What?" She stared in dismay. "It was Adonis Zenner. Not Derringer."

"The bomb had all of Zenner's trademarks. Plastic explosives, braided wiring, remote detonator, backup timer. But John could have duplicated Zenner's style. Or he could have been collaborating with him."

"Why would he collaborate with the man who ruined his career?"

"Who knows? Maybe the assassination in the Canary Islands wasn't a mistake on Derringer's part. Maybe he and Pluto were coconspirators. If so, Derringer would have been terrified that Sully might find out. Once Sully killed Pluto, Derringer could be next. So he made it look like Pluto's son killed Sully. Or worse, he helped Adonis get revenge."

"Wow."

"This is ninety-nine percent speculation, of course. The only link the CIA found between Derringer and the murder was that Derringer was in San Francisco the day before Sully was killed. Airport tapes showed him arriving from Paris. He was traveling under a fake passport."

"They were looking at those tapes to find Adonis, and found Johnny instead?"

"Exactly. Still, it proves nothing. The CIA didn't follow up on it for that reason. But it has always stuck with me. Such a coincidence, don't you think?"

She remembered Johnny's sincere smile and shuddered. "If it's true—if he and the Zenners have been partners in the past—Adonis could be part of Shelby's kidnapping. Which means Zack needs to know about this."

Theo shook his head. "You were right about him, Breezie. That temper is his downfall. And ours, too, if we're not careful. It was your father's only reservation about him. Hot blood, Sully called it."

"Maybe a little hot blood is what we need to fight such cold-blooded monsters," Sabrina said softly. "I think we should tell him."

"Tell him what? My suspicion is probably unfounded." Theo stood and began to pace. "You don't realize how close those young men were. As angry and disappointed as Zack was when John disappeared and started pulling jobs, I think he still has a soft spot for him. Like the prodigal brother or whatever. But if he ever suspected John hurt Sully—well, the sense of betrayal would send him into a rage. We can't afford that. We need him to focus on saving Michelle, not avenging Sully." Stopping in front of Sabrina's chair, he rested his hands on her shoulders. "Trust me on this, honey. I know him pretty well."

Her gut told her it was a mistake. Flaws or not, Zack was their advance man on this mission. He needed every scrap of intel available. If Zenner really was involved, that added to the list of potential motives behind the kidnapping, not to mention the list of memories Derringer might be trying to access in Shelby's mind.

"Sabrina? You do trust me, don't you?"

"Of course!" She stood, then touched his cheek in apology. "It's not a question of that. I promise."

"You had me worried. After what you said under hypnosis…"

"Hmm?"

"When Zack asked if you trusted me, you said 'sometimes.'"

"Did I?" She winced. "Who knows what I meant by that? Meanwhile, would I have come here if I didn't trust you? I'm putting Shelby's future in your hands. That says it all." On impulse, she gave him a hug. "Okay?"

"I'm glad to hear it," he admitted, removing his glasses again and wiping his eyes with the back of his hand. "If you really feel that way, there's something I'd like to try. Something that might help us find Shelby."

"Anything."

"Good." He put his glasses back on and smiled encouragingly. "I'd like to hypnotize you again."

"Hmm?" She tried for a neutral expression, although the suggestion struck her as odd. Almost creepy.

"I have a lot of respect for Zack, but he's young. And his training was cut short by Sully's death. I saw your father in action more often, and I have a feeling my technique is a little more sophisticated."

"Really?" Sabrina licked her lips, trying to remember if Theo had ever really been involved in the field operations side of Perimeter. According to her father, it had been a fairly clean divide. Theo handled the business end, investing Perimeter dollars shrewdly, monitoring expenses, payroll, et cetera. Sully handled everything else.

Still, there was a lot she didn't know. And there was no reason for Theo to lie, was there?

Which brought them back to his original question: did she trust this man—this old friend of the family—or not?

It's not a question of that, she told herself warily. *It's just plain creepy. Because of those stories they told you about DT3. Because you know Johnny's out there, alone with Shell, playing with her head. You're just spooked. But this is different. This is Uncle Theo! You let that hothead Zack do it, didn't you? So why not Theo?*

"What exactly would you be doing?" she asked, still trying not to show her reluctance.

Theo smiled. "I'd like to do a progression. Zack should have done one. It basically involves walking you through the various stages of your life. Asking questions that might prompt a memory. It's similar to what Derringer is probably doing, although of course we won't be using DT3, so our work will be mild and noncoercive in comparison."

"But Derringer knows what he's looking for. You don't."

"It's a long shot," Theo agreed. "The theory is that the memories that come most easily to you are either very strong, or unresolved, or recently evoked."

"Recently evoked? You mean, the memory that Johnny tried to get from me might still be fresh in my subconscious mind? That makes sense, I guess." She coughed lightly. "Why didn't you tell Zack to do that?"

"I thought he'd do it on his own. And once he didn't, I was reluctant to criticize him. He already feels like I'm second-guessing him too much."

"That's true," she admitted.

"And quite frankly, I thought you were anxious for him to leave. There seemed to be a lot of friction between you. Not that I blame you for that. He made some hurtful remarks when you first arrived."

"I'm beginning to understand his frustration with me," she said, choosing her words carefully. "Shell and I took the money and the heart out of the company. And because of us, Zack couldn't hunt for Adonis. That would be hard on any guy, much less a hot-blooded one."

"I'm glad to see there are no hard feelings." Theo smiled. "He's been a lifesaver for me and for the company. Single-handedly put us back on our feet. And then he got us a multibillionaire client with a limitless security budget."

Sabrina nodded. "Some king in Texas, right?"

"How did you know?"

She bit back a smile, remembering that Theo hadn't heard about the music room caper yet. "Zack mentioned it before he left. Something about a birthday party?"

Theo nodded. "Once a year, King Dominik gives his son Nikolo a party. Glitterati galore. And there's always a political aspect because each year rumors circulate that the king is going to relinquish the throne to the prince as a present."

"That's some present." Sabrina rolled her eyes. "Does the title mean anything, or is it just ceremonial?"

"Dominik has been happy in exile. But Nikolo is different. The monarchists in Delphinia are hopeful that he might want to return and claim his so-called rightful place as head of the country."

"Who rules it now?"

"The military. It was a popular coup fifteen years ago, but according to our sources, the monarchists have a fair amount of support these days. In any case, Dominik tells Zack that the rumors of his abdication are completely unfounded. Still, the possibility of an assassination attempt, while remote, is something Zack needs to treat seriously."

"Some client," Sabrina marveled. "Dad would have loved that kind of challenge."

"So?" Theo eyed her hopefully. "Shall we give the progression theory a try?"

"I'm a little tired," she hedged. "Do you mind if we wait till after dinner? I'd like to unwind a little. And maybe watch that video. But after that, sure. Why not?"

He seemed about to argue, then he nodded instead. "We'll have more success if you're rested and well-fed. Why don't you give your eyes a break and go upstairs to bed for a while?"

"Good idea." She gathered up the new files. "I'll take these just in case I can't sleep." She smiled as she reviewed the names on the labels. Zack. Johnny. Connor. Plus three other males: Derek, Carlos and Roger. The next generation of Perimeter.

"Uncle Theo? Is Paul Hanover still with the company? I'm guessing he isn't, or you would have put him in charge instead of Zack." She frowned as she added, "The whole crew can't be gone, can they?"

Theo cleared his throat. "You remember they were down to four men even before your father died. And most of them were talking about retirement. That's the reason he was training Zack and John and the others."

"So Paul retired? Was he really that old?"

"Paul and his family went into RAP, just like you and Michelle. His wife was sure Zenner would target them next, since he was your father's right-hand man."

"Wow. Do you think they were really in danger?"

"No. Paul was miserable over quitting, but she gave him an ultimatum—her or Perimeter."

"That sounds like Marilyn Hanover, all right," Sabrina admitted, remembering the spoiled, demanding woman well. The day she had married Paul Hanover—a widower twice her age—had been the day Sully's close friendship with Paul had become strained and formal.

"Where do they live now?"

"He killed himself a few months ago, Breezie. I'm sorry."

"Oh, Uncle Theo." She sank into her chair again. "How awful."

"He left a letter saying he was torn between his old life and his love for Marilyn, and couldn't take it anymore."

"Ouch. I almost feel sorry for her. Do we know what happened to her?"

"She stayed in her new identity. That's all I know."

Sabrina pursed her lips. "That's weird, don't you think? Maybe I should talk to her."

"I have no idea where she is, or what name she uses. That was part of the protocol for RAP."

"But you knew everything about us?"

Theo smiled. "That's because they subcontracted your security to Perimeter. We made them one of those offers they couldn't refuse, namely, that we'd do it for free."

"Another way I almost bankrupted the company?" She shook her head. "I'm so sorry about Mr. Hanover. What about the rest of Dad's crew?"

"They got other jobs. Consulting, mostly. They could have retired—your father made sure they put money away for all those years—but like you said, they were still in their early fifties."

"They weren't worried about Zenner coming after them though?"

"No. It was a long shot, even for Hanover."

"I guess I can't blame Marilyn for being afraid. But staying in RAP seems extreme."

Theo arched an eyebrow. "Interesting subject, actually. What are your plans? After we find Michelle, I mean."

She smiled, grateful to him for assuming they would find her sister. "If she's healthy and unharmed, I guess we'll see. But if she's not, that's another story." Taking a deep breath, she added wearily, "I can't think about any of that right now."

"Go upstairs. Try and get some sleep."

"Okay, thanks. I'll come down around five-thirty or so for the video. And after that, we'll have dinner."

He laughed. "Dinner and a movie. My first date in months."

She laughed, too, then stood and hugged the files close to herself as she hurried out of the room, telling him silently, *If your dinner-and-a-movie dates end with putting the poor girl in a trance, it's no wonder you haven't had any recently.*

She wasn't sure why it bothered her so much, but it did. Theo had been against the hypnosis idea completely at the beginning. And then he had cautioned Zack to make it quick. Now suddenly he wanted to probe her mind in detail?

Once in the guest room, she dumped the files on the bed. Then she dug in her suitcase until she found her father's bag of tricks. Switching on the global positioning device, she smiled to see that it was working perfectly.

Zack was a tiny red blip on the screen, and as she enlarged his location on the map, she could see that he was just outside Stockton. Rummaging further, she found her cell phone and Zack's business card, and dialed him without giving herself time to change her mind.

"Zack Lansing."

"Hi, Zack. It's Sabrina Sullivan."

"Hey, what's up? Did you hear from your sister?"

"No." Sabrina sighed. "Any news on your end?"

"Not much. What's wrong?"

"Nothing. I just have a question. About Paul Hanover."

"Oh…" He coughed. "Theo told you about that?"

"Yes. You don't happen to know the new identity of his wife, do you? Or what town she's in?"

"Yeah. I've got all that."

"I was thinking we should talk to her."

"Right. It's on my list."

Sabrina was impressed. "I want to be there when you question her."

Zack was silent for a moment, then he said, "That's not prudent."

"I met hcr a couple of times. I'm hoping she'll relate to my dilemma. My concern for Shelby."

"We'll see."

She knew he was just placating her, but decided to let it go. For now. "Hey, Zack? Can I ask you something?"

"Sure."

"First you have to promise not to tell Theo."

"Okay, shoot."

"Wait. You also have to agree not to overreact. Or to read anything in to this at all."

"Why don't I just agree to let you cut my balls off? Wouldn't that be simpler?"

Sabrina laughed. "So much for not overreacting."

To her surprise, he laughed, too. "What's the problem?"

"It's not a problem. Just an odd thing. I'd like to get your take on it." She took a deep breath. "Theo wants to hypnotize me again."

"He *what?*"

Sabrina bit back another laugh. "So? It seems odd to you, too?"

"Tell me what he said."

"Well… How can I put this delicately? He thinks you weren't thorough enough. He wants to try something called progression theory."

"Screw that. It's a waste of time. You can tell him I said so."

"Except I don't want him to know we talked about it," she reminded him. "His feelings were a little hurt by what I said under hypnosis, that I only trust him sometimes. So now, if I don't let him do it, he'll think it's because I really don't trust him."

"So? You agreed to let him?"

"Yes. I put him off till after dinner. But then I guess I'll do it."

"After dinner? Like, three hours from now? Good. Stick with that plan. I'll take care of everything in the meantime."

His words were accompanied by the sound of tires squealing, and Sabrina's gaze went to the GPS screen, where to her disbelief she saw that he was now headed south, back toward Monterey.

"I didn't mean for you to turn around!"

"How did you know I turned around?"

"The screeching wheels were a dead giveaway."

"You've got your dad's hearing," he congratulated her.

"I mean it, Zack. I don't need to be rescued from my own uncle. I just wanted a second opinion."

"Fine. My opinion is, you're stubborn." He chuckled. "I was debating whether to come back anyway. For another reason. So just stick to your plan till I get there."

She grumbled her consent and started to say goodbye when he interrupted her with, "Hey, Sabrina?"

"Yes?"

"Don't drink anything but clear liquids till I get there. Okay?"

"Okay," she murmured. Then she disconnected the call and stared at the little red dot working its way relentlessly back toward the Howell mansion.

In a strange way, it made her feel better. Not because he was coming back, but because he had cautioned her about the liquids. Didn't that mean he was suspicious of Theo's motives and boundaries, too?

Flipping open Zack's personnel file, she studied his photograph with interest. He was young in the picture— probably twenty-three at the most. From his start date, she could see that he had worked for Perimeter for just about ten years. Five with Sully. Five without.

Unlike John Derringer's file, this one did not contain a Perimeter job application. Instead it held a photocopy of Zack's application to work for the CIA. Sabrina assumed there was a story there somewhere. Thumbing through it, she located the spot where Zack was asked why he wanted to work for the agency. His answer had two parts: to serve his country and to follow in his father's footsteps.

She scanned the rest of the file until she found the spot where he was asked about other family members. Both parents were listed as deceased. No siblings were listed.

It rang a bell with her, and she reached for Johnny's file, where his Perimeter application asked many of the same questions. And the answers were surprisingly the same: an only child. Specifically, an orphaned one. But in the Reason for Applying section, Johnny hadn't written about service to his country or honoring his elders. Instead he had scribbled, "All the fun of espionage with a better retirement plan."

She bit back a smile. That sounded so much like the playful guy who had returned her cat to her one moonlit night three weeks earlier. Then she reminded herself that that "playful guy" was holding her baby sister hostage, and she shook her head.

He won't hurt her. If he wanted to, he would have done it right away. Plus, he just isn't the type...

Unless, of course, Theo was right and John Derringer was her father's murderer.

She surprised herself by actually dozing off for an hour or so, awakening in time for her "date" with Theo. Marietta had set out some hors d'oeuvres along with a decanter of red wine and two graceful goblets on a tray table near the leather sofa in the study, and Sabrina tried not to notice the rich, dark, DT3-masking color of the beverage. Instead she wandered over to the bookcase that housed Theo's collection of framed photos.

Virtually every shot contained Sully's smiling face, sometimes alone, sometimes with one or both daughters. Sabrina's favorite was a picture with five-year-old Shelby in the foreground building a sandcastle on the beach near Theo's house, while Sabrina fetched a bucket of water from the ocean in the background under Sully's careful supervision. She remembered that day distinctly, because they had gone to the cemetery first to visit her mother's grave on the first anniversary of her death.

"There aren't any pictures of Mom," she murmured without thinking.

"Pardon?"

She felt her cheeks warm. "I was just thinking of something Zack said before he left. That he hadn't ever seen a picture of my mother. And I guess that's true, although I'm surprised Dad didn't have one on his desk at work."

"He had one for years," Theo assured her. "I don't remember how it was at the end. It's not like Sully spent much time in his office in any case."

"True." She smiled, remembering how dynamic her father had been. Then she remembered Paul Hanover's suicide message—that he wasn't meant for a desk job. "He and Paul just loved to go out on jobs. I wonder what would have happened if they'd lived. Would they ever have retired?"

"I doubt it." Theo cleared his throat. "I'm sorry I don't have a picture of her, Breezie. You know how it was with Sully. Until she died, he never once brought you girls, or Jenny, to this house. He wanted to keep business separate from family life, in large part because *she* was so intent on that."

"I didn't mean it to sound like a complaint," she assured him. "You're absolutely right. Until the day Mom died, I barely knew you. And I guess you didn't know her, either."

"I knew she made your father happy. That made her a princess in my book. And then she gave me two beautiful nieces. It's unforgivable that I don't have at least one picture of her. I'm going to remedy that right away."

"How?"

His brown eyes began to twinkle. "All of your father's things—and yours and Michelle's, as well—are stored in my garage. You're not the only one who looked forward to the day you'd leave RAP and come back where you belonged. I kept everything for you. I'm sure there are dozens of beautiful pictures of Jenny out there."

Sabrina resisted an impulse to dash out the door toward the garage, reminding herself that she didn't really know if she was "home" yet. If Shelby was unharmed, it was possible they might go back to Sacramento. To teach. To resume their lives as Briana and Shelby York.

"Sabrina?"

"Hmm?"

"I don't blame you for being uneasy about the hypnosis. Not after what Derringer did to you. So…" Theo exhaled sharply, then opened a drawer in his desk and pulled a slender black bottle into view. "I want you to use this on me."

She accepted it gingerly. "Is this…?"

"DT3. The last dose I own. I'm not allergic, so it will give you an idea what Michelle is going through. And you can ask me anything you want. Anything."

Embarrassed over having made him feel the need to make such an offer, and ashamed that she had called Zack about it, Sabrina stuffed the bottle back into his hand. "This isn't necessary, Uncle Theo. I trust you."

"If you change your mind—"

"I won't."

"Well, then…" He returned the bottle to the drawer, then picked up a DVD and inserted it into his home theater system. "Time for the show. But first I'll pour us some of that wine."

"That sounds good, except red gives me headaches," Sabrina told him, trying for a casual tone, again embarrassed by her persistent distrust of everyone and everything. Her father had taught her to be careful, not paranoid. But to be fair, Adonis Zenner and John Derringer had given her reason to be extra cautious, at least until Shelby was safe again.

"I'm sure I have something you'll like," Theo was assuring her. "Excuse me just a moment."

She shook her head as she watched him leave the room. How silly to think he would slip her a hypnotropic mickey, knowing she'd then vomit all over his new hardwood floor! But Zack had had the same concern, hadn't he? Which only meant they *both* should be ashamed of themselves.

Still, she was quick to accept the glass of pale gold Chardonnay that Theo brought her. And to compensate for her disloyalty, she gave him a quick peck on the cheek when she joined him on the sofa.

He used one remote to dim the lights, another to start the video. The opening scenes brought a lump to Sabrina's throat as scores of mourners, dressed in black, filed past a small altar containing a poster of Sully Sullivan's handsome, reassuring face.

Too late, she remembered that there was no coffin or ash-filled urn. Zenner's bomb hadn't just killed her father, it had obliterated him from existence.

Or maybe Johnny had done the honors.

"Who are all these people, Uncle Theo?" she murmured.

"More than half are from the CIA. Either they knew him way back when, or they attended classes he taught at Perimeter. Remember, product development was big for us for a number of years. Sully trained hundreds of people in government and private enterprise on the use of our products."

The video photographer seemed intent upon capturing every face in the crowd, and Sabrina finally realized why that was. "This is surveillance footage?"

"In part," Theo said with an apologetic smile. "Some of us thought Adonis might be bold enough to show up. In disguise, of course. And we wanted to be ready."

"Good idea. Hey, there's Zack! Oh, Lord, look how young he was." She bit her lip, touched by the defiant jaw and dark glare that were belied by red-rimmed eyes. But no five-o'clock shadow, which along with his sharply pressed black suit told her something else. His respect for Sully really did know no bounds.

"Another reason for the comprehensive photography was that I thought—and some of the company men agreed—that John Derringer might have the nerve to show his face. We weren't after him per se, but if he had shown up, believe me, we would have nabbed him."

"Johnny spent five years training with Dad before that assignment in the Canary Islands went haywire. Don't you think it's possible he was grieving, too? I mean, assuming he didn't plant the bomb."

Theo gave her a surprised look. "There was a time when I would have thought that was possible. That was before he drugged your sister and kidnapped her."

"Right." She cursed herself for having said something

so stupid. Then she straightened a bit, realizing that the formal ceremony was about to begin.

"You had it outside? Not in a church?"

"Does that bother you, Sabrina? He wasn't particularly religious—"

"No. It's fine," she murmured, although in her heart she was disappointed. She had pictured a huge cathedral filled with statues and incense and sobs that reverberated from the rafters.

But this was nice, too.

"It was Zack's idea to have it outside," Theo insisted weakly. "In case we had to fire a weapon."

"Good thinking," she admitted. "It was absolutely a good choice. But you're wrong about Dad, you know. He was very religious."

"I never saw that side of him."

Sabrina shrugged, remembering that she had seen it most clearly when her mother was still alive. But even after the automobile accident that had claimed Jenny Sullivan's life, Sully had worshiped in his own way. If nothing else, he had been quick to remind his daughters that miracles surrounded them. One simply had to be humble enough to recognize them.

On the screen, Theo Howell walked up to a podium then looked out over a sea of mourners seated in white, wooden, folding chairs. He looked haggard yet also commanding, and Sabrina bit her lip, in awe of the simple truth that kept slipping from her mind—that Theo had regarded Sully as his brother, friend and godsend, and had been truly devastated, spiritually and emotionally, by his death.

"Oh, Uncle Theo, I'm so sorry," she whispered, cuddling closer to him. "I wish I had been there."

"In spirit, you were there. So was little Michelle," he said, his voice choked with emotion.

On screen, he began to speak. "Thank you all for coming. Wherever Sully is, he knows we're here. And he appreciates it. He always appreciated us, didn't he? I think that's the reason we loved him the way we did. Because he made us feel as though we mattered, to him and to the world. This brave man, who knew no bounds, inspired each of us to test our own limits. And we did so in hopes that he would be proud of us. Proud to call us his friends."

Tears streamed down Sabrina's cheeks as she acknowledged the truth of Theo's words. To earn her father's pride—to know he admired or respected her. Wasn't that *her* reason for being? Her motivation in everything that counted? Her singular focus, no matter the cost?

On screen, Theo's voice was gently serenading the crowd. "We each have our Sully Sullivan story to tell, and I hope each of you will come to this podium and regale us with yours. Mine is a rather simple one, and one most of you know already." He took a deep breath. "I inherited a burglar alarm company, which I tried to transform into a full-service security company called Perimeter. I thought I had succeeded beautifully. We had the best technology money could buy. We had terrific personnel. And thanks to the uncertainty of the times, we had boundless opportunity. But we didn't have a heart. We didn't have a soul. And we didn't have a genius.

"What we *did* have was the Venice peace summit. Thanks to my efforts and the mediocrity of our competition, Perimeter was awarded a contract to protect the greatest diplomats of our time. We devoted endless hours to the task. We tried to think of everything. But at 10:00 p.m. on the second day of the peace talks, we came face-to-face

with our humanity. Some of you were there that night—
the night a sophisticated bomb was discovered in the boiler
room below the conference hall. The timer was set for ten
minutes. There was no time to evacuate. We just stood
there, knowing that disaster was upon us. We were dead.
That was a forgone conclusion. But the future of the world
was dead, too. And that made us stand as if rooted to the
floor. Even if escape had been possible, I doubt if any of
us would have run away that night. We needed to stand
there. To bear witness to the end."

Theo's eyes began to shine. "Then a young man in
baggy khakis strode into the room. He was six foot six, but
he seemed much taller. Maybe it was the cocky smile on
his face, or the irreverent twinkle in his blue eyes. He was
a kid—twenty-five if he was a day. And he strode right up
to me and said, 'Are you in charge?'

"And I said, 'Does it matter?'

"And then Sully said—" Theo's voice became choked
with sobs—" 'Don't worry, buddy. This is the reason I get
up in the morning.'"

Tears were streaming down the eulogist's face and Sabrina was openly sobbing. Then she looked over at Theo
on the couch beside her and ached with compassion, seeing how truly devastated he was at reliving these strange,
life-defining events.

Then the speaker at the podium composed himself and
explained, "Sully went to work then. It was the most amazing thing I ever saw, or ever will see. He studied that bomb
as though it were a crossword puzzle. Then he solved it.
He pulled a pair of tiny clippers from his pocket and
snipped one wire, then another. Then another. Then he
looked up at me and said, 'You can breathe now, buddy.
We're not gonna die tonight.'"

Theo Howell's video image was nearly luminescent. "I hired him on the spot. And every day, from that day forward, he did the same thing. Infused everything he did—everything he touched and everyone he met—with raw energy and raw optimism and raw talent. I invite each of you to take your turn. To tell your story. But before I do, I have a message for the animal that did this to Sully. And to us."

The camera panned from Theo's face to the six mourners in the first row of the audience. Sabrina recognized two men who, along with the absent Paul Hanover, were left from Sully's original crew, and Zack, who stood tall and straight and painfully respectful, flanked by two other grim-faced young men in new black suits.

"Adonis Zenner, you've robbed us of our hearts today." Theo's voice from the podium was insistent. "We will despise you until our dying breaths. But I promise you today—I swear to you—that this vendetta is at an end. All of you have noticed that Sully's angels—the daughters that mattered more to him than life itself—are not here. We've hidden them away. They are *civilians*, Adonis. Respect that. Be satisfied with the carnage you have wrought. And in return, I give you my word, not one resource of Perimeter will be used to pursue or apprehend you.

"The government will come after you—and selfishly, I pray they destroy you—but we will not be a part of that. We will cooperate with the government—we have no choice in that—but not one Perimeter man-hour, not one Perimeter dollar, will be used against you. In return, I ask that you spare Sully's daughters your twisted vengeance. They are your insurance policy. But harm one hair on their heads and we will rain our fury down on you."

The words were electric, but it was the look on Zack's

twenty-seven-year-old face that mesmerized Sabrina. He was visibly stunned by Theo's promises. Stunned and then infuriated. And she knew why. He had been promised his vengeance—"Give the girls time to go safely into RAP, then you can hunt this murdering asshole"—but now Theo was taking that from him, and it was as though life itself were being sucked from his gut.

As his look of stunned disbelief faded, only anger blazed in his emerald-green eyes. Then his upper lip curled with contempt and he shoved past the young man to his left, elbowing his way viciously until he'd reached the end of the row. Then he stormed off into the distance.

"In my defense," a cool voice informed them from the study doorway, "that was five years ago. I've adjusted my attitude since then."

Chapter 5

Sabrina had been so mesmerized by the funeral video, she had honestly forgotten Zack's impending arrival, and she spun toward his voice in surprise. Then she was surprised again, this time by the fact that he was smiling. Not a warm smile by any means, but reassuring in its own way.

She smiled back, realizing that her view of him had changed, partly because she now knew he had lost his father to a sniper's bullet at a young age, but mostly because he had loved Sully—a surrogate father—who had been ripped from his life just as violently.

No wonder he was angry so much of the time.

From this vantage point, he looked taller to her than before. Taller and sharper. More dangerous. Was that just because she knew his father had been CIA, like hers? Or maybe it was because he had turned his car around for her.

Or maybe he's just a hunk, she thought, laughing at herself. *You just didn't notice it before because he was insulting you.*

"What are you doing here?" Theo asked, a trace of annoyance in his tone.

"I did some thinking and decided on a change in strategy. Is that a problem?"

"No, of course not." Theo cleared his throat. "Come on in. Have a glass of Merlot with us. It's superb."

"Merlot?"

"I'm having Chardonnay," Sabrina explained quickly, holding up her glass so that he could see she hadn't been drugged.

She kicked herself mentally again for having ever suspected Theo of an ulterior motive in suggesting a second hypno session. His taped eulogy—such an incredible outpouring of love and pain—had reminded her of the simple truth. Theo Howell had worshiped Sully Sullivan as surely as had Zack or the daughters.

"Come and sit with us," she urged Zack. "Tell us about the change in strategy."

Ignoring the fact that she had scooted over to make room for him on the couch, he ambled to the desk and leaned against it, facing them. "It's simple, really. John doesn't know Shelby left the second message, so he doesn't know you're worried, much less that you've come to us and discovered his true identity. That gives us an advantage, right?"

"Right."

"The last thing we need is for him to find out you're on to him. So I started thinking, what if he's working with a partner? Someone who's keeping an eye on you. Assuming you weren't followed—"

"I wasn't," she insisted. "You'd have to know how it was

with us, growing up, to know I would have noticed some-one following me for that length of time. From the day I got my driver's license, Dad used to follow me just for kicks. If I discovered him or, even better, evaded him, I got gas money. If I didn't, I got grounded. Those habits never go away."

Zack laughed. "Maybe so. Anyway, like I said, they wouldn't know you were worried, so they wouldn't see the need for round-the-clock surveillance. But they'd check in on you, maybe once or twice a day. If you're gone for too long at a time—or worse, overnight—they'll realize some-thing's wrong. You need to go home."

"She won't be safe there," Theo protested. "She abso-lutely has to stay here."

"I doubt John will come back for her, now that he knows she's allergic to DT3. But I'll post a guard there just in case."

"Which Johnny's accomplice—if there is one—will no-tice right away," Sabrina objected. "Plus, I'm not going to just sit home while that creep plays with Shelby's head. I'm not staying home, and I'm not staying here. Not for long. I have to start searching for my sister. Sorry, Uncle Theo, but that's the way it is."

Zack scowled. "You'll just get in the way, all your games with Daddy notwithstanding. Leave it to the profes-sionals if you really want to save your sister."

She glanced at her watch. "I've left it to the profession-als for almost five hours. So far, the results are under-whelming. Have you made any progress at all?"

"No," he admitted. "So far, all we know is that she hasn't used her passport. And there's no record of her fly-ing under her own name on any commercial airline. I'm assuming she'd be suspicious if Derringer suggested she use a fake name. Correct?"

Sabrina nodded.

"We have a description of the car they left in—"

"His gray Lexus," Sabrina interrupted, trying not to sound as though she were gloating. "One of the neighbors confirmed for me that they left in it. I can describe it in detail if you want. I even know part of the license number—713, which is Shell's birthday. That seemed so romantic until today," she added with a sigh.

Zack gave her an amused look. "I heard about that Lexus. Apparently, John used it every time he visited Shelby. Until that last day, when he showed up in *another* dark gray sedan—similar in color, but definitely *not* a Lexus. A Ford Taurus."

"But I asked Shell's neighbor…"

"Mrs. Grant? Yeah, my guy talked to her, too. She didn't notice the switcheroo. But her grandson—a sixteen-year-old car zealot—noticed the difference right away." Dropping the facetious tone, he added, "One or both were probably rentals. My crew's canvassing all the companies in the area that carry both makes."

"Shelby would have noticed the switch," Sabrina told him.

"Right. But he would have said the other one was his sister's. Something like that. I'm guessing John switched vehicles yet again at some point, to an SUV maybe, selling the switch to Shelby as part of his romantic surprise. He wanted to keep a low profile, so we're guessing he didn't use any commercial transportation at all. And he wanted to get going immediately with the hypnosis, so they probably only went a short distance. He had promised her a tropical island, so to be consistent, he had to take her someplace beautiful. Maybe on a lake. So we're thinking Tahoe. Or Donner. Or maybe up to Shasta. Yosemite at the outside. Remote—no neighbors—but still romantic. My guys are headed to the major locations as we speak. Connor's team is still checking train records and private jets, but we figure she's in the mountains."

"That makes sense," Sabrina admitted. "I'm impressed."

"Why?"

"Airport checks. Passports. You've got connections. That's what I came here for."

"But you were worried when you found out who was in charge?" Zack surprised her by laughing. "It probably didn't help matters that Fred let you drive up here without checking your ID, right? Just because you said the magic word—Sullivan? And Marietta didn't alert us, either."

"She wanted to surprise Uncle Theo," Sabrina murmured.

"Yeah, well, instead, *they* got a surprise. In the form of a lecture from yours truly. Believe me," he added, his tone becoming a displeased drawl, "it won't happen again."

"Tahoe-Donner. Plus Yosemite. Plus Shasta. And let's not forget the whole northern California coastline. That's a huge amount of territory for us to cover," Sabrina said half to herself.

"I don't see him on the coast," Zack countered. "He wouldn't show his face here in Monterey for obvious reasons. He knows I live in Santa Cruz, so that's out, too. And he grew up in San Francisco. Believe me, he doesn't hang out there for fear of being recognized. There are other beautiful spots, but it would take time to get there. My money's on Tahoe—two hours from Sac and one of the most scenic places on earth."

"That makes sense. If they didn't take a private jet somewhere, I'll bet you're right. So let's head on up to Tahoe."

"I just told you, you need to be home so they won't get suspicious."

"Assuming there is a 'they,' which is unlikely, don't you

think?" She grimaced and added, "You don't think he's working with Adonis Zenner, do you?"

Zack shook his head. "No way. If I implied that, I'm sorry. There's no reason to think Zenner's involved in this."

Sabrina arched an eyebrow at Theo, and when he ignored the prompt, she murmured, "We have to consider every possibility. Don't we, Uncle Theo?"

The older man licked his lips, then nodded.

"Fine." Zack exhaled in clear exasperation. "I've considered it, and I've decided it's nuts. Now let's move on."

Sabrina glared at the cocky young man, but she knew most of her frustration was actually aimed at Theo for not sharing the information about Derringer's presence in San Francisco the day before the bombing of her father's house. Apparently he was going to keep that secret from Zack forever, and expected Sabrina to do so, as well.

She was sick of being caught in the middle—on this issue *and* the progression hypnosis one. If they were going to be a team, albeit a dysfunctional one, they at least had to be honest with one another.

As if he had read her mind, Zack asked carefully, "Did you get any rest at all this afternoon, Sabrina? Any side effects from the hypnosis? You should have felt refreshed, but it's possible it stirred up memories that Derringer was trying to access, which could be disturbing."

Grateful for the opening, she said, "No side effects at all. In fact, if you want to do a follow-up session, feel free."

Zack pursed his lips as though considering it. "I don't have anything else at the moment. Theo? Can you think of anything I might have missed?"

Keeping her own expression neutral, Sabrina searched Theo's face for any sign that he suspected a conspiracy, but instead he seemed uneasy, as though he was concerned Sabrina would share his hypno plans with Zack.

When he finally spoke, the older man said simply, "I can't think of anything you missed. And even if I could, Marietta will shoot us if we're late for dinner. She's been cooking up a storm all afternoon in honor of Sabrina's homecoming." Glancing at his watch he added, "Should be ready anytime now."

"Great. I'm starved." Zack started out of the room, then surprised Sabrina by saying, "Come on, Sabrina. Keep me company while I get the rest of my stuff out of my car."

"Okay." She gave Theo a sheepish smile. "We'll just be a minute."

The older man was clearly surprised and admonished them with, "Don't be too long."

"Okay." She pecked him on the cheek, then followed Zack into the hall, trailing in silence until they'd stepped through the front door and out into the evening air, which was crisp and cool thanks to a strong breeze from the adjacent beach.

"Well, *that* was awkward," she murmured. "He's going to wonder what we're talking about, and I really, really don't want him to know I called you."

"He doesn't suspect a thing," Zack assured her. "I meant what I said, you know. I was thinking about coming back anyway."

"Good, because I feel terrible for calling you behind his back. Or for suspecting him of *any*thing, even for one second. Watching that funeral video—hearing that eulogy—reminded me of how much he loved Dad. He'd never do anything to endanger me or Shelby, or to take advantage of us."

"Yeah, he loved Sully to an extreme. And he hates John

Derringer just as obsessively. He's convinced John single-handedly destroyed the company."

"When we both know I'm the one who destroyed it?"

Zack scowled. "Is there any point in my apologizing again?"

"Probably not."

"Then I won't bother." Zack popped open the trunk to his black convertible, then turned back to Sabrina. "The problem with Theo is, he's got Sully's death mixed up in his mind with John's bad behavior. Don't ask me why."

"I don't have to ask. I already know why," Sabrina told him. "Uncle Theo thinks Derringer helped Adonis Zenner kill Dad."

"He said that to you? Based on what?" Zack's eyes flashed. "I'm as disappointed in John as the next guy, but he'd never do anything like that."

"He drugged me and my sister. He kidnapped her, and you yourself said she might not survive."

"Yeah." Zack exhaled wearily. "You're right. I don't really know what Derringer's capable of. The fact that he's endangering Shelby is almost incomprehensible to me. But killing Sully? Working with Zenner? I still think *that's* out of the question."

Zack exhaled again, then leaned against the car and crossed his arms. "Anyway, we're not talking about John. We're talking about Theo."

"Please don't be too hard on him," Sabrina said soothingly. "He misses Dad so much. And he's worried about Shelby. He's been part of the Sullivan family ever since the night of my mom's accident. Did you ever hear the story?" When Zack shrugged, she explained, "Dad got a call from the hospital, saying Mom was in a coma. He didn't have anyone to leave us with, so he dumped us on Theo—a man we hadn't spent any time with up till then. But he took us in without hesitation and kept us for that whole week so Dad could stay at her bedside."

"Yeah, Sully always said that cemented his loyalty to Theo," Zack agreed. "And to Perimeter. Otherwise he might have just taken you girls and gone off somewhere. Started over. But the company was having growing pains around that time—losing some clients, getting other ones—and he had to scramble to keep things going. He felt he owed it to Theo."

"It was good for him. For all of us." She smiled. "We'd better get back inside. Don't tell him what I said about him suspecting Johnny of working with Zenner. And don't mention the hypnosis anymore, either, or he'll get suspicious."

"In other words, you don't want me to talk at all?"

"If only," she drawled. Then she bit her lip. "What should we say if he asks what we talked about out here?"

"Just tell him I put the moves on you and you shut me down."

She flushed. "After the way we've been arguing, he'd never believe that."

"Sure he would." Zack gave her an encouraging smile. "He probably won't even ask, but if he does, just add 'sexual predator' to the list of complaints you have against me. I guarantee you he'll buy it. For one thing, you look unbelievable in that dress." When Sabrina just stared, he advised lightly, "It's a guy thing. Don't overthink it."

She sighed. "Even if you're right, I hate the idea of lying to him again, when he's being so sweet and hospitable."

"So? You're asking me to really come on to you? So it won't be a lie?"

"What?" She saw too late that he was joking, and tried for a lighter response. "I'd rather lie. Thanks anyway."

Zack laughed. "Go on inside. I'll be there in a minute."

Completely flustered, she turned away and headed toward the house as he had suggested.

Get a grip, she advised herself. *You keep telling him you can play with the big boys. I think that was your first test, and you flunked it!*

Half expecting to see him grinning from ear to ear, she spun back toward him and saw him pacing with his back to her, his ear pressed to his cell phone. And from the way his free arm was gesturing wildly, she had a feeling the person on the other end of the line—probably the hapless Connor—was getting a tongue-lashing.

Grateful at least that his attention was off her for the moment, she hurried up the steps and into the house. With any luck, she could steal away to the guest bedroom for a few minutes to debrief herself.

But Theo was waiting in the hall for her. "Is something wrong?" he demanded. "Did you and Zack have another argument?"

She hesitated, then said, "Even better. He actually had the nerve to hit on me. Can you believe that?"

Theo surprised her by chuckling. "With Zack, I've come to expect the unexpected. You said it yourself—he's a hothead. Apparently in more ways than one."

When Sabrina's only answer was a scowl, Theo added teasingly, "Don't be too hard on him. You look awfully pretty in that dress."

"So I'm told. I'm thinking of having it bronzed," she muttered.

Her surrogate uncle arched an eyebrow. "Do you want me to have a talk with him?"

"No. Please don't." She gave him a rueful smile. "I'm pretty sure I made my feelings crystal-clear."

"I'll bet you did," he said with a chuckle. "I don't need to call the paramedics for him, do I?"

"He'll live."

"I hope he can still eat," Marietta interrupted from the dining room doorway. "Because dinner is served and I made enough to feed a small army."

After five years of taking care of herself and Shelby, Sabrina was touched by the overprotective antics of her honorary uncle during dinner. Theo was clearly keeping an eye on Zack, ensuring that the young man's unpredictable ardor didn't erupt again no matter how nice Sabrina looked in her sundress.

And Zack did a good job in his new role, as well. Slightly subdued, more respectful—quieter, actually, than she had seen him thus far. He listened intently as Theo questioned Sabrina about her time in RAP, and while she knew that both men were already familiar with most of the details, thanks to the reports Connor had filed, she answered each question fully and honestly as a way of making up to her host for the deceptions earlier that day.

Five years of finishing college and becoming teachers like mom rather than security specialists like dad; of becoming Shelby and Brianna York instead of Michelle and Sabrina Sullivan; of settling in Sacramento in separate houses a mile apart—little houses on a greenbelt that stretched from a park to the private school where Brianna taught third grade while Shelby shepherded a kindergarten class; of leaving their hefty trust fund—supposedly a legacy from "grandma"—virtually untouched, despite Shelby's protests, because Sabrina wanted to buy their way back into Perimeter as soon as possible...

Five years of waiting for the moment when Adonis Zen-

ner was either arrested or killed—preferably the latter—
so that they could return to their real lives.

"I couldn't wait to be Sabrina Sullivan again," she admitted with a sigh. "And Shell was anxious, too. You
wouldn't believe how many times she wanted to just pick
up the phone and call you, Uncle Theo. Every time something went wrong, or one of us got sick, or even if she just
felt nostalgic. I wouldn't let her of course. It would have
negated everything we went through and put her in danger of being hunted by Adonis." She shuddered, then added
with a smile, "I have to give her credit, though. She made
more of our exile than I did. I think she liked being Shelby
York in some ways—she loves kids, and those kindergart-
ners really got to her. She got that from Mom, I guess. And
she made friends, which was tough for me, since I figured
at any minute I might have to say goodbye to them, the
way we had to say goodbye to our old life when we went
into RAP.

"But Shell didn't let that stop her. She dated a *lot*—as
your guy Connor mentioned on the phone this afternoon."
Sabrina laughed fondly. "I'll never forget the day she told
me she wanted to keep the name Shelby, even when we finally got to be Sullivans again. She wasn't going to let that
part of her just disappear. I admire that. She wanted to live
every minute to the fullest…" Sabrina paused, horrified
that she was talking about her sister in the past tense, and
added softly, "When you meet her, Zack, you'll understand. She's so full of life. We *have* to find her."

His green eyes were filled with compassion. "Sully used
to tell us stories about the two of you. Remember when
Connor asked me which one was missing, the warrior or
the con artist? That's what we used to call you guys. Because of the stories. Shelby was always the rascal, right?

The lovable one. And you were the amazing one. You should have heard the way he talked about you."

"And every word was true," Theo insisted. "The girls showed talent at such a young age. And Sully found ways to encourage it. Remember, Breezie? That game you used to play with him, where you memorized a room, then had to answer questions about it? Like you did this afternoon? Tell Zack about it."

Sabrina nodded, then explained it to Zack.

"Sounds like fun."

"Games with Daddy," Sabrina reminded him. "Nothing special. So—" she moistened her lips "—con artist and warrior? Because...?"

Zack cleared his throat. "It just fit. You were direct, right? Shelby was manipulative. For example, Sully told us about the day you got your driver's license, and immediately wanted him to buy you a car. You told him—in a very straightforward manner—that if he expected you to keep your little sister safe, you needed to be mobile. As opposed to Michelle-slash-Shelby. She took another approach."

"Did she? I don't remember," Sabrina confessed.

"She said she wanted to be able to visit the cemetery any time she felt a need to be with her mommy."

Sabrina bit back a smile. "That's right. I forgot, but yes. That's pure Shell." Her spirits fell and she admitted under her breath, "I miss her."

"She's fine," Theo insisted with unexpected force. "I've been giving a lot of thought to what Zack said, and I think he's right. Derringer has no reason to suspect that you've come to us. His plan is to get what he wants out of little Michelle's memory, then take her home, safe and sound, and break off his affair with her. He has no idea that his ruse won't work. No idea that we'll be waiting there for him, or that he's finally going to get what he deserves."

"Thanks, Uncle Theo."

"I don't think he has a confederate watching you, either," Theo added. "Why bother? As far as he knows, you trust him implicitly. He thinks you believe that he and Michelle are off on a tropical island having a safe, harmless romantic adventure."

Sabrina gave her uncle an encouraging smile. "But if he *did* have a confederate, who do you think it would be?"

She wanted him to mention Adonis Zenner so that he and Zack could finally air their differences on this issue. But Theo disappointed her again, this time by murmuring, "I have no idea."

She looked at Zack, but he was concentrating on his prime rib and mashed potatoes. So she turned to herself instead. Did *she* think Adonis was Derringer's accomplice?

No. Not really. She didn't know much about the assassin, but suspected he rarely played second fiddle. Not to anyone, and certainly not to someone as small-time as Johnny. So if there was an accomplice, it was someone else.

"What about Connor?" she asked carefully. "If what I read in his file is true, Dad didn't think he could cut it as a crew member, much less a crew leader. And you seem to share that assessment, Zack. For good reason, apparently. John Derringer visited me and Shelby every day for two weeks right under his nose. Is there any chance he took the easy way out? *Sold* out?"

There was stunned silence at the table for almost a full sixty seconds. Then Zack's expression darkened. "No. There's no chance. So drop it."

She leveled a stare directly into his dark green eyes. "I

understand this is difficult. But we need to be thorough. Connor has a lot in common with John Derringer."

"No he doesn't."

"Sure he does. Dad didn't think Connor could cut it. And you've confirmed that opinion. Derringer's a little different, obviously. Dad thought he walked on water. Then he proved he wasn't up to the challenge."

"What John proved—ultimately—is that he couldn't be trusted. Connor's loyal to the bone." Zack turned to their host and insisted, "Theo, tell her."

"Connor's loyal," Theo murmured, adding ruefully, "I'm beginning to think he's a little lazy, but loyal nonetheless."

"Not lazy," Zack corrected. "He just lacks the proper motivation, as Sully would say."

"His paycheck isn't motivation enough?" Theo asked dryly. "Where else could he make this kind of money?"

"Not everyone measures their worth by the money they make," Zack retorted. Then he explained to Sabrina, "Connor isn't materialistic. It's one of the things I admire about him. Your father admired it, too."

"So? What does he care about?"

"Sports." A reluctant smile played over Zack's features. "He's a nut for all that stuff. You claim you were trained from birth to be a spy? Well, Connor was raised on baseball and football and basketball. *Any* kind of ball. He had dreams of being a pitcher. Was a superstar in high school and college, then he fractured his shoulder in a car wreck and the dream ended. But that doesn't stop him from living vicariously—and without bitterness—through every game he watches." Zack gave a halfhearted chuckle. "He drives me nuts, but he's a great guy. And a good friend."

"Okay, okay." Sabrina took a deep breath. "Let's move on to our next suspect. Adonis Zenner. If half of what I've heard and read is true, he's a loner. And an egotistical mastermind. I don't see him playing second banana to Johnny. Watching my house while Johnny runs off with Shell. Do either of you?"

She turned to Theo, who took a long, leisurely drink of Merlot as if to dismiss himself from the inquiry.

"Zack?"

"I don't see Zenner and John coexisting," he confirmed. "On the other hand, John and Shelby—*that* makes sense. Two con artists, working together."

Sabrina set her fork down and stared at him. "Pardon?"

He shrugged. "We're going down the list, aren't we? So let's do it right."

"He *kidnapped* her."

"Originally. But like you said, she might figure it out. The question is, what would she do then?"

"That's enough," Theo said with an authoritative growl.

"No, let him finish." Sabrina eyed the younger man intently. "What are you suggesting?"

"I'm not suggesting anything. I'm eliminating suspects, just like you are." His expression softened. "Does she ever resent your role in her life?"

"My role?"

He shrugged. "From all accounts, she didn't want to go into RAP. She wanted to go after Zenner. You vetoed that. She wanted to spend the money, but you said no. She wanted to call Theo, but you said no. Barely two years difference in age, but *you* were completely in charge."

"Hardly," Sabrina drawled. "I never would have let her take off with a guy."

"Not just any guy. A con artist. Just like her. He rebelled against Sully and Perimeter. Isn't there the slightest possibility she would find that attractive?"

"No. If he tells her who he is—*what* he is—she won't be his girlfriend anymore. Just his prisoner."

Zack cleared his throat. "I guess I'm saying I wouldn't blame her."

"Why? Because I'm so controlling?"

"You're more or less the bossiest female I've ever met," he admitted.

"What? Oh…" She grimaced. "You're kidding again?"

Zack grinned, and even Theo chuckled before murmuring, "Shelby was lucky to have you all these years, Breezie. You've dedicated yourself to watching over her and keeping your skills up."

"Judo," Zack interrupted with a laugh. "That'll come in *real* handy. If you're ever in a James Bond movie, that is."

"Well, there's no danger of *you* being in a James Bond movie. That's for sure," Sabrina retorted.

Zack laughed again. "Probably not."

She shook her head, annoyed with herself for having fun while her sister was missing and in danger. "Let's hit the road," she suggested abruptly. "But don't try to keep up with me, unless you like the taste of dust."

"I'm sure it won't be a problem."

"My car's amazing," she told him with a proud smile. "And speeding is my only vice. You, on the other hand, drive like an old lady. You were gone six hours round-trip this afternoon and you didn't even make it to Sac."

"For your information, I stopped at the office in San Jose." Zack shook his head. "But if you do happen to get to your house before me—"

"Let me guess—you want me to wait for you? No way. I can protect myself from anyone unlucky enough to be waiting for me."

Zack exhaled in frustration. "I was going to say, just give

me a quick call before you go inside the house. One of my men is watching the place. It shouldn't be a problem, but humor me, okay?"

"It's a waste of manpower," Sabrina assured him. "That guy should be looking for Shelby."

"I agree. Once we get there, he can join the others in the mountains."

Frustrated that he had agreed with her twice in a row—what kind of tactic was *that?*—she turned the tables by imitating his casual tone. "Whatever. Call me when you get to Sac so I don't blow your head off when you knock on my door."

"Right. Anything else?"

"Are you planning on sleeping at my house?"

"Absolutely not," Theo interjected, adding an apology in Zack's direction by explaining, "If someone's really watching Breezie's place, they'd be suspicious of a strange man sleeping there."

Zack seemed to agree. "I'll crash at the surveillance house. It's two doors down on the other side of the street. Close enough to be useful, but not arouse suspicion."

"The Morrison house?" Sabrina winced, remembering that the place had been vacant for over a month. "Your crew is there?"

"Just one guy. And Connor has a guy watching Shelby's place. Everyone else is in the Sierras or up at Shasta, with the exception of a few that are detailed to Dallas to guard our premier client."

"Okay." She stood and nodded. "See you in Sacramento."

"Right. Try not to get a ticket."

Chapter 6

A few minutes after dawn officially broke through the darkness on Wednesday, Sabrina peeked through the slats of her living room miniblinds, her gaze fixed on the not-so-vacant house across the street and two doors down. It seemed too early to call Zack for a progress report, but he had said call *anytime*…

He's actually being a pretty good sport, she had to admit. He hadn't once lost his temper on the phone on the drive up to Sacramento the night before. Of course, they hadn't talked much at all. She had used most of the drive to process the day's events, such as returning to her old life after five long years of exile, seeing Theo and Marietta, and meeting her father's successor at Perimeter. And she had also tried to deal with the avalanche of bizarre information she had received about John Derringer, aka Johnny Miller, aka Shelby's abductor.

Zack had called her twice during the drive, mostly to tell her to slow down and to remind her to be careful going into her house. She had scoffed at both pieces of advice, but had had her Glock in her hand when she finally stepped onto her front porch at 10:30 p.m. Of course, all had been well, just as she predicted. Her only complaint was that Zorro wasn't there to greet her, since she had left him with neighbors for safekeeping that morning. It was too late to retrieve him, and for all she knew, she'd be taking off again in the middle of the night if Zack called with a lead or Shelby called with a plea for help, so she decided to forgo the much-needed cuddling and leave the cat where he was.

A judicious ten minutes later Zack had arrived at the Morrison house, and while she had been tempted to invite him over so that she could pump him for more information, she had decided it could get awkward, socially, so she had just murmured, "Good night," into her cell phone when he called, then spent the next three hours poring over the files on Johnny and company.

Only when her eyes truly began to cross had Sabrina finally stumbled off to bed, where she had promptly and predictably begun to fret about Shelby. And to curse herself for having failed in her one mission in life: to keep her little sister safe. Hardly a restful few hours, despite the fact that she managed to doze between self-recriminations.

At least you had a bed, she scolded herself as she sipped her morning coffee. *Zack and his associate probably had to sleep on bare floors over there. You should have invited them to use the sofa bed.*

The least she could do was make them breakfast, she decided, reaching for her cell phone and hitting the redial button.

Zack answered on the first ring. "Hey, sleepyhead. I expected you to start hounding me hours ago."

"I figured the more sleep you got, the less grouchy you'd be. So? Do you and your friend want some breakfast? I'm not fancy, but I can scramble eggs and make toast."

"My friend? Do you mean, my crew member?" Zack drawled. "He took off for Tahoe last night. The lure of a room at one of the casinos with a real bed, I guess. But if the offer's open to just me—"

"Of course it is." She grimaced. Did he think she was afraid to be alone with him? "Come on over."

She hurried to the kitchen and surveyed it for embarrassing paraphernalia, but everything was nice and neat. Not like the living room, which was knee-deep in files, not to mention the notes she had taken during the night. She had also compiled a list of vacation rental agents in the Tahoe and Donner areas. As soon as business hours began, she would start calling them.

She had come up with the plan on the ride home, anxious for some way to contribute to the search. Her theory was that Johnny had expected to get the information— whatever it was—quickly. When it had begun to take too long, he had needed to arrange the impromptu "romantic getaway." If they were lucky, he had begun making calls to rental agents, looking for a secluded, scenic, luxurious spot. The odds of finding the exact agent with whom he had dealt were low, but maybe some of the others would remember such a call, which would at least help to identify the area in which Johnny had been looking. Between that and Zack's effort to locate the rental car company, they might just be able to pinpoint a location.

Meanwhile she headed for the bathroom to splash water

on her bloodshot eyes. Then she pulled her hair out of the French braid she'd worn to bed, and brushed it vigorously. It looked pretty nice, she decided with relief. Soft and wavy—not as straight and styleless as it had been the day before. And her outfit—soft fleecy shorts and a matching gray T-shirt—was just the right look. Casual, sporty, but also flattering.

It's not a date, she reminded herself, sheepishly acknowledging that she wasn't sure how she wanted to look or relate to Zack. She needed his help—needed to get along with him. No more fighting. A little less competition. A lot more mutual respect.

A knock sounded at the back door and she hustled to the kitchen to admit him. To her amusement, he looked completely different than he had in Monterey. For one thing, he had shaved. For another, his green eyes were hidden by aviator-style sunglasses.

"What's the password?" she demanded playfully.

He took off the glasses and looked her up and down, then arched an eyebrow. "It's a little early for flirting, don't you think?"

"Be quiet," she advised. "And come on in. Do you want some OJ? Coffee?"

"Both if it's not too much trouble." He commandeered a bar stool at the island in the center of the room. "Nice place."

"Thanks."

"How are you holding up? Get any sleep?"

She poured his juice and served it to him, then reached for a coffee mug from a nearby rack. "A few hours. I spent most of the night reading about Johnny." She eyed him hopefully. "No news, I assume?"

"Sorry, no. We'll have the satellite photos by noon, though. Maybe we'll catch a break with those."

"I made a list of vacation rental agents in the mountains," she told him, then she quickly outlined her plan.

"Sounds great," he said, nodding. Then he added softly, "I've given it a lot of thought, and I think she's gonna be just fine. It's an ordeal because of the DT3, but because of the DT3, she doesn't know what's going on. She'll survive. She's Sully's daughter, which means she's tough. And John's not a killer. I'm almost sure of that."

"I hope you're right." Sabrina popped two pieces of bread into the toaster, then poured six beaten eggs into a sizzling skillet. "I'll never forgive myself for misjudging him so completely. He sat right there where you're sitting and bullshitted his way into my heart. And worse, into Shelby's."

"That's his specialty."

Sabrina eyed him intently. "Were you jealous of that?"

"Nah. Competitive, maybe, but not jealous. I was a card-carrying believer, remember? He was the closest thing to a best friend I ever had in adulthood."

"You first met him through Dad, right?"

Zack nodded. "John and four other guys—including Connor—applied for an opening with Perimeter. Sully wrote the job description and made it sound like cloak-and-dagger meets high-tech toys. I didn't actually apply, but I ended up being a contender."

"Because Dad recruited you? The impression I got from your file was that you applied for the CIA and Dad hijacked your application."

"Exactly. He lured me over to Perimeter, then made me compete with five other guys for one opening on his crew."

Sabrina enjoyed the twinkle in Zack's eyes for a moment before observing, "It must have been pretty cutthroat."

"It would have been, but John gathered us all together

and made a suggestion. That we make a pact not to under-cut one another. His theory was, Sully was looking for a team player above all else. So we should act like a team, and may the best man win. That sort of thing.

"I was impressed," Zack admitted. "Skeptical but impressed. And I found out quickly that John really meant it. The first guy who undermined a weaker opponent, John was right there, protecting the underdog."

"I'm sure it impressed Dad, too."

Zack grinned. "John admitted that was part of his strategy. And it worked. More importantly, four of the six of us became good friends. The other two refused to follow John's plan, and they competed with us instead."

"And? Who got the position?"

"The two backstabbers got cut within two weeks. After that, one of the group—Derek Coleman—dropped out to form his own bodyguard service, which was more along the lines of his interests anyway. We all stayed friends with him. In fact, he went to Sully's funeral." He took a deep breath, then finished the story. "John and I got positions on your dad's crew. Connor got redirected into Perimeter's IT division."

"So?" Sabrina set a plate of eggs and toast in front of him. "Dad lied when he said there was only one spot?"

"He claimed it wasn't a lie. That he really only intended to hire one of us, but made an exception because he wanted all three of us. Who knows?"

Sabrina surveyed him intently, imagining how her father must have felt, confronted with Johnny—who could charm the birds right out of the trees—and Zack, a guy who even at twenty-two must have vibrated with passion and integrity. The son of a hero. Between the two of them, they must have presented an impossible choice, and because

Sully believed there was *always* a choice, he had simply hired them both.

"And he hired Connor, too," she observed quietly. "But not for field work."

"Your father respected him for being such an upfront guy. We all did. In return, Perimeter got Connor's everlasting loyalty. And believe me, after Sully died, loyalty was at a premium. Theo needed someone to send to RAP as the Perimeter representative to protect you and Shelby, but couldn't spare me or the other experienced guys. So he used Connor. And after a few years, when RAP was considering disbanding their surveillance of you girls completely, Theo offered them Connor and a skeleton crew, practically as a gift." He arched an eyebrow in defense of his unmotivated friend. "We knew Zenner would try to find your location. And we knew for a fact that Connor wouldn't betray you. He earned our trust. And frankly, he earned yours, day in and day out, even if you didn't know it."

"He sounds like a great guy," Sabrina said, soothing Zack without stating the obvious—that Johnny had seemed like a "great guy," too, right up till the time he started robbing mobsters and abducting innocent women.

He seemed to sense the implied criticism and leveled one of his own. "Sully would have a cow if he saw that knife block on your counter."

"Hmm?" she turned in the direction of Zack's gaze and saw the block of wood from which five substantial ebony handles protruded.

"All that training, and you have a kitchen that could double as a horror movie set?" Zack arched a teasing eyebrow. "If a bad guy broke in here, he'd be armed within seconds. And you'd be slashed to ribbons."

"Slashed by what?" She strolled over to the counter,

picked up the block, and carried it to Zack. "I defy you to slash me with one of these."

He frowned, pulled out one of the handles, then burst out laughing when he saw that there was no blade attached, just an inch or so of wooden slat to anchor the implement in the block.

Sabrina laughed, too. "Dad always told us—make your opponent feel overconfident. If a quote-unquote bad guy broke in here, he'd go for the knives, right? Whereas I'd go for this." She reached under the island and pulled out a compact pistol from the shelf she had installed under the counter's lip.

"Dang, that's cool."

"That's my childhood," she replied proudly. "Some girls learned about eyeliner and ballet. I learned to kill in the kitchen."

Zack laughed again, then shrugged to his feet. "You're in capable hands while I run my errands then. Make your phone calls, and I'll be back around one with those satellite photos. And thanks for the breakfast. It was terrific."

"Wait." Sabrina shook her head. "Not so fast. What errands?"

He cleared his throat. "They're probably dead ends. I don't want to get your hopes up. Just make the calls to the real estate agents, okay?"

"If you're going to see Paul Hanover's wife, I want to go, too."

"Listen." He stepped close to her, then looked down with a firm but compassionate smile. "You're worried about your sister. I understand that. But you have to let me do my job, my way. That's our best shot at finding her in time."

"Protecting Shelby is *my* job, not yours. I'm willing to let you help—I'll appreciate it until the day I die—but this is my sister. Ergo, my problem."

"Ergo, your mission?" Zack shook his head. "Man, Sully really overdid it with that, didn't he?"

Sabrina pulled back, offended by his patronizing attitude. There was obviously no point in reasoning with this guy. He was a chauvinist who would always see her as Sully's little girl, with her make-believe mission and games-with-Daddy training.

Meanwhile, Shelby's life was at stake. It was time for this nonsense to end. "Go ahead then. If you get any leads, give me a call, okay?"

"Absolutely." He winced. "If I came on too strong—"

"I guess it's that time of the month for me, right?" she told him coolly. "I'm an overly emotional female, or whatever. Just go."

"I didn't say any of that." He exhaled in frustration, then backed toward the door. "The sooner I get going, the sooner I'll be back."

"I'll count the minutes."

His eyes narrowed, then he shook his head and strode toward the back door, adding over his shoulder, "Call me if you hear from her. Otherwise, stay put."

She watched through the slats of her living room blinds until Zack had crossed the street, climbed into his sports car, and roared away. Then she located her handheld global positioning monitor and set it on the coffee table to track his movements while she simultaneously entered a string of telephone numbers into the address book of her cell phone. Twenty Tahoe-Donner rental agents. She could call them from her car as she tailed Perimeter's arrogant head of operations from a judicious distance.

The little blip on the screen moved north until it reached Interstate 80, then he headed west, toward San Francisco. Sabrina wasn't surprised. Marilyn Hanover had always been a style-conscious, status-conscious woman. Given her choice of places in which to relocate, she would definitely choose the cosmopolitan city by the bay.

Sabrina's plan was simple. She'd follow Zack, then wait until he was done questioning Marilyn—or whatever her name was now. Once he was gone, she'd talk to the widow. Get her to open up. With any luck Zack would never realize what had happened—a key part of her strategy if she wanted to use the GPS tactic more than once.

After changing into neatly pressed jeans and a navy-blue silk blouse, she hit the road in her powerful white convertible. It was still a little early to make business calls, so she spent most of the drive perfecting her plan for the day, the most important component of which was to stop fighting with Zack. It wasn't productive, and whether she wanted to admit it or not, she needed him, or rather, she needed the information his crew would be feeding him all day long. Anything they could tell her that would narrow the search was worth its weight in gold. They might even discover that Derringer and Shelby had gone to a tropical island after all, by means of a private plane.

Sabrina just needed the location. Then she could do the rest on her own. In fact, she was beginning to realize she *had* to do it on her own. Because Zack was right about one thing, at least: they had an advantage as long as Johnny didn't know Perimeter was involved. By now he might be expecting Sabrina to come after him, but alone. He'd be ready for that, ready to try to recharm her. Or tie her up. Or whatever. Still, he wouldn't panic.

But if he caught sight of Zack, or any other Perimeter employee, he'd realize the stakes had grown astronomically and he *would* panic. He might even kill Shelby on the spot.

So it's official, she told herself. *You'll use Zack to narrow things down. Then you'll cut him loose. He'll argue, but you'll win, because she's your sister, not his.*

She felt a twinge of guilt, knowing he had already become personally invested in the search. On the other hand, he was the originator of the panic theory—the need to keep Perimeter's involvement secret. And he had a king to protect in Dallas. So maybe he'd be easy to convince.

It didn't really matter. All that mattered was her sister.

Just hold on a while longer, Shell, she told her absent sibling firmly. *Cooperate with Johnny until I get there. Then we'll take him down together, just like Dad taught us to do.*

When Shelby opened one eye that morning the sun was already streaming in the window of the cabin's luxurious master bedroom. Delighted, she reached for Johnny, then frowned when he wasn't there.

It just wasn't like him. He loved making love in the morning. Almost as much as he loved it at noon, at dusk, at midnight…

She smiled mischievously, imagining that he might be in the shower, a scenario with definite romantic possibilities. But she would be able to hear the water, wouldn't she? Especially since the door to the bathroom was wide open.

Sliding to her feet, she bundled a soft robe over her wisp of a nightgown and wandered to the window. There he was, in a clearing behind the cabin, talking to the antisocial caretaker.

"Ugh," she said out loud as she watched them. "Johnny's so sweet to put up with that guy. We're probably paying a fortune for this place, and we have to let a pervert roam the premises, just because he's the owner's brother. If it were up to me, he'd be gone."

Of course, the pervert and his ever-present hatchet had their uses, given the fact that the place was reportedly crawling with rattlesnakes. The phenomenon wasn't typical of the Donner Lake region, but Johnny had explained that they were having an unusual summer. And since he hadn't known about Shelby's irrationally strong fear of *all* snakes, poisonous or otherwise, he hadn't realized what a damper it would put on their vacation. No long walks down to the lake, no erotic games of hide-and-seek among the pine trees. Thanks to her paranoia, they were virtual prisoners in the cabin.

Fortunately it was a pretty posh place.

She remembered how Sabrina had laughed at the irony of it on the phone the day before. "Paradise, except for the creepy crawlies," she had teased her little sister. And Shelby had just sighed, sensing that Sabrina was a little jealous of her. It had become more and more evident with every phone conversation over the last few days. Sabrina had seen Johnny first, but it was Shelby who had snared him.

They had never competed for a guy before, and if Shelby had realized sooner what was going on, she might have told Johnny it couldn't work between them. But Sabrina hadn't shown her jealous streak until the couple had already left for their romantic getaway. And now Shelby's crush had morphed so completely into love, there was no question of giving Johnny up.

Poor Brie. She just needs to find a hunk of her own. She's so sure we'll be going back to Perimeter any day now, she never lets any guys get close to her. Maybe seeing me with Johnny—even if it stings a little—will be a good example for her, she told herself philosophically. Meanwhile, the strain of the last few phone chats made her a lot less anxious to talk to her sister, despite Johnny's insistence that they keep in touch.

As Shelby watched, the caretaker turned and began walking away, down the hill toward the lake. Johnny stared after him for a minute, then stretched his arms as though greeting the warm rays of the sun filtering through the trees. He looked so sexy—broad-chested, golden-haired, tanned and toned—and Shelby felt a thrill of desire ripple through her.

Maybe it was time for a little lovemaking in the pines after all, she decided mischievously. There wasn't a snake in sight—it was probably too early for them, she imagined—and the caretaker wouldn't be there to spy on them. So she shrugged out of her robe, brushed her hair and her teeth quickly, then headed, barefoot and bare-legged, down the stairs and out through the kitchen until she was standing on the back deck. Then she sneaked along the edge and down onto the needle-strewn dirt path that led to where Johnny was standing, unsuspecting and sexy as could be.

"Hey, Boy Scout. Wanna earn a wildlife badge?"

"Huh?" He turned to stare at her, clearly not believing his eyes as they scanned her filmy, thigh-length nightie, and the body it failed to obscure, even just a little. "Goddamn it! Get back in the house!"

Shelby pulled back, stunned by the tone, the words, the expression of outrage on his face. Then she turned toward the house, intending to run to her bedroom and lock the door and then…well, she had no idea what she'd do then!

But it didn't matter because Johnny caught up to her before she took her first step. Grabbing her in his arms, he hoisted her into the air and carried her toward the cabin, insisting hoarsely, "Are you nuts? Do you know how you look in that outfit? Sheesh, baby, if that crazy man saw you like this, who knows what he'd do?"

"Put—me—*down!*" She slammed her fist into his jaw and was pleased at the cracking sound, even though some of it came from her crushed knuckles. She didn't care. It didn't hurt one bit. Not compared to the way his words had hurt her.

"Shit!" His head flew back from the impact and he almost dropped her, but he managed the last few steps to the doorway and dumped her over the threshold before rubbing his face. Then he smiled ruefully—a smile only Johnny could manage under such circumstances—and insisted, "Man, you've got a helluva punch. Where'd you learn that?"

"From my sister." She tried to back away in disgust, but without warning her legs buckled under her and, for a moment, day turned to night—a deep black, star-studded night. "Uh-oh…"

"Shelby? Hey!" He picked her up again, this time more tenderly, and carried her up the stairs to the master bedroom, setting her gently on the bed. "Are you okay? Say something."

"I'm dizzy again," she admitted.

"What do you mean, again? Goddamn it! There weren't supposed to be any side effects. Here, look at me. How many fingers am I holding up?"

She brushed his hand away. "Side effects from what?"

"Huh?" He coughed. Then explained, "From the altitude."

"I've been at higher altitudes than this," she told him.

"Yeah, but not in the summer, right?" He stroked her cheek. "How do you feel now?"

"Pretty awful."

"Still dizzy?"

"No. Still mad."

"Oh." He grinned. "Yeah, I'm an ass. I saw you standing there, naked as the day you were born, and all I could think was, that pervert's gonna start stalking her now for sure."

"He's not here. I saw him leave. So did you."

"He went to get some firewood. He could be back any second." Johnny stroked her face again. "I'm serious, baby. The guy's unbalanced when it comes to things like this. Man..." He rocked back on his heels, his expression forlorn. "I wanted this to be the most romantic week of your life. Instead I give you snakes and a stalker and altitude poisoning. And to make it worse, I bite your head off when all I really want to do is kiss you senseless. Forgive me?"

She brushed his hand away again. "I never saw that side of you before. You were so angry."

"Scared, not angry. If anything ever happened to you—"

"I can take care of myself. If that creep ever dared lay a hand on me, I'd clobber him the same way I clobbered you." She eyed his jaw hopefully. "Does it hurt?"

"Do you want it to?"

"Oh, yes," she assured him. "More than anything in the world."

"Man, you're tough. What can I do to make it up to you?"

"Nothing," she murmured, resisting an impulse to tell him the truth—that he had shocked her. That for one unsettling moment, she had believed he wasn't in love with her after all, and it had devastated her. She still wasn't sure what to think about it. He was being so sweet now. But to erupt over a measly little caretaker, when either one of them could take him with one hand tied behind their back? It wasn't as though Johnny ever left her alone long enough for the pervy guy to get near her in any event. So what exactly was the problem?

"Come on. Ask me to do something for you," he coaxed. "Anything to make it up to you. The sky's the limit."

She was tempted to suggest they go into Truckee for dinner, but she suspected she only wanted to say that to hurt him by ruining his silly incommunicado love affair. He'd been so careful to shut out the rest of the world. Except Sabrina, of course. Even Johnny knew better than to come between sisters.

"Anything?" She pursed her lips. "Do you have any single guy friends?"

"Huh? You want me to set you up with someone else?" His face fell. "That's the one thing I won't do. Not ever. You're stuck with me and my crummy attempts to protect you."

She smiled. "I was thinking about Brie. She sounds so lonely when I talk to her on the phone. She wishes she had what we have, believe it or not."

His smile returned, this time tinged with relief. "That's a tough one. A guy for Brianna. I get the feeling she's pretty choosy."

"I wonder why," Shelby drawled, adding more seriously, "It's funny. You never talk about your guy friends. Don't you have any? You said there are lots of lawyers at your firm. Do you hang out with any of them?"

"I've got a couple of good friends. One named Connor—he wouldn't last a day with that Banshee sister of yours. But there's another guy, named Zack. He doesn't scare easy. Maybe he could handle her."

"Zack?" she murmured, warming to the subject. "Tell me about him."

"He's intense. A great guy—solid as they come—but

temperamental. Now that I think about it, they might kill each other." His eyes twinkled. "Want to hear a story about him?"

She nodded.

"When I first met him, we were both in law school. It was a demanding environment, and by the time Saturday night would roll around, I always needed a break. So I'd drag Zack to bars near campus with me. Guess why?"

"You're gay?"

"Just the opposite," Johnny said with a grin. "I didn't just want to meet a girl. I wanted to meet them all. That's where Zack came in. Between the two of us, we could attract just about any female in the place. The ones who didn't go for me went for him. I'm the charming boy-next-door, right? And he was the edgy, brooding one. If they were looking for love, they wanted me. For danger, they were all over Zack."

"A bad boy? That sounds promising." Shelby touched his face. "You wanted all the girls, not just one? Maybe that's the problem."

"There is no problem."

She shrugged. "You're so social. Here we are, virtually stranded together, just the two of us. Cut off from the rest of the world, thanks to the snakes and the pervy caretaker. Maybe that's why you were so—well, so not-yourself a few minutes ago."

"I know I sounded tense. I just didn't want him to see you dressed like that."

"No," she corrected him. "You weren't worried. Not about me, at least. You were upset. Like I was making your life difficult or something—"

"No, Shell."

"Just listen." She touched his cheek again. "We barely know each other. Coming up here was a pretty big step in our relationship. Maybe a premature one."

"I love being alone with you," he told her, his voice soft with emotion. "I'm so in love with you—"

"Are you? I'm not sure anymore. The way you looked at me outside. Like I was the last person on earth you wanted to see—"

"Oh, God, I'm so sorry." He cupped her chin in his hand and stared directly into her eyes. "If you knew how much I love you—God, I'm such a jerk! If I screw this up, I'll never forgive myself. Just give me another chance. Please? I love you, Shell. I swear I do."

She was flattered by his intensity. Pleased by his sincerity. And seduced by his devotion. Licking her lips, she slipped her arms around his neck. "I love you, too, Johnny. Make love to me."

"That's all I want," he whispered, then without warning he tugged her nightgown up and over her head. Throwing the flimsy garment to the floor, he buried his face in her breasts, kissing them frantically.

Shelby leaned back onto the bed and moaned with delight as he tenderly, passionately dedicated himself to her. For all the times he had made love to her, this one was the most amazing. The most vivid. The most perfect.

Nothing had ever felt this right. This real, or honest, or true. She couldn't believe she had doubted their love, even for an instant, and she promised herself never, ever to question his feelings—or motives—again.

According to Sabrina's rough calculations, she was just about five minutes behind Zack. He seemed to travel between seventy and seventy-five miles an hour, which she found unbearably frustrating. Couldn't he hear the relentless ticking of the clock that was more like a time bomb? Didn't he realize that every precious minute put Shelby closer to the time when Johnny might be finished with her, either because he had gotten what he wanted from her brain or had fried it with too much DT3?

It was a relief when nine o'clock finally arrived and she could busy herself with making calls to real estate agents. Her routine was a simple one.

"I hope you can help me. My sister and her new husband are honeymooning up there in your area," she told them. "He made all the arrangements and kept them secret so none of us would bother them, which *would* have been wildly romantic, but—well, my other sister had an accident. Not fatal, but I really, really need to get hold of Janie. And all I know about the place they rented is that it's remote and isolated—very luxurious, and with a gorgeous view, but the kind of place where they won't encounter another soul the whole week. He left the reservations to the last minute, so I'm just hoping—praying, really—that you remember getting a call from someone—a guy—asking about a place like that within the last three weeks."

So far, the responses had been friendly but not helpful, which alone told Sabrina something, since she had started with rental agents on Tahoe's south shore and was working her way north. If no one in that area remembered such a call, she could focus her attentions on North Shore agents, and if that failed, turn to those in the Truckee/Donner Lake area.

And at least it gave her something to do to keep unproductive worrying at bay as she followed Zack. She was so sure they were going to San Francisco that she almost didn't notice the little blip exiting Interstate 80 at Emeryville. Changing lanes quickly, she managed to maneuver off the freeway, then pulled onto a frontage road and studied the GPS screen with concern.

He was headed into a commercial and light industrial area, and while there were apartment buildings nearby, Sabrina doubted Marilyn would ever consider living in one of them. The Hanover house in Denver had been stately and elegant—and a strain on the couple's finances, according to Sully. But Paul had been so hooked on his beautiful young wife, he had cheerfully gone into debt for her.

And then, apparently, into exile, too. But this time, not so cheerfully.

"What are you up to, Zack?" Sabrina murmured, noting that the little red light had stopped on the screen, indicating that he had probably parked. She needed to be careful now—to catch up without him spotting her. She drove slowly, finally edging up to where his now-empty car sat in front of a modest brick building that bore the sign Derek Coleman Security Services.

Derek Coleman. One of the original six considered by Sully for the coveted spot on his crew.

What was it Zack had said?

We all stayed friends with him...

All? Did that mean Coleman was still friends with John Derringer?

Salivating at the prospect of such a direct link to her sister's whereabouts, Sabrina popped open the glove compartment and grabbed her Glock, which she stuffed into her blue canvas purse.

Just in case a little extra persuasion was needed.

Chapter 7

To Sabrina's amusement, Derek Coleman's receptionist was as ill-suited to the security business as the guard at Theo's gate had been, and in less than a minute, had buzzed her in through the heavy glass door leading to the waiting room.

"You're Zack's partner? Lucky you," the pretty woman told her with a smile.

"Thanks for trusting me," Sabrina replied, flashing her identification again as she'd done from the other side of the glass partition, then stuffing her wallet back into her purse. "I can't believe he forgot to tell you I'd be joining them."

"I didn't realize he was here on business, but it's so hard to tell with Zack. He's so private."

"I'd better not keep them waiting. Do you need to announce me or...?"

"I guess I'd better." The receptionist picked up the

phone and pressed a button. "Derek? Zack's partner, Ms. York, is here."

Sabrina held her breath, and was relieved when she was instructed to "go right on in." Then she shifted her bag to her left shoulder, flashed another smile, and pushed open the door to the inner office.

Zack was scowling in her direction, but she strode right past him and extended her hand to the nice-looking, non-scowling man behind the desk. "Mr. Coleman? Thanks for seeing us. I understand you knew my father."

"I'm sorry, I didn't catch your last name," he murmured, accepting the handshake.

"I'm Sabrina. Sabrina Sullivan."

"Sullivan? Damn, you're Sully's kid? Hey, nice to meet you. I thought you two were in hiding or something. This is great!" He turned to Zack and seemed to notice the expression on his face for the first time, so he cleared his throat and murmured, "What's going on?"

Sabrina looked from one man to the other. "Zack didn't tell you yet?"

"Tell me what? Something about Sully? I thought this was about John Derringer."

Zack eyed Sabrina coolly. "I was just telling Derek I thought six years was long enough to hold a grudge. So I wanted to mend fences with this guy named John that Derek knows. I used to work with him at Perimeter."

Sabrina groaned inwardly, admitting that Zack's approach had been a pretty smart one, seeking information about Derringer without revealing that Sabrina had contacted Perimeter.

"What's going on?" Derek repeated.

She turned back to him and moistened her lips. "We need your help, Mr. Coleman. Desperately."

His eyes warmed. "I can see the resemblance. Man, your dad was such a terrific guy. I'd do anything for you." To Zack, he added cryptically, "Which one is she?"

"You mean, am I the warrior or the con artist?" Sabrina gave him a smile she hoped was dazzling. "Which one do you think I am?"

He laughed. "You could con *me* out of anything, so I guess that's my answer."

"So much for pleasantries," Zack interrupted. "Obviously, I didn't just come here to square things with John. But I do need information on how to contact him. And I need you to keep this meeting confidential—from everyone, especially him."

Derek grimaced. "We've been down this road before, buddy. You're both my friends—"

"Your so-called friend kidnapped my sister," Sabrina interrupted.

"What?" The bodyguard looked to Zack, who nodded.

But Derek shook his head. "That's not possible. John would never hurt one of Sully's kids. He'd never hurt a female, period. No way."

"He drugged me at my house," Sabrina assured him. "Then he drugged Shelby and kidnapped her. I was there, Mr. Coleman. Believe me, it happened."

"Why would he do such a crazy thing?"

Zack held up a hand to stop Sabrina from answering. Then he said, "When the girls went into RAP, we liquidated Sully's share of Perimeter and put it in trust for them. Millions of dollars, just sitting there. Easy pickings for your larcenous good-for-nothing friend. We figure that's got to be the motive."

Derek chewed his bottom lip. "So? You want me to tell you where he is? I don't know. I swear, Zack. We talk on the phone sometimes—and we had a drink about six months ago when he came through town—but he always makes the contact, not me."

Zack's eyes narrowed. "You're telling me you don't have any information? Not even a cell phone number?"

"I swear I don't. Not a number. Not an address. Nothing." Addressing Sabrina, Derek insisted, "I'd help you if I could. I'd do it for Sully. And I'd do it for John, to clear his name, because I *know* this is some kind of mistake."

"How do you think he makes a living these days?" Zack demanded. Then he shook his head as though completely discouraged. "You swear you don't have a number?"

Derek nodded.

"If he contacts you—"

"If he contacts me, I promise I'll help straighten all this out," Derek insisted. "But he probably won't. We only talk a few times a year, and if he's busy—"

"Busy holding Sully's daughter captive?" Zack drawled. "Yeah, he's got his hands full these days. And if you do anything to facilitate that—if you even breathe a word to him that I came here with Ms. Sullivan—"

"I won't say a word about this visit. I promise." Derek's tone grew sterner. "Give me some credit, will you? *You're* the one who lied to *me,* remember? You weren't going to tell me about the alleged kidnapping at all. You were going to use me to get to him. Right?"

"The fewer people who know the details, the safer the little sister is," Zack explained. Then he stuck out his hand. "I know you'd help if you could. If I offended you, I'm sorry. Let's keep in touch, okay?"

"Definitely. And keep me informed about this. I'll…I'll pray for your sister, Ms. Sullivan."

Right, she told him in silent disgust. In fact, she was disgusted with both men. It was so obvious that Derek was blind to Derringer's faults. And Zack was blind, too—believing that Derek didn't have any clue as to the kidnapper's whereabouts.

"Come on, Sabrina. Let's go home."

"You go on ahead," she told him quietly. "I'll be right behind you."

Zack hesitated, then shrugged. "I'll be in my car."

"Thanks." She waited until he had left the room, then she said to Derek, "I've seen Zack's temper firsthand. Believe me, I know why you don't want to admit to him you have John's number. He'd say you've been holding out on him all these years. Protecting a criminal. Blah, blah, blah. Right?"

He laughed. "You know him pretty well."

"I've been on the receiving end of those scowls," she confirmed. Then she walked around to Derek's side of the desk, her expression as trusting as she could manage. "If you give me the number—or any information at all that you have—I promise I won't tell Zack where I got it. I need your help desperately, Mr. Coleman. If you won't do it for my poor, innocent sister, do it for my father. You went to his funeral. I know because I saw you on the video, crying your eyes out." Her own eyes were stinging with tears. "Please, please help me?"

Derek bit his lip again. "If I could help you, I would. But I swear, Miss Sullivan. I don't know anything. And John would *never* hurt your sister."

"Really?" She inhaled deeply, then released the air slowly. Then she reached forward and grabbed the bodyguard by his neck, forcing him flat up against the window with one hand while pulling out her Glock and jamming it into the side of his face with her other. "Enough with the stupid excuses. I want that phone number. Now!"

"Shit!"

She locked gazes with him. "In case you're wondering,

I'm the warrior. Now *talk* to me. And don't say you can't help me, because if you do, I'll shoot you."

Derek's gaze shifted to the doorway and he murmured gratefully, "Zack. Thank God. Call her off, will you?"

"Can't help you, buddy. When she gets this way, it's better to just do what she asks."

Relieved, Sabrina tightened her grip on the bodyguard's throat.

"Okay, okay. There's a number. I've never used it. I have no idea if it's current. It's in my top desk drawer. In my book. Under J, not D."

Zack strode over and opened the drawer, pulling out a leather-bound address book and flipping through it. Then he said, "This is a cell number, right? With a Los Angeles area code? Is that where he lives?"

"I have no idea where he lives. He moves around. Lives in hotels. Or at least, that's what he tells me."

Sabrina released him and backed away to stand by Zack, all the while keeping the gun pointed at the bodyguard's face. "I have another question for you. Did he ever talk to you about his childhood?"

Derek was rubbing his neck. "His childhood?"

"He lived in San Francisco, right? Do you know where his family went on vacations?"

He nodded. "They went to Europe a lot. Something about his grandparents living there."

"Any place in California?"

"They went to Shasta. Rented a houseboat and fished. Is that what you mean?"

"Yes. That's what I mean." She arched an eyebrow. "Don't call him. Is that clear? And if he contacts you, *don't* tell him we were here."

"She's right, Derek," Zack added. "We're not sure what

John's going to do. He might be willing to let the little sister go if Sabrina agrees to pay him what he wants. But if he finds out Theo and I are involved, he'll panic and kill her. You don't want that on your conscience, do you?"

"No." Derek walked over to a couch on the far side of the room, sat and buried his face in his hands. "This is nuts. I'll never believe he kidnapped that girl. Or asked for a ransom. Or any of this." Raising his eyes to look at Zack, he added vehemently, "He was your friend once, too. You know he's not capable of this. Stealing money—yeah. I guess he does that. But only from other crooks. He'd never hurt an innocent woman."

"Yeah, well, he's doing it. And I'm going to stop him before he goes too far. If you care about him, you'll wish me luck. Because if I don't find him in time—if he hurts a hair on Michelle Sullivan's head—I won't stop till I kill him. Unless Sabrina here does it first."

"My money's on her," Derek muttered.

Sabrina gave him a sympathetic sigh. "Thanks for the phone number. We'll call you as soon as we know Shelby's safe. In the meantime, you said you'd pray for her. I'm going to hold you to that."

Derek stood slowly, then crossed to her and patted her arm. "If she's with John, she's safe. If she's not—well, she's Sully's kid, too, right? Maybe she'll beat the crap out of the kidnapper like you just did to me."

"That's such a sweet thing to say," Sabrina told him with a wry smile. Then she turned to Zack. "I'll meet you back in you-know-where."

"Hold up, Sabrina. I need to talk with you." Grabbing her by the elbow, Zack pushed her toward the door, adding over his shoulder, "Take it easy, buddy. We'll get together when all this is over."

Sabrina waved to the receptionist but allowed Zack to propel her through the waiting room without stopping. Within seconds, they were on the porch. Zack motioned toward the concrete steps leading to the street and suggested, "Let's talk."

"Before you say anything, admit that I got the number."

"Sit."

After she had complied, he sat beside her, then surprised her with a weary smile. "Nice work."

"Really?"

"Sure. Like you said, you got the number."

She eyed him, suspecting a trap. "But I also let him know you were after Johnny. With *your* approach, that wouldn't have happened."

He nodded. "Derek's been wanting to repair my friendship with John for years. I was hoping he'd take the bait— give me the number if I said I wanted to get in touch with him and mend fences."

"Are you so sure Johnny wants that?"

"Yeah. He made it clear to me after he left Perimeter that he wanted to keep the friendship going. Called a half dozen times."

"But you told him the only way it would work would be if he what? Stopped pulling jobs? Turned himself in?"

"Stopped pulling jobs would've been enough before your father was killed," Zack admitted. "After that—when John didn't even bother coming to the funeral—I was sick of him for good."

Sabrina could hear the hurt behind his words. "It was a good plan. But I don't think Derek would have given you the number. He would have insisted on making the contact himself, I'll bet."

Zack nodded. "If he made the call, we'd have picked up

the number. We've got every kind of trap and register known to man on Derek's phones."

"Oh." She licked her lip, acknowledging again that his plan was fairly solid. "That might have worked. But now you don't need to intercept it, because I *got* you the number."

"Right." He rubbed his eyes. "Absolutely."

"He won't call John now, will he? That would make him some sort of accomplice or accessory, right? So we're in good shape. And we can eliminate the Shasta Lake area now, right? Even though it wasn't really ever a focus."

Zack nodded again. "Yeah. He'd never hide her somewhere he could be recognized. I'll call my guy back from there, so we can use him somewhere else."

"So all's well that ends well."

"Except Derek knows more than he should. Which is okay, because I think he'll keep it to himself. But you need to be more discreet, Sabrina. You almost told him about the DT3, right?"

She was surprised by the question. "Why would that have been so bad? It would have shown him the seriousness of all this. And it's our proof of Johnny's bad intentions, right? Since I experienced it firsthand, it's not just speculation, like everything else. It's the reason we know for sure they aren't off on a romantic vacation."

"Derek doesn't know about DT3. It's the biggest secret Perimeter has, outside of your RAP identities and location, and we guard it religiously. Only three people know. Four now, including you."

"Connor doesn't know?"

"Right. It's incendiary information for a lot of reasons. If it were up to me, the formula and all remaining supply would have been destroyed long ago. But Sully and Theo couldn't bear to part with it. Then when John left, and took the secret with him, Theo believed we had to hold on to it in case some of the formula turned up on the black market. Shit," he added, pushing back his dark hair with frustrated fingers. "It's all such a god-damned mess."

"But we have a good lead, right? Speaking of which, don't you need to give the phone number to someone who can use it to track Johnny?"

"In a minute. First, I want your word. I don't know how you managed to tail me without me knowing it, but don't do it again. You could compromise my efforts, or put yourself at risk. That won't help get Shelby back."

Sabrina pursed her lips, admitting that he was right about one thing: it didn't make sense to let too many people know that one of the Sullivan sisters had come out of hiding and was hanging around with the head of Perimeter operations. It could get back to Derringer, who might panic and do something deadly. Or it could get back to Adonis Zenner…

Zack seemed to be reading her thoughts. "You see the risk?"

"Zenner?" She chewed her bottom lip thoughtfully. "After all these years, do you really think he cares anymore?"

"After all these years, I thought you girls were safe. I was wrong. You have to keep a low profile. If not for your own sake, for Shelby's."

He was smart to put it in those terms, she told herself. And maybe he was even right, just a little. Around the edges.

"Are you still planning on visiting Marilyn Hanover?"

"I'm going there next. Hopefully without a tail." He eyed her grimly. "She's the last person we can trust with confidential information. The woman's a flake."

"If you don't tell her what's going on, how will you get her to give *you* confidential information?"

"She likes men. A lot."

Sabrina bit back a smile. "Are you saying what I think you're saying?"

"I'm saying she used to flirt with us. All of us. It was disgusting."

"Did she flirt with Dad?"

"Yeah. Once. He set her straight about it, believe me. We all did. Paul was one of us. A great guy." He exhaled, then slipped his arm behind her, resting it on a step. "What did Theo tell you about Paul and Marilyn? About their years after Sully died, I mean."

"Not much. They went into RAP like me and Shell, but Paul felt torn between his old life and Marilyn. Eventually he committed suicide. She stayed in hiding."

"Yeah. I figured that's what he said. But they didn't exactly go into RAP. And he didn't exactly commit suicide."

"What?" Sabrina calmed herself down, then murmured, "Why would Uncle Theo lie to me?"

"Guilt, I think. We both felt pretty crappy about what happened." His green eyes clouded. "Marilyn was hysterical after your father was killed. She was sure Zenner would come after Paul next and she demanded that they go into RAP, too. But the risk was imaginary, so RAP wouldn't accept them. Paul designed a new life for them— new IDs, the works—using his retirement fund. Anything to make his sexy wife happy."

"Wow."

"Yeah. Five months ago, on the fifth anniversary of Sully's death, Paul came to Monterey. He said he felt disloyal for running off, leaving you and Shelby unprotected. He asked for his old job back. And to be assigned to protecting you."

"What about Marilyn?"

"He was going to leave her. And believe me, he was sick over it."

"Oh… Poor Paul."

"Yeah. Theo was going to go along with it, but I had a suggestion—a lousy one as it turns out." Zack stood and stared into the distance. "I said maybe Paul and Marilyn could go to Dallas. Take over security for King Dominik. I figured it would appeal to her."

"That was a good idea."

"Ya think?" he drawled. "Anyway, Paul loved it and ran back to Marilyn, who apparently threw it in his face and gave him an ultimatum. One so cruel it broke him. He started writing a suicide note, and had his pistol ready, but he had a heart attack before he could kill himself."

"Oh, Zack."

"Yeah. Loyalty to Sully versus lust for Marilyn. The struggle literally killed him. I felt like crap. So did Theo."

"It would have happened no matter what."

"Maybe not. Maybe guarding Sully's daughters would have given his life enough meaning to leave Marilyn. And *he* would have spotted John Derringer, that's for sure." He sat and put his arm behind Sabrina again. "If Marilyn has information about John, I'll do my best to get it. But I doubt he ever stepped foot in San Francisco again once he left Perimeter."

"She lives over there? I knew it." Sabrina hesitated, then patted Zack's hand. "You're wrong, you know. The CIA caught Johnny on videotape at the San Francisco airport five years ago."

Zack cocked his head to the side as though he wasn't quite sure he had heard correctly. "Five years ago?"

"The same day Dad was killed."

"That's why Theo connected him with…?" Zack's face fell. "Damn."

"For what it's worth, I don't think it's true," she murmured. "I mean, it's true that Johnny was in San Francisco. But if he was working with Zenner, wouldn't I be dead? Wouldn't Shell?"

"You were safe as long as you stayed out of the business," Zack reminded her. Then he cupped her chin in his hand. "The guy loved your dad once. Things went sour, obviously. But there's no way John would have helped Adonis murder Sully. And for sure, not with a goddamned bomb. Adonis ruined John's reputation—his life—that day in the Canaries. He wouldn't have forgiven him for that. Even if Adonis offered him all the money in the goddamned world, no way."

"No way?" she echoed, pulling her face free gently. "That's what Derek said when we told him Johnny kidnapped Shelby. You both need to wise up. And so do I, right? Which means I should let you interview Marilyn alone. Although at this point, I don't see what we hope to gain."

She bit her lip, then continued. "When I first heard Paul died so recently, I thought maybe Johnny had paid him a visit. Used DT3 on him and got information about Dad, which led to the suicide. But now…"

"Now you know what really upset him."

"Right."

Zack nodded. "I figure it's a wild-goose chase, too. But for five years, things were quiet. Then Paul dies within four months of Shelby being kidnapped. I can't just let that go without checking it out."

"You're thorough. Like Dad was. Like your dad, too, right? He was on a bomb squad, like my father, wasn't he?"

"Yeah." He jumped to his feet. "Drive home carefully. No one's watching your place, so be cautious when you enter. If you see anyone, do to them what you did to Derek."

She smiled and stood to face him, pleased that he now saw her as a capable partner. "I'll see you in Sac, then. Have a good time with the merry widow."

He grimaced. "Funny. And just in case you have any ideas about following me, I'm going to escort you to the freeway entrance. Once I know you're going north, I'll go south."

She almost laughed out loud at the useless precaution. It was so convenient, having the GPS beacon at her disposal. And while she didn't intend to intervene in his questioning of Marilyn, she did intend to follow him again, just to get the address, in case she needed it in the future.

"It hurts that you don't trust me," she told him with a mock pout.

"Don't play con artist with me," he said, laughing. "Come on. Let's get you safely on your way."

Driving across the Bay Bridge to San Francisco a discreet distance behind Zack, Sabrina thought about Derek Coleman's loyalty to John Derringer. It seemed to be the theme of the week—blind loyalty. Derek had it to John, Sabrina had it to Shelby, Shelby had it to Johnny, Zack and Theo had it to Connor. And *everyone* had it to Sully. Unless of course no one did!

It would almost be refreshing to see Marilyn Hanover, a woman who had loyalty to no one, including her husband.

Be fair. She's a widow now. Maybe she's regretting all the slutty innuendo and out-unendo, Sabrina chastised herself as she followed the red blip through Golden Gate Park until the Pacific Ocean came into view. By the time she made a left turn to where the blip had come to another resting place, she was beginning to think maybe Marilyn had the right idea. It was such a beautiful spot. Who wouldn't want to change identities and move here!

Zack had found a parking space, and was already walking up the steps of a lovely blue Victorian home. The only spot left for Sabrina was in front of a fire hydrant—not the best for someone traveling incognito—but she had the location, so she began to turn around in a driveway, ready to head home.

The she saw Marilyn step onto the front porch of the Victorian. The curvaceous redhead was wearing white denim pants, cropped to just below the knee, a red tube top and red sandals.

"Go, Zack," Sabrina murmured, ignoring a twinge of confusion—almost jealousy, but not quite—at the sight of him with another female.

He walked right up to the widow, so close that Sabrina could feel the heat between them, even from a distance.

Go home, she advised herself. *You don't want to see this. How will you ever look the poor guy in the eye again?*

She put her car into Reverse, then realized that things weren't going according to Zack's plan. Far from falling into his arms, Marilyn was getting hysterical—and not in the good, nympho way he'd been anticipating.

The widow Hanover was waving her arms. She even seemed to be yelling, although Sabrina couldn't hear any sounds, other than a dog barking in the distance, which she refused to attribute to Marilyn's high-pitched voice.

She's not going to talk to him, Sabrina realized in amazement. *Because she's so scared of Johnny, or Zenner, or both, that she can resist a sexy guy like Zack.*

Grabbing her canvas handbag—with the gun still in it, although she had no conscious desire to shoot Marilyn on other than general principles—Sabrina turned off her car, abandoned it in the driveway of a stranger's home, and strode toward the pair, determined to get the information that would save her sister.

"Marilyn?" she called as soon as she was within range.

The redhead and Zack turned in unison, and both winced, which made Sabrina smile and wave.

Marilyn stared in dismay until Sabrina had climbed the steps. Then she demanded, "What are *you* doing here? You're not you anymore! And I'm not me."

"And yet, here we are," Sabrina told her cheerfully. "I have one question. Answer it and I'll go away."

"This is insane. You're going to get me killed."

"By whom?" Zack demanded. "Who are you afraid of?"

"Go away."

"One question, or we camp on your doorstep," Sabrina told her.

Marilyn's gaze scanned the neighborhood as though she were convinced it was filled with enemies, then she motioned Zack and Sabrina to go inside the house. "Hurry!"

They followed the hostess through a narrow entryway and into a pink-and-white-striped drawing room. Then Marilyn demanded, "Are you crazy?"

"Thanks for agreeing to answer a few questions," Sabrina replied, trying not to crack a smile.

"Just hurry. But I can tell you right now, I don't know anything."

Big surprise, Sabrina quipped silently, and again she suspected herself of being jealous, just a little. At the age of thirty, Marilyn Hanover had been a beautiful bride. Now with five more years and some excellent plastic surgery behind her, she was drop-dead gorgeous.

Zack gave Marilyn an encouraging smile. "When was the last time you saw or spoke to John Derringer?"

"Who?"

He produced a small photo from the pocket of his black polo shirt.

"Oh. The friendly one. Not like you," Marilyn added with a pout. "You called me a whore."

"Did I? I'm sorry," Zack murmured. "You were married then."

Marilyn began to melt before their eyes. "That's true. But I'm a widow now. That changes everything. Is that what you're saying?"

Sabrina knew she was cramping Zack's style, and wondered if she should make a graceful exit. But he handled the situation differently, telling Marilyn, "The reason we're asking about John is that he always had a crush on you."

"Really?"

Zack nodded. "And like you said, you're a widow now. So we thought maybe he had paid you a visit. We need to find him right away."

"I haven't seen him in years." Marilyn shot Sabrina a curious look. "You're supposed to be in hiding."

"I am."

"Then go back where you came from. If you don't, I won't be responsible for the consequences."

"What are you afraid of?" asked Sabrina. "Has someone threatened you?"

"Thanks to you and your father, I'm always in danger. Paul tried to protect me, but now he's gone and I have to protect myself."

Zack stepped close to her again. "I'll protect you, Marilyn. No one will hurt you if you cooperate with us."

Marilyn's eyes glazed over with lust-tinged gratitude,

and Sabrina wanted to tell her to have some self-respect. But Zack's mojo was working in Shelby's favor, so she did her best to fade into the woodwork and let him do his thing.

Marilyn seemed about to capitulate, then she visibly roused herself and told him, "You have to leave. I'm not afraid of anyone but you. You and your kind. Just get out of here."

"Marilyn, listen." Sabrina stepped forward. "If someone's threatening you—"

"As if you care about me. I've been safe. Safe and happy and prosperous. Then you dare to show up, with your ugly CIA ties and horrid memories. Now I'm *begging* you to go away. But I know I can't make you. If I threatened to call the cops, you'll threaten to reveal my true identity. I can never win with people like you. All I want is to be left alone!"

Sabrina bit her lip, intimidated by the idea that she herself had become the very sort of menace from which she had tried to hide Shelby. "We aren't here to scare you. Or change your life. We just have one last question. What happened to Paul? Did someone visit him? Scare him? Threaten the two of you? Is that why you're so upset?"

The redhead stared at Sabrina, hatred in her eyes, and then she told her in a clear, contemptuous voice, "The only person I'm scared of in the whole world is you. I ran away—changed my name, gave up my life—so that your father's stupid vendetta wouldn't get my husband killed. But Sully's reach was too strong. Even from the grave, he taunted Paul. Made him feel like less of a man because he chose me over Perimeter. Now Paul's dead. But you still won't leave me alone. It's like you won't be satisfied till we're *all* dead. You, too," she told Zack. "You were one of Sully's men. Do you think he's going to let you live?"

"He? Do you mean John? Zenner?"

"Zenner?" Marilyn's eyes widened. "Who said anything about *him?* I was talking about Sully. Oh, my God, this is a nightmare."

Sabrina rested her hand on Zack's arm. "Let's go."

He nodded, but stepped forward and handed Marilyn a business card. "If you're hiding something, and your conscience starts to bother you, call me. I give you my word we'll protect you. *I'll* protect you, with my life if necessary, if you help us."

When the widow stepped into him, imperceptibly but with heat-seeking need, Sabrina grimaced. But could she judge this woman? Marilyn obviously hadn't had a man like Sully for a father. No one had prepared her for this crazy life.

So she spoke up with the same humility and compassion Zack had shown. "Call Zack if you're scared, okay? Or call me here…" She took his card from Marilyn's hand and scribbled her own number on the back of it. "It'll be okay. We promise."

Marilyn gave her a surprised look but didn't smile or nod. Instead she told her quietly, "You shouldn't have come here. If anything happens—to me *or* to you—it'll be your fault. I tried to warn you."

"That's enough," Zack said, his voice close to a growl. Grabbing Sabrina by the arm, he ushered her down the hall and out onto the porch, muttering, "Ignore her. She's the same self-centered bitch she always was."

"She's scared to death, Zack."

"Yeah? What about you? Are you scared?"

"No—" she began.

But he assured her, "You should be. How the fuck did you tail me?"

Sabrina gulped. "Dad taught me—"

"Bullshit. You tagged me, right?" A smile was brewing behind his angry eyes. "Where is it?"

"Hmm?"

The smile became a full-fledged laugh. "Never mind. I'll find it. Geesch, you're something else."

"So are you," she admitted. "Thanks for defending me in there."

"Like you needed it?" He looked down the street. "That neighbor doesn't seem too happy with you. Better run and get your car before he has it towed."

"Oh! Okay. See you at home." She paused to ask playfully, "Do we have any more errands?"

Zack burst out laughing again. "No. But I'm gonna stop and pick up the surveillance photos from Connor on the way back to your place. So remember what I said—pay attention when you get there. Use your gun if necessary."

"Okay." She sprinted down the steps, then turned to tell him sincerely, "We know a lot more now than we did this morning. Thanks."

He gave a curt nod.

"When you talk to Uncle Theo, tell him I think he made a smart move, picking you as Dad's successor," she suggested, then she turned away and hurried toward her car, uncertain whether she wanted to see how he reacted to that tribute. Knowing Zack, it would tick him off for some reason, but she didn't care. It was true. He was really good at his job.

Unfortunately she still wasn't sure whether he was good enough. Or whether *she* was, for that matter.

But somehow, they just had to be.

There was no one skulking around when she returned home, which didn't surprise her. John Derringer had moved on to Shelby, and wouldn't show his face in Sacramento again. And the idea that he was working with a partner seemed dubious, given his history. Still, she dutifully checked every room, then she threw her bag and gun on the bed and changed into shorts and a tank top to better survive the predicted 103-degree Sacramento afternoon. She was feeling discouraged, despite the progress they had made that morning. They still didn't know where Shelby was, and only two and a half days remained before Derringer would be forced to make a decision—bring her home and break off the affair or...

You're just tired from talking to all those real estate agents on the way home, she consoled herself. *Just remember, by eliminating all the South Tahoe agents, you're closer to zeroing in on Shell. And maybe Johnny'll use his cell phone and Zack can pinpoint their location that way.*

She also reminded herself that Shelby probably didn't know she was a prisoner. She was making love with Johnny, enjoying the beautiful view, eating delicious meals, being pampered. If Johnny's plan was working, Shell had no idea that she was being hypnotized—that her mind was being probed. That at least was a blessing.

Despite Sabrina's need to do something active, she knew she had to continue laying her groundwork, which meant phoning the agents in North Tahoe and Truckee, and maybe calling some of the private party newspaper ads for vacation rentals, as well. The Sunday paper always had a full column of prospects, and the worst that could happen was that people would hang up on her.

And once Zack arrived, they could look at the satellite images, as well, although she knew he was correct—until they narrowed down the possible sites substantially, the chances of finding anything that way were practically nil.

He had called her during the drive home to tell her that John's cell phone provider was cooperating, but that the phone was turned off and therefore untraceable for the moment. But they'd be monitoring it now—their best lead so far. Zack had sounded encouraged. Almost upbeat, at least for him. He had even offered to pick up lunch as well as the satellite photos, and Sabrina had gratefully accepted.

The least you can do is set the table and find something cold for him to drink. Maybe even a beer, she told herself as she padded in bare feet toward the kitchen. At moments like this, she missed the cat, she decided with a wistful smile, knowing that Zorro would be playfully attacking her toes at each step of the way.

Maybe she'd take a few minutes this afternoon to visit him. She might even drop him off at the vet's for a check-up on his leg. Unless of course, she and Zack were on their way to rescue Shelby by then.

Her pulse raced at the thought of going after Johnny. Of sticking a gun in his face the way she'd done to Derek Coleman that morning. That would be such a rush!

Rounding the corner, she gasped to see that she wasn't alone in the house anymore. And as quickly as they had come, thoughts of Derringer vanished as her brain snapped to attention, remembering that there were men in the world so evil, so depraved, they made John Derringer look like a choir boy.

Her platinum-haired visitor had been lounging against the island, but now straightened and uncrossed his arms so that she could see the gleaming silver pistol in his hand. Then he gave her a mock bow and murmured, "I've been looking forward to this moment for five years, Miss Sullivan. Adonis Zenner, at your service."

Chapter 8

For a moment Sabrina couldn't breathe. Couldn't believe this was happening. For all her fears these past twenty-four hours, she truly hadn't believed she was up against this monster. She had been so sure she and Zack could handle the situation, because Derringer was ultimately handleable.

Adonis Zenner was not. He was an international assassin. A professional on a level only a handful of men and women had attained. Just looking at him—the ebony eyes, so filled with nothing, the relaxed posture, even within seconds of a kill, the utter contempt for danger, because danger feared *him,* not the other way around.

Forcing herself not to freeze, she walked up to him, ignoring the gun, and said simply, "I'll cooperate with you. Anything you want. Just let my sister go. Then you can do whatever you want with me. If there's something in my memory, it's yours. You don't need drugs or guns to get it."

She took a deep breath, then repeated firmly, "Just let Shelby go, and I'll give you everything you want."

"Interesting," he admitted, moistening his lips. "Your sister is missing? When did this happen?"

Sabrina winced. He seemed genuinely surprised, but then again, he was a master. "You know exactly what I'm talking about. And the fact that you're here shows you haven't been able to get what you want from her. So just prove to me that she's alive—deliver her safely to Theo Howell in Monterey—and I'll do whatever you ask. You have my word. On my father's grave."

"There wasn't enough of him left to warrant a grave," Adonis reminded her with a playful smile. "Why not swear on the stratosphere? His pulverized remains are still floating up there somewhere, I'm sure."

Sabrina's temper flared, and with it, her courage. "Just cut the crap and tell me where my sister is. Now."

He cocked his head to the side. "Sounds like we need to talk. Come and sit with me." He motioned to the eating area, and when Sabrina didn't move first, he shrugged his shoulders, then took a seat at the head of the table, laying his pistol on the place mat in front of him.

Forcing herself to take regular breaths, in and out, Sabrina joined him, sitting directly across from him and his gun. "Tell me what you want."

"I came here for information," he explained. "About you. Specifically, I've heard you're back in the game, and I wanted to verify that. But this business with your sister makes it a little more complicated than I thought."

"You really didn't know about her?"

He shook his head. "Tell me what happened."

"Someone took her. I didn't think you had anything to do with it at first. But now here you are."

"To see if you're still a civilian," he reminded her.

"You're saying you somehow heard I'm in touch with Perimeter? That was awfully fast. Do you have someone working inside there?"

"Wouldn't that be convenient?" Adonis laughed. "Unfortunately my spies are on the periphery."

"The periphery? Oh!" She felt a wave of disgust. "Marilyn?"

"Very good. And don't blame her too much. She'd love to have me out of her life. But I had a feeling she'd be useful, so I've kept in touch with her. That paid off today." He leaned forward. "If she hadn't called me right away, I would have killed her for holding out on me. So as I said, don't blame her."

"I can't believe she told you where I lived."

"I've always known where you live," he assured her. "What she told me was that you're running around with Lansing, asking questions."

"You killed Paul, right? Scared him into having a heart attack, then covered it up with a staged suicide?"

"Did I?" Adonis shrugged. "All I remember is asking him a simple question once. I heard he was coming out of retirement, and I wondered if maybe Sully's daughters weren't doing the same thing. And now I have that question again. Surely you're aware of my bargain with Theo Howell. I don't touch you, Perimeter leaves me alone, and you and the other one stay out of the game."

Sabrina folded her arms across her chest. "We'll gladly keep our part of the bargain. But I have to be able to protect my sister or what's the point?"

"Tell me who took her. You mentioned information in your memory—that's the motive? Information about Sully?"

"We don't know. That's our best guess." Sabrina shook her head, trying to make sense of her situation. She was chatting with Adonis Zenner—a man she had hated, had dreamed of killing for five miserable years.

"How did you let it happen?" Adonis asked gently. "You've been so protective up until now. How did this man get close enough to her to abduct her? Tell me everything, Sabrina. Maybe I can help."

"Help?"

He laughed. "I understand your confusion. To you, I am your father's killer. Nothing more. Nothing less. But our relationship is much more complicated than that."

"Actually, it's not. And you should go—"

"I'll go when I'm ready."

She tried not to flush at the cold reality behind his boast. "Zack's going to be here soon. If you really only came to see if I'm a civilian—if you're still willing to keep your bargain with Theo Howell and Perimeter—then this meeting is over. But believe me, if Zack walks in and sees you—"

"He'll try to kill me? Yes, I think that's probably true. 'Try' being the operative word. The truth is, you'll both be dead in an instant if that happens, so let's be quick, shall we? Tell me who took your sister."

"A man named John Derringer."

"The Perimeter reject? That makes sense," Adonis admitted. "I'm just surprised he waited so long to get his revenge."

"Revenge for what? If he wanted revenge against anyone, it should be you, right?" Sabrina demanded. "When you and your father assassinated our client in the Canary Islands, you ruined Derringer's career. Shelby and I didn't do a thing to him."

"There are so many different versions of the truth," Adonis mused. "Who knows what Derringer thinks? Does he blame *me?* I doubt it. He blames Perimeter. And you, my dear, *are* Perimeter, because Sully and his precious company were synonymous for so long. When he died, you and your sister were all that was left." Dropping the philosophical tone, he added, "The good news is, Derringer is a small-time buffoon. Give me the information you and Lansing have gathered so far, and I'll have your sister back for you by tomorrow morning."

"Even if I believed you could do it, I don't believe you would. Why? We're your enemies."

"As I said, it's not that simple. Yes, in the sense that your father killed my father, we are enemies. But Sully and Pluto were more than enemies, and so are their children. We inherited their relationship, which at times was one of profound mutual respect."

"That's not true. Not on my father's part, at least."

Adonis smiled. "You're wrong. Pluto and Sully were the best, respectively, at what they did. The world knew that. *They* knew that. Haven't you ever wondered why Pluto only tried to hit Perimeter clients twice on Sully's watch? Twice in more than twenty years. Quite a tribute."

"Twice?" Sabrina bit her lip. "The Canary Islands assassination, obviously. I didn't know there was another time."

Adonis cleared his throat. "That was indiscreet of me. I assumed you knew Pluto planted the bomb at the peace summit. The bomb that started it all, so to speak."

"We suspected as much," Sabrina murmured. "But that wasn't really Dad's watch, was it? He didn't work for Perimeter yet."

Adonis's black eyes flashed. "You're being too literal. In the grand scheme of things, that day was the day Sully and Perimeter became one living, breathing, amazing entity. The day he earned Pluto's respect. Twenty years passed thereafter, and it was only because the Canary Islands job was so irresistibly lucrative that we finally hit Sully. We knew he'd hit back. We knew one of them—the two most worthy opponents in the world—would die."

Leaning forward, Adonis insisted, "I took no pleasure in avenging Pluto's death, Sabrina. Sully was a hero of mine. I know you don't believe it, but it's true. The very fact that Pluto feared him told me what a great man he was. Still, he killed my father. I had no choice but to kill him in return. Pluto's spirit demanded vengeance, and the community would have thought me weak if I didn't follow through in spectacular fashion."

When she just stared, he added softly, "Why do you suppose I accepted Theo Howell's bargain? I didn't want to kill you or the little one. But I would have had to, had Howell not given me an excuse to leave you alone. You were civilians. He pledged not to avenge Sully by coming after me. It worked for everyone. That's why I was so unhappy when I heard you were running around with Lansing. I thought I'd have to kill you after all. I'm pleased to hear that I don't. And even more pleased that we've taken this first step toward mutual appreciation."

Sabrina struggled to digest the information, and when she didn't respond right away, Adonis smiled. "You're still skeptical? Let me prove it to you by rescuing the little one."

"No." She forced herself to speak with respect. "There's something you don't know. Johnny didn't really kidnap Shelby. At least, not in the classic sense. He seduced her. Whisked her off with him on a romantic vacation. It was only after they left that I found out who he really was. Like you said, someone with a grudge against Dad. Our best guess is he's trying to find out something—winning Shell's trust so she'll talk to him about Dad. We think there's a good chance he'll let her go at the end, as long as she doesn't suspect anything. But if he realizes I know what's going on—and if he realizes I involved Perimeter—he'll kill her."

Adonis nodded. "Interesting. She was safer when you were ignorant. When you believed he was a handsome stranger."

"Probably," Sabrina admitted. "Of course, there's always the chance he's going to kill her no matter what. That's why I want to try and find her before the week is over. But it's very important that he not find out I'm on to him. If he hears inquiries are being made—by you or anyone else—he might panic and kill her right away. So I'm asking you to stay out of it. I know you can find him—obviously, you're better connected that I am, even with my Perimeter resources. But we're doing a good job of keeping this on a low profile—except for the meeting with Marilyn of course—and I'd like to handle it myself." She gulped and added, "Thanks for the offer though. It's bizarre but…well, I appreciate it."

He gave her a warm smile. "It's going to take you a little time to understand our new relationship. But I predict it will be worth it. Our legacies are amazing, yours and mine. We have so much in common. Descended from Titans, you see? Sully and Pluto—the best the world has ever known. Now it's our turn."

"For what?" she asked, curious in spite of herself. "My legacy is to oppose you. Professionally. But then I wouldn't be a civilian anymore and you'd try to kill me. And vice versa."

"That's the danger," he agreed. "Unless I save your sister. Then the balance shifts. Suddenly we'd be on the same side—Zenner and Sullivan. Rather than canceling one another out, we'd join forces. And then, who could defeat us? Do you see the possibilities?"

"You killed my father," she reminded him.

"But only because *he* killed *my* father. Why turn it into a vendetta? The two killings cancel one another out. We can start with a clean slate, you and I. Build something more interesting than a feud. For now, we have our truce. The status quo. But someday, it can be more. An alliance. An unstoppable one."

When Sabrina shrugged, the assassin cocked an eyebrow. "What will you do if Derringer murders your sister?"

"What?"

He smiled. "You'll want to go after him, won't you? You won't rest until he suffers the way he made her suffer. By happy coincidence, I do that sort of thing for a living. I'll be at your disposal, and you'll accept my help then. Do you know why?"

"Because nothing would be able to stop us?"

"There's nowhere he can hide that I can't find him. There's no law-enforcement agency or security company that could outwit us. He wouldn't get a trial. Just a death sentence."

Sabrina licked her lips, admitting to herself that she would want Johnny dead—not just imprisoned—if the worst happened.

"So?" Adonis flashed a grin. "You admit it's possible that we may one day form an alliance? That's progress, at least." Shrugging to his feet, he picked up the pistol and shoved it in a holster strapped to his chest under his suit coat. "The next step is allowing me to help prevent the tragedy rather than just avenge it. I'll respect your wishes and stay out of it for a while. Twenty-four hours, shall we say?"

"And then what?"

"You'll call me. You may be desperate enough by then to let me help, don't you think?"

She had to admit it was true. If she and Zack hadn't pinpointed a location by then, she might just be willing to let Adonis take over. For Shelby's sake. "How can I reach you?"

"Here." He handed her a business card that appeared at first to be blank. Then she noticed that a series of numbers were embossed on it. "I'll look forward to hearing from you."

"Okay." She forced herself to smile again. "Thanks. And don't forget. You aren't going to do anything until you hear from me, right? I can't take the chance yet that Johnny might hear you're after him."

"He would definitely panic, and possibly harm her if he suspected that," Adonis agreed. "Yes, you have my word. No inquires until we've spoken again."

His word? She wanted to throw that back in his face. To tell him his word was worth nothing to her. That she hated him! But there was one grain of truth in all these lies. This man did indeed have the resources to find Shelby. He hadn't exaggerated when he'd said he—and Pluto and Sully Sullivan—were men in a different league. They could do anything they put their minds to, with ease and speed outside the reach of normal men and women.

She needed a man like that if she was going to save Shelby. As much as she had come to respect Zack, she knew he wasn't there. Not yet, at least. With another five or ten years of experience, she believed he might reach that level. Might be everything Sully had been in his late thirties and early forties. Maybe he'd even surpass him! But that would be too late for Shelby.

"If we had time, and champagne, I'd toast our new bargain," Adonis told her, taking her by the hands and urging her to stand and face him. "Instead, we'll just have to seal it with a kiss."

"Go kiss Marilyn," she advised him, stepping back and folding her arms across her chest.

He laughed. "I might do just that. But I'll be thinking of you. And waiting for your call."

He bowed again, murmured, *"Ciao, bella,"* and strode out the door and onto the back porch without glancing back even once. She stared after him, wondering without really caring if he would walk around in broad daylight or hug the shadows and slither away. If Zack saw him coming out of the house he'd go after him like a bulldog. And if Zack suspected for one minute that Sully Sullivan's daughter had consorted with such a monster, he'd never respect her again.

She couldn't really blame him. It was disgusting. Revolting. And yet, to save Shelby, she knew she'd do much worse. She only hoped the need never arose.

"Then you click here, see? And you can zoom in and out on any part of the grid. Just remember to go back out before you download another one. But admit it, Sabrina," Zack insisted. "Isn't this unbelievable? We can download any satellite image we want, right from your living room, and with the clarity and capability of this screen, it's ten times better than hard copies. But if you still want hard copies, Connor gave us a high-tech printer, too. It's out in the car. Just let me know."

Sabrina smiled weakly. Zack was turning into a geek right in front of her eyes, drooling over the forty-thousand-dollar laptop Connor had supplied to him for viewing shots of the mountains via satellite. And she had to admit it was an amazing instrument. And his enthusiasm and commitment were just as amazing.

The whole thing made her feel like a rat. Had she dared question Connor's loyalty? Or Zack's fitness to run Perimeter? At least they weren't in cohoots with Adonis Zenner!

"What's with you, anyway?"

"Hmm? Oh sorry. I didn't sleep much last night, you know. What were you saying?"

Zack hesitated, then knelt in front of where she was curled up on the couch. He took her hands in his own. "I know it seems like we haven't made any progress, but we have. We'll find her in time. I promise."

"You've done a wonderful job," she told him with a sigh. "I must seem like the world's biggest ingrate, but believe me, I know we're getting close. Thanks to you."

He winced. "You're not going all sweet and helpless on me, are you?"

"Hardly."

"Good. I like the warrior." He jumped to his feet. "Maybe you're just hungry. You hardly touched your sandwich."

She smiled again, thinking of the huge bag of assorted goodies he'd brought with him, explaining that he figured he'd buy enough for lunch and dinner. To which she had replied, "For you and me and an army?"

Her appetite had left with Adonis, it seemed. And the embossed business card in the pocket of her shorts was enough to make her slightly nauseous all by itself, but she had forced down half a turkey sub for Zack's sake.

"I had plenty." She stood to face him. "I'll just get going on those phone calls again. You handle the photos, okay? If you find anything interesting, let me know."

He scowled and she knew he was offended on the computer's behalf. "I'll play with you and your new toy when I'm ready for a break."

"That's more like it." He chuckled. "Do you want a beer? I think I'm going to have one."

"Let me get it for you." She headed for the kitchen before he could object. She hadn't stepped foot in the room since Adonis left, and she knew she couldn't keep avoiding it. Of course, she'd never be able to eat off that table again, but other than that, she had to let it go before she drove herself crazy.

Pausing in the doorway, she fixed her gaze on the seat at the head of the table. After all her fantasies about tracking down Zenner and killing him, she had had him right here. But had she even considered going for his gun? Nope. Instead she had conspired with him.

You've got a perfect record. First you have Derringer right under your nose, and you let him drug you and kidnap your sister. Now you let Zenner go. Nice work, Sabrina.

An empty towel rack on the side of the sink caught her eye, and she absentmindedly located a clean towel from the laundry room and hung it there. Then she got Zack's beer and a pilsner glass and returned to the living room.

"Thanks." His green eyes twinkled. "Did you notice anything different in there?"

"Pardon?"

"Did you?"

"No. Why?"

He grinned, then reached under the cushion of a nearby chair and produced a hand towel. "So much for gestalt."

She burst out laughing. "Don't you have anything better to do than test me?"

"You flunked."

"Did I? Go look."

He studied her suspiciously, then stalked into the kitchen, returning in a few seconds, a sheepish look on his face. "You're a freak."

She smiled. "You should see Shelby in action. It's really uncanny."

"Come on." He took her by the hand and led her back to the sofa. "Tell me more about the training Sully did with you two."

"Why?"

"I like seeing you smile," he admitted. "Plus, it's nice to have someone to talk to about him."

"You really miss him, don't you?" She sighed. "I like talking about him, too. He was so much fun."

"He taught you to shoot?"

She nodded. "And some basic martial arts and boxing moves. And the ones we've already talked about, like tailing people."

"Speaking of which, I found that GPS sensor," he drawled.

She smiled. "I won't need it anymore, will I?"

"No. You're in the official loop from now on. So? What else did he teach you?"

"The attitude, I guess. He had a million sayings. Like, 'Panic is an agent's worst enemy.' Or, 'Your first instinct is your truest instinct.' Or my favorite, 'Sometimes the problem *is* the problem.'"

"I never liked that one," Zack confessed.

"Why not? It just means, if you can't find the answer you need, maybe you're asking the wrong question."

"Yeah, I know. That's the one he always got me with. I have a habit of asking the wrong question, I guess."

"Me, too." She smiled. "Did he really teach all those platitudes to you guys, too?"

"Yeah. It got on my nerves, but now I miss it."

"It's funny," she said, smiling sadly. "He was wrong about the instinct thing, at least where Johnny was concerned. We all instinctively liked him at the start."

"Not really," Zack told her. "My first reaction was negative, actually. But he won me over. And yours was understandable—hormones, not instinct. There's a difference."

When Sabrina scowled, Zack laughed. "Let's face it, the guy has a way with women. And the statistics back it up, by the way. He used to brag that he could get a date with eighty percent of women in any given situation. His theory was…"

She tilted her head to the side, intrigued by the hesitation. "Go on."

Zack flushed. "That the other twenty percent went for me, actually. We used to test it by going to bars sometimes, and damned if he wasn't right. He liked the fact that we could have one hundred percent success between the two of us."

"Only twenty percent? I'm sure it's higher."

"Who cares?" he scoffed. "It's just our bad luck that you and Shelby both fell in the eighty percent camp. Otherwise maybe one of you would've been a little more suspicious."

Hormones. She knew he was right about that. Hormones mixed with loneliness. So maybe she'd let herself off the hook for having let Johnny get his hands on Shelby. And as for Adonis Zenner—well, she had an excuse for that one, too, didn't she?

One thing was certain, she never wanted to have to use that embossed telephone number. The next time she talked to Adonis Zenner, she wanted it to be in connection with his apprehension and trial.

"There are extra pillows and blankets in the hall closet if you need them."

"I'll be fine. Thanks. This beats the floor across the street by a mile." Zack clapped his hands down on Sabrina's shoulders. "We made a lot of progress today, thanks to you. You've pretty much eliminated South Tahoe from contention, which narrows the search. And John's bound to use his cell phone at some point. If he does, we've got him. Sully would be proud of you."

"He'd be proud of you, too. You're so much like him. It's crazy that I didn't see it from the start."

Zack flushed. "Thanks. Are you going to be able to sleep?"

She shrugged, then picked up a stack of files and walked toward her room. Pausing in the doorway to watch him settle back down in front of Connor's laptop, she murmured, "Hey, Zack?"

"Yeah?"

"Just for the record..." She took a deep breath, then admitted, "I was pretty lonely the day Johnny showed up here."

He arched an eyebrow, but didn't say a word.

"Anyway," she continued sheepishly, "if the circumstances had been different—if I'd been sitting in a bar, for example, and you and he walked through the door, I'm pretty sure I would have been in the twenty percent camp."

"Yeah?"

She nodded, then repeated, "Just for the record."

"Definitely good to know."

She could feel her cheeks warming, so she waved as she backed into her room. "See you in the morning."

"Right. Good night, Sabrina."

"Good night, Zack."

Chapter 9

Sabrina's thoughts that night were a jumble, keeping her awake as she cycled through her dilemmas. First there was Shelby's predicament, aka, the mission. Zack was right about that—she was a freaking fanatic on the subject. But missions aside, Shelby was her sister, and she wasn't going to leave her in John Derringer's clutches for one minute longer than necessary.

"But at least Johnny isn't working with Adonis Zenner," she muttered to herself again and again as she tossed and turned. "Just the opposite in fact. *You're* working with Zenner! Of course, you're also working with Zack. And flirting with him, too. Have you lost your mind? He's right in the next room! You invite him to sleep on the couch, then tell him how lonely you are? And how attracted you are to him? He's probably wondering what he's supposed to do now. Follow you in here and have sex with you? Run for the hills?"

It seemed that no matter where her mind wandered, there was trouble. And meanwhile, in the very back of her mind, a warning light was flashing, courtesy of her Sullivan instincts. She kept trying to ignore it, since she didn't understand it, but that light was just bright enough to keep her awake, reminding her of something Adonis Zenner had said to her.

It's a tribute to Sully that we only hit Perimeter twice on his watch...

Twice. Once in the Canary Islands, and once...when?

Adonis had offered a plausible explanation and she might have bought it if he hadn't been so darned precise about everything else he said. He just wasn't the kind of guy to make a careless comment.

The peace summit—yes, Sully had been there, but only as part of a CIA team. It hadn't been "on his watch" Perimeter-wise. Did that mean the Zenners had assassinated—or at least tried to assassinate—another Perimeter client sometime during Sully's twenty-something-year-long tenure?

It jibed with another problem she had been wrestling with in the back of her mind—the mystery as to why the Zenners had left Perimeter untouched for so many years. Adonis's explanation—that it had been out of respect for, or even fear of, Sully Sullivan—just didn't cut it for Sabrina.

Sometimes the problem is the problem...

This was one of those times. Sabrina was sure of it. She was asking the wrong question. And while logic told her it didn't matter because the Zenners had nothing to do with Shelby's abduction, her instincts were telling her something very different.

They were telling her that somehow, in some way, if she could just find the right question, she'd also find her sister.

* * *

When her cell phone blared at her from the nightstand, she bolted out of a sound sleep and grabbed it, certain it must be Shelby. It matched with the dream she had just been having—of Shell overpowering Johnny, stealing his keys and driving home at breakneck speed down a treacherous mountain highway.

"Shell?"

"I'm sorry. I was trying to reach Linda Meyers."

"Oh, that's me!" Sabrina sat up, sheepish yet alert at the sound of her newest alias. She had used it when leaving messages for agents whose phones had rolled over to answering machines. She had been reluctant to take this approach, for fear the agent might contact Johnny with the news of his bride's sister's accident, but as time passed and certain agents had been otherwise unreachable, she'd had no choice.

Of course, she had taken extra precautions. The alias, for one. And she had also ended each message with an entreaty to "Please, please let me be the one to break it to them. My sister's health isn't good, and the wedding was already such a strain. All I need is for you to call me back. Then we can decide together the best way to break the bad news to them."

Apparently this agent had cooperated, so Sabrina took a deep breath and said, "Thanks so much for calling back. May I ask which agency you work for?"

"I'm Annette, from Truckee Travel Pro. I'm sorry to say I can't put you in touch with your brother-in-law. But you said I should call if I spoke with him at all, even if we weren't able to supply a property to him."

"Right." Sabrina gulped. "You're saying you spoke with him?"

"Well…" Annette's tone was wary. "I spoke with a gentleman two weeks ago who was trying to make last-minute arrangements for a remote cabin with a view. For a honeymoon."

Sabrina steadied her voice. "That's him. Oh, thank God. You said you're in Truckee? Did he want a river view? Woodsy?"

"He wanted Donner Lake."

Oh Lord… Shelby, just hang on…

"But like I said," Annette continued, "we couldn't accommodate him. I suggested he try some private party listings in our local paper, but at this time of year, that would be a long shot, too. Still…" She paused to laugh lightly. "He was very determined. And willing to pay a hefty premium for just the right property."

"You said remote. Do you happen to remember the size he requested?"

"He didn't care about size, but he wanted all the amenities. Fireplace, hot tub, et cetera. And a nice deck. That sort of thing. His main request was that they be left absolutely alone. It all sounded very mysterious and romantic."

"Well, Annette…" Sabrina's voice was soft with sincere gratitude. "I can't thank you enough for taking the time to call me. Now at least I know they're probably in the general area of the lake. That helps enormously. I'm going to send you the biggest bunch of roses you've ever seen, so make sure someone's around the office this afternoon, okay?"

"Wait. Don't you want to verify the name?"

Sabrina gasped. "You remember his name?"

"I jotted it on my calendar. Zack Lansing, right?" Annette paused, then murmured, "Miss Meyers? Isn't that your brother-in-law's name?"

"Yes. Zack Lansing. That's him. I'm just so…" Sabrina

shook her head, then insisted, "I'm just so happy. And so grateful. Goodbye, Annette. Have a really, really nice day."

Zack was already stationed in front of the laptop at the coffee table when Sabrina walked into the room. He gave her a teasing smile. "Did I hear your cell phone? Thank God, something finally woke you up."

"You've been awake for a while? Was the sofa bed comfortable?"

"Better than the floor." He seemed to notice her expression for the first time, and asked warily, "What's going on? Who called?"

"A rental agent in Truckee. She got a call from a guy two weeks ago. Looking for a remote cabin with a lake view." Sabrina held up her hand to prevent him from interrupting her. "The guy said he wanted to be completely undisturbed because he was going to be honeymooning. And guess what? She even remembered his name."

"Unbelievable."

"I know."

"So?" he demanded. "Was it John Derringer? Johnny Miller? What?"

"It was Zack Lansing."

He stared for a second, then his green eyes boiled over. "That asshole used *my* name? God*damn* him!" He began to pace, waving his arms wildly. "He's probably doing that all over the goddamned town! Wait till I get my hands on him. He's a dead man."

Zack stopped in front of Sabrina, seeming to remember for the first time that she was there. Then he demanded, "So? Why are you so quiet? Don't tell me you think I'm somehow involved with this!"

She smiled and slipped her arms around his neck. "I

just wanted to see you go ballistic. It's been hours. I needed a fix."

"Huh?" He cocked his head to the side, then returned the smile. "You're flirting with me for real this time?"

"I'm just so happy," she whispered. "It's Donner Lake, Zack. We've got him now. We can go up there—it's doable, right? We'll take the laptop and focus on that area. And we'll ask around. We've got him. We've got *her*. And we did it in time. Thanks to you."

"Me?"

"I would have concentrated on tropical islands. But you're so good. So talented. I'll be grateful till the day I die." Pulling free, she wiped the mist from her eyes and insisted, "Let's get going."

"Wait." He planted his hands on her hips and pulled her back against him. "We need to talk for a minute. And then we need to kiss. Then we'll hit the road, I promise."

She laughed and backed away. "We'll talk and kiss later. I guarantee you. But I can't stand still, Zack. We have to get up there. Pack the computer, okay? I'll get the rest of those sandwiches and we can eat them on the road. We'll take my car—*please* ride with me? I promise not to go too fast on the twisty parts. I just want to ride in the same car with you for once."

"Sabrina?"

She winced at his serious tone. "What?"

"I want five minutes. Now. We can spend it talking or we can spend it arguing about talking. Your choice."

She grimaced, then nodded. "Okay, but make it fast. I'm going to explode if we don't jump on this lead right away."

"Sit down."

She grimaced but complied, settling onto the sofa. He didn't sit beside her, but rather, began to pace.

"Obviously this is great news. We'll get there in time. She'll be fine. We'll have her back safe and sound by tomorrow. So? Where does that leave us?"

"What?"

He gave her a demanding glare. "If we hadn't found her on time, I know what would have happened. We'd have hunted John down together. And after he was in custody or dead, we'd have gone after Zenner. Together. It's not like I wanted that to happen, but at least I knew. But this—we haven't discussed this. And now I want to know. Next week, are you going to be Sabrina Sullivan? Or Brianna York?"

"I don't know. Why do I have to decide now?" She squirmed, impatient. "It depends if she's perfectly healthy, I guess. And if Johnny gets away, well, that's a factor, too."

"And? Am I a factor?"

"Oooohhhhh…"

His glare softened. "Come on, Sabrina. Don't pretend you haven't noticed. Like it or not, we're friends. And we work well together, don't you think? That's what I'm telling you. I want to work with you. Hang out with you. *Make* out with you." He flashed a rueful smile. "Does any of that interest you?"

She nodded. "It all does. Obviously. But Shell and I went into RAP for a reason, and that reason hasn't changed. The day we're not civilians anymore is the day Zenner comes for us."

Zack nodded, clearly prepared for the objection. "I've got that covered. We'll hit him first. Shelby can stay with Theo. We'll beef up security in Monterey until we're sure it's impenetrable, then we'll leave my crew there for good measure. Then you and I will contact the CIA and offer to work with them, the way Sully did when he was chasing Pluto. They'll be happy to have us since we come pretrained and with our own financing." He finally joined her on the couch, his smile cocky. "We'll get Zenner together. That alone has got to be a pretty decent incentive for you. And if half of what I've heard about Shelby is true, she's gonna be on my side. Except she'll want to go after Zenner with us, of course."

"She's always wanted to do that. So have I. But we had to be practical. And when this is over," Sabrina warned him, "I have to be practical again. Strong enough for both of us. And by 'us,' I mean me and my sister."

The statement seemed to hit him right between the eyes, but he recovered quickly. Jumping to his feet, he said, "Okay, that's settled then. Get your gear together while I call Connor and fill him in."

"Zack—"

"Drop it, Sabrina. Let's get on with your mission."

She wanted to say more—to tell him about Adonis Zenner's visit. Then maybe he'd understand how crucial it was for her and Shelby to return to "civilian" status as soon as possible. As much as Zack liked to mock her "mission," it wasn't a joke.

On the other hand, the idea of going on the offensive, of hunting Zenner with Zack, was appealing on so many levels. She did love working with him; she would love to hang out with him. To make out with him—

Her telephone rang, and she sent him an apologetic smile, then reached for the receiver on the end table. "Hello?"

"Breezie? It's Uncle Theo. Did I wake you?"

"Of course not. Wait a minute. I'll put you on speaker. Zack and I have some great news." She pushed the button and returned the receiver to the base, then said loudly, "Uncle Theo? Guess what? We have a lead on Shell's location. They're in the Donner Lake area."

"Are you sure?" Theo murmured.

"Almost positive."

"The reason I ask is…" Theo's tone was uncharacteristically tentative. "I think I saw them here in town this morning."

"What?" Sabrina demanded. "You saw Shelby? In Monterey?"

"Not Shelby. I thought I saw Adonis Zenner. In fact, I'm sure I did. And he was with another man who looked a lot like John Derringer."

Speechless, Sabrina looked to Zack, whose eyes had narrowed with concern. "Are you sure, boss? Zenner? Where exactly did this happen?"

The older man cleared his throat. "There's a new exhibit at the aquarium. I wanted to be there when the doors opened, and I had Sebastian take me to a café on the wharf for a light breakfast first. That's when I saw him. Zenner, I mean. Sebastian had dropped me off and was looking for a parking space. I saw Zenner come out of the café and get into a car driven by a man in a baseball cap. But it was John. I'm practically sure of it. They sped away before I could get Sebastian's attention."

"Did they see you?"

"No. I don't think so."

Sabrina's heart was pounding. "Was there anyone else in the car, Uncle Theo? Maybe she was in the back seat?"

"I don't think so, Breezie. But the windows were tinted, so I suppose it's possible. I'm sorry," he added, his voice cracking. "I should have done something, but I was frozen to the spot. Can you forgive me?"

"Don't be silly. You're not trained for that sort of thing," she told him shakily. "Did you notice what kind of car it was?"

"A black BMW. I didn't get the license plate, though. It all happened so fast."

"That's okay, boss," Zack interrupted. "Are you back home yet?"

"We're pulling up to the gate now."

"Okay. Stay put. We'll be there in a couple of hours."

They barely spoke for the first half hour after Theo's call. Instead they packed up quickly, taking the laptop and sandwiches, along with paraphernalia of their trade—Sabrina's Glock and Sully's bag of tricks and Zack's duffel bag, which he moved from the trunk of his car to Sabrina's. Then he climbed into the passenger side, allowing her to drive as she had requested. He even told her between gritted teeth to "go as fast as you want."

She did just that, her pulse racing in time with the engine. This nightmare was so real—so stunningly out of control—she didn't know what to think. How to plan. How to banish the feelings of guilt so that she could be effective.

And she knew Zack was going through the same miserable exercise, upbraiding himself for having dismissed the possible connection between Zenner and John. For having concentrated on the mountains instead of the sea coast and probably for a million other errors, real and perceived.

When he finally spoke, the frustration in his voice was second only to the remorse. "We wasted thirty-six hours because of me. I'm really sorry, Sabrina. You and Theo tried to tell me—"

"Actually, I made the same mistake you did. I didn't want to accept the fact that a monster like Zenner had her."

"Yeah." The muscles in his jaw were tensing visibly. "I was so full of myself. So sure John wouldn't show his face in Monterey. But he outsmarted me. He picked that location on purpose, knowing I'd never, *ever* consider it. It's like he read my mind, the bastard. He even made calls to rental agents, knowing we'd ask around. That's why he used my name, you know. To taunt me. And I *still* fell for it."

"Well, if it makes you feel any better, I made the biggest, most arrogant mistake of all."

"Trusting me?"

She sighed. "No. If I had trusted you—really trusted you—I would have told you about Zenner's visit to my house yesterday."

She was glad Zack wasn't driving, since the announcement seemed to hit him with the force of a grenade. "What?"

"Go ahead and yell at me. I deserve it. I've been wrestling with it since it happened, and now I see how blind I was. How I let him toy with me—"

"Did he touch you? I'll fucking kill him with my bare hands!"

"No, no. It's nothing like that." She gave him a grateful smile. "I thought you'd be strangling *me* right about now."

He shook his head. "When did this happen? What did he say? Jeez, what are we, complete idiots? Sully must be having a cosmic cow right about now." Taking a deep breath, he repeated more calmly, "What did Zenner say?"

She gave him a complete rundown of the visit, then murmured, "Just the thought of Shell with him terrifies me. At least Johnny has a gentle side—phony but still gentle. But Adonis is so cold. So dead inside."

Zack patted her arm. "On the bright side, his visit tells us she's still alive."

Sabrina turned to him, surprised and grateful. "Really?"

"Watch where you're going! Jeez…" He gave a half-hearted smile. "We can't save her if we're road kill, so take it easy."

"Tell me why you think she's still alive. Please?"

He shrugged. "He says he came to ask you if you're still in the game. And he pretended to be surprised about the kidnapping. But obviously he already had the information. The fact that they're in Monterey means they wanted to keep an eye on Theo's place. To see if you went to him for help. Right?"

"Go on."

"So he knew you were working with us. With me. Marilyn just confirmed that our investigation was progressing slowly. And then he confirmed that with you. And convinced you he wasn't involved, to throw you further off the track. Why bother doing any of that unless he wanted to see how much time they had left to pick her brain?"

"That makes sense. Except…" Sabrina bit her lip. "If she's still alive, would they risk leaving her alone? Wouldn't one of them stay with her at all times?"

"Not necessarily. John probably drugs her a lot. He'll go back to their romantic hideaway, then use DT3 to convince her he's been with her all morning, making love, talking, whatever."

"Oh, God, I hope so."

"She's still alive. I'm sure of it. Because of me, we wasted thirty-six hours checking out the mountains, but on the bright side, Monterey is a better place for us. I know it like the back of my hand. And they can't really hide there as well as at Donner. It's more open, and much more developed."

Sabrina tried to take part in his new optimism, but the knot in her stomach wouldn't quite let her. Even if he was right, and Zenner's visit to her house meant Shelby was still alive, the corollary was equally true. As much as the bad guys wanted to keep probing her brain for the mysterious information until the last possible minute, there was no doubt now what they ultimately intended to do. Zenner had just been taunting Sabrina with talks of alliances and of admiration for Sully. He was going to take great pleasure in killing Shelby Sullivan.

"Do you think he'll use a bomb?" she asked, half to herself.

"We're gonna find her before that happens. We have the upper hand now."

"What universe are *you* in?"

He laughed. "They don't know Theo saw them this morning. So Adonis believes we're still on the wrong track. The very fact that they left Shelby alone this morning shows that they're letting their guard down, doesn't it? They're underestimating us, and probably underestimating her, too."

"Her? You mean, Shell?"

"Right. If Zenner's hanging around in the background, she'll sense it eventually. She's a Sullivan, right? Even if she's consciously falling for John's line, a part of her must suspect the truth. Which means it's not just the two of us anymore. We've got someone on the inside. Remember what your dad always said about that?"

She bit back a smile. "Even the best security system can't keep an insider out?"

"Right."

She stared into his green eyes, greedily absorbing his confidence. "I like that. And even though things are much, much worse than we thought, at least we're finally asking the right questions. Right? The problem isn't the problem anymore."

"Yeah. The only thing keeping us from complete success is your driving. So slow it down, will you?"

* * *

"I trust your instincts," Zack was telling her as they drove down the road leading to Theo's gatehouse. "But I still don't see the connection between Shelby's kidnapping and the number of times the Zenners hit—or didn't hit—Perimeter over the years."

"Neither do I," she admitted. "Maybe it's tied into the information they're trying to get out of Shell's memory."

Zack pursed his lips. "Yeah. I'd like to figure that out. But again, is it necessary? What we need is the exact location where they're holding her, pure and simple."

"Well, as soon as we get inside, you can have a nerd-fest with satellite images of Monterey and its surrounding areas. There can't be more than a zillion black BMWs around here, right?"

He started to laugh, but the sound died on his lips, and Sabrina realized his alert gaze had focused on the guardhouse. "What's wrong? Oh…" She could see now that the position wasn't manned. "Maybe he's on a break? The gate's still closed. That's a good sign, isn't it?"

"Stop here. Stay in the car." Zack pulled his pistol from its shoulder holster and opened the door, then pointed the weapon while warily crossing the two hundred yards to the guardhouse.

Furious with herself for leaving her Glock in the trunk with the rest of her gear, Sabrina forced herself to stay in the car, watching in every direction for signs of intruders. Then she saw Zack drop to one knee beside the doorless entry to the gatehouse, and she knew he had found a body. She only hoped the guy was still breathing.

He signaled for her to drive up, and as she did so, he triggered the pedestrian gate. Then he walked back to her and motioned for her to stop again. "Let's get your stuff. Do you have your own vest?"

"No."

"I've got an extra."

She popped the trunk, then followed him to the rear of the car. "Is the guard hurt bad? Shouldn't we call someone?"

"He's dead."

"Oh, God, are you sure? Is it Fred?"

"Yeah." Zack's eyes were blazing with anger. "They got him right between the eyes."

"Why? Why would they come here? It's crazy."

He helped her into a thin shock vest, fastening it tight across her chest. "I need you to follow my lead. Just this once. Back me up, okay?"

"I will."

"We'll leave the car here and go along the windbreak." He looked deep into her eyes. "Be prepared for anything. Theo might be dead already. Marietta and Sebastian, too. You're going to have to deal with that later. Not now."

She nodded.

"Okay." He took a deep breath, then inclined his head toward the trees. "Let's move."

She followed his lead in more ways than one, adopting his cool, almost-detached attitude as they made their way to the back of the house, entering through the servants' quarters, which led to the kitchen. There was no sign of Marietta or Sebastian, and Sabrina hoped they might be at the store or otherwise safely away from the scene of the burglary.

They began to move noiselessly down the hall leading to Theo's study, and they saw the cook lying motionless, a deep gash on her head.

Zack held his finger to his lips, then dropped down to

check Marietta's pulse. Sabrina could see from his expression that he was relieved.

"Stay with her," he mouthed.

When Sabrina shook her head, he scowled but nodded, then gestured for her to continue following him. The doors to the study were wide open, and Zack hugged the wall with his back as he moved toward it, his pistol raised. Sabrina did likewise, listening intently to the voices emanating from the room.

She couldn't make out any words, but still she felt a wave of relief. Theo was alive. There was no mistaking his voice, even though it was soft and tremulous. Zack seemed to think so, too, flashing an encouraging smile, then holding up three fingers.

When Sabrina had nodded that she understood, he made a fist, then raised one finger, mouthing, "One," at the same time. Then, "Two." Then he raised the third finger and they burst into the room, side by side, their weapons aimed toward the desk as Zack shouted, "Freeze!"

"Oh, God," Sabrina whispered, her gaze traveling from Theo's terrified face to Zenner's sneering one.

Theo was sitting in his chair, with the assassin right beside him, holding a gun to his temple.

"Drop it, Zenner," Zack ordered him.

"Relax, Mr. Lansing." Adonis gave Sabrina a cheerful smile. "Twice in one week. What an unexpected pleasure."

"Uncle Theo? Are you hurt?" she asked, ignoring the taunt.

"No," Theo told her, but she could see from his eyes that he was terrified, and she remembered Paul Hanover's heart attack. Was this a replay of that event? Adonis Zenner, scaring a wonderful man to death?

"Put the weapon on the desk and move away," Zack insisted. "There's no way you're getting out of here, Zenner. If you want to live, you'll cooperate. At least you'll get a trial, which is more than you deserve."

"You're saying you won't shoot me the minute I'm unarmed?"

"That's what I'm saying. It'll kill *me* not to kill *you*, but you've got my word. That's how it'll go down."

"I have a better idea," Adonis told him. "You put down your weapons, and you'll have my word I won't kill anyone. Or should I say, anyone else?"

Sabrina glanced at Zack, whose jaw was clenched. And she knew he was thinking about Fred, lying in a pool of blood.

Stepping forward, she demanded, "Where's my sister?"

"That again?" Adonis laughed. "I'm wounded. After all we've meant to each other? What made you begin suspecting me again?"

"Uncle Theo saw you this morning with John Derringer."

"I beg your pardon?" Adonis seemed genuinely offended. "Didn't we establish that he isn't in our league, darling? At least now I understand why you broke your promise."

"My promise?"

"It's been twenty-four hours. You never called. So I decided to take matters in my own hands and find the little princess for you."

"By coming here?" she murmured.

"I wanted information about Derringer. This seemed like a good place to start. But Howell here told me you have the files. The only copy. That seemed unlikely, so I've been trying to persuade him to cooperate."

"I did take the only copy," Sabrina admitted. "I left it in Sacramento." Confusion fogged her brain. "Uncle Theo saw you with Derringer this morning."

"That's impossible, since I've never met the fellow."

"I said it looked like him, but I wasn't sure," Theo reminded her, his voice shaking. "He was wearing a baseball cap, but he was definitely the right size. The car windows were tinted."

"Where was this?" Adonis asked.

"Down the street from the aquarium."

Adonis's eyes twinkled. "I did meet with an associate today. But I assure you, it wasn't a two-bit criminal like Derringer."

"Okay, that's enough," Zack interrupted. "You came here for information about John? I don't buy it. You killed one of my men—"

"It's what I do." Adonis grinned. "I can kill this quivering boss of yours, too. It's up to you. Or you can put down your weapons and I'll leave quietly."

Sabrina glanced at Zack, wondering what he was going to do. There was a cold gleam in his eyes and she guessed he was calculating the odds. Wondering if it wasn't best to sacrifice Theo to save Sabrina and avenge Sully.

Zenner seemed to be sensing something, too, because he insisted suddenly, "There is a third solution. Mr. Howell, reach into my left pocket, won't you?"

"Wait." Zack scowled. "What are you up to?"

"A solution, as I said. No one else gets killed today. And you and I play a harmless little game. How does that sound?" Before Zack could answer, he added with a growl, "Do what I say, Howell, or I'll air-condition your skull."

Theo stuck his hand into Adonis's jacket pocket, pulling out what looked like a complicated set of handcuffs.

"What's that?" Zack demanded. "Theo, be careful. Put it on the desk. Gently."

"You've got your father's instincts," Adonis congratulated him. Then he arched an eyebrow. "That's right. I know all about him. Nasty way to die, isn't it? But he asked for it. So did Sully. You don't want to be next, do you?"

Sabrina stared at the device in disbelief. It was so slender. Could it possibly be a bomb? That's what Zack and Adonis seemed to be saying, wasn't it?

"Unhook the two pieces from each other, Howell. And like your man there said, do it gently. Good. Now put the cuff around your wrist and snap it shut."

Sabrina watched in morbid fascination as Theo followed Adonis's directions. The assassin then told him to very, very carefully hand him the second piece.

Adonis held up the device. "Do you know what this is, Lansing?"

"A remote detonator."

"Very good. If I push the button, Howell loses an arm. Which might not be so bad, but it'll probably take a piece of his chest with it. Very messy. I've really never tried this little gem out, so we're just speculating. But I predict it will function well." Dropping the bantering tone, he explained, "This detonator has a range of two hundred yards. It shouldn't take me long to cover that distance. In the meantime, you'll be busy disarming the device. From the moment Howell snapped it shut, the timer began to count down. It started at five minutes. The sooner I leave, the sooner you can get started."

Zack took a step forward, his eyes narrowed with contempt. "Disarm it yourself. *Now.* Or you're the one who'll lose a chunk of chest."

"Tick, tick, tick," Adonis told him with a shrug.

"Zack, let him go," Theo pleaded. "We don't have time to play games."

Adonis grinned, then started to edge away from the

desk. In his right hand he held the remote detonator. In his left, the pistol, which was now aimed at Sabrina. "Get to work, Lansing. You've got four minutes."

"Zack," Sabrina whispered. "Let him go. We'll figure out some way to get that off Uncle Theo's wrist."

"Smart girl. Listen to her," Adonis advised. "Tick, tick, tick."

"Shut up," Zack told him. "Put down the detonator and disarm that fucking thing."

"Tick, tick, tick."

"Fuck!" Zack shoved his pistol into its holster and strode over to the desk. "Sabrina, cover him until you're sure he's out the house, but don't follow him. Come back and help Marietta. Stay out of this room. Is that clear?"

She nodded, focusing completely on Adonis, who gave her a cheerful wave, then ambled into the hall, adding over his shoulder, "Tell Lansing there's a trick to it."

"What kind of trick?" she demanded, trailing him with her gun pointed at his head.

"A mnemonic. I always use them with experimental devices. Tell him the acronym is GROW—G-R-O-W. But the trick is, should he reverse it?"

"I don't understand," she murmured. "Reverse what?"

But Adonis just waved her away, saying, "Your boyfriend needs the information. Go on. Here's hoping we meet again soon."

He darted through the front doorway and out onto the porch. She wanted to run after him—to make him explain what he meant by reversing it—but there was no time, so she spun and ran back to Zack instead.

Chapter 10

Theo was still sitting in his chair, his cuffed arm resting on the desk. The cover of the explosive device had been removed, revealing an intricate maze of wire and metal. Also on the desk was a row of delicate-looking silver instruments arranged in a black leather case. And Zack was standing over all of it, like a surgeon, probing carefully at the bomb with a slender, pinlike tool.

She approached quickly but noiselessly, giving Theo an encouraging smile. Then she whispered, "Zack?"

"Get out," he told her without shifting his gaze. "Take care of Marietta."

"Adonis said there's a mnemonic. It's an acronym. GROW—G-R-O-W. Do you have any idea what that means?"

Zack gave her a quick look, then turned his attention back to the bomb. "Grow?"

"Adonis said you might have to reverse it."

"Reverse what? Damn, this thing is bizarre."

"Two minutes," Theo said, his lip trembling. "If you can't do it, you should both just go. Call 9-1-1. Maybe it won't do as much damage as—well, maybe it won't kill me."

"Theo's right. Get out of here, Sabrina," Zack insisted. "Call an ambulance. Take care of Marietta. Just stay clear of this room." To his employer, he added boldly, "I want all the glory for myself. Don't worry, boss. Two minutes is a nice, long window. I'll have you out of this in ninety seconds tops."

Sabrina watched, transfixed.

Then Zack murmured to no one in particular, "An acronym? For the colors maybe?"

"The colors?" She moved closer, then nodded, amazed. Green, red, orange and white. Grow. It was so obvious, she wondered why she hadn't seen it right away.

The only problem was, there were *two* white wires. And Zack might need to reverse the process, which made no sense at all.

"Okay, folks." Zack reached for a pair of tiny silver clippers. "Here goes nothing. Sabrina?" He looked up at her and instructed grimly, "Stand the hell back. I can't think clearly with you there."

She took two steps back, then watched as he began snipping wires. First one white one, then the other. Then he gave Theo a reassuring wink and cut the orange wire.

"Fuck," he whispered. "I think that asshole told us the truth. Hold on to your hats, folks. We got the W and the O. Here's R." He cut the red one, then exhaled in relief and sent Sabrina a mischievous smile. "Want to cut the last one?"

"Just do it!"

He laughed and complied. "Looks like you're gonna live, big guy."

Theo buried his face in his hands and moaned, while Zack clapped him on the shoulder. Sabrina moved quickly around the desk to embrace the older man, then she looked up at Zack. "You were amazing."

"He gave me the acronym," Zack said with a shrug. Then he strode toward the doorway. "Stay with him. Call 9-1-1. I'm gonna check on Marietta."

Two hours later the last of the police and FBI had left the premises, taking the bomb with them, along with statements from Theo, Zack and Sabrina. The three witnesses had been candid in their identification of Adonis Zenner, whose name the authorities had recognized, knowing that the notorious killer had had run-ins with Perimeter in the past, most notably, when he'd murdered Sully Sullivan in nearby Santa Cruz.

But no one—not Theo, not Sabrina, not Zack—said a word about Shelby's predicament, nor did they talk about Zenner's interest in information about John Derringer. Instead they vaguely mentioned that Adonis had come in search of confidential files, but Sabrina and Zack had arrived before he was able to secure any.

Sabrina took a few minutes to freshen up—and to order roses for Annette of Truckee Travel Pros—before joining Zack in the study where he had set up his laptop. "Thank God things have finally settled down," she told him with a sigh.

"How's Theo?"

"Kind of a wreck. The paramedics gave him a sedative, so hopefully he'll doze off soon." She walked over to him and peered at the screen. "Donner Lake, I presume?"

"Yeah. Unless you think Adonis was lying again, and he really is part of the kidnapping."

"That doesn't seem likely. He came here for information about Johnny so he could track him down, right?"

Zack shrugged. "So he said."

"At least he didn't lie to us about that acronym. Speaking of which, I took some pictures of the bomb before the FBI confiscated it. Here." She handed him a digital camera. "Can you load them onto the screen?"

"Why?" he asked, closing the file he was working on and interfacing the camera with the laptop.

"I want you to show me how you knew which wire to cut."

Zack retrieved the first picture, which clearly showed the inner workings of Zenner's explosive cuff. "It was easy. Like you said, he gave me the answer."

"But you still had to know whether or not to reverse the letters. Plus, there were two white wires. How did you know which one to cut first?"

Zack exhaled in mock exasperation. "You can't learn this stuff from a picture, Sabrina."

"Humor me."

"Okay. Look at this white one. See what it's hooked to?" He used a pencil point to indicate the spot. "That's a receiver. For the remote detonator. If Zenner had triggered it, the bomb would have gone off instantly. So I figured his acronym probably called for him to cut that one first. After that, it was downhill, right?"

"I guess." She tapped the screen. "What about this green one? It leads from the timer to the explosive, right? So why not make *that* your second cut? Without the remote detonator or the timer, the bomb would never go off. Right?"

Zack grinned. "Why didn't I think of that?"

"Come on, Zack! Teach me."

"I'll teach you later." He pulled her into his lap. "Right now I just want to enjoy the fact that we're still alive."

"Thanks to you." She rested her hands on his shoulders. "My hero."

"Yeah—which reminds me, what part of 'Do what I say' don't you understand?"

"Hmm?"

He laughed. "I told you to stay with Marietta. You didn't. I told you not to come back to the study after Zenner left. You did it anyway. I ordered you to get out, but you stayed."

"But otherwise, I did exactly what you wanted," she reminded him, then she suggested softly, "Order me to do something now. I promise I'll do it."

He licked his lips, then caressed her face before gently covering her mouth with his own. Sabrina gave an appreciative moan and returned the kiss while threading her fingers through his dark curls, enjoying the feel of him without even considering the consequences.

"Nice," he murmured when they finally came up for air.

She nodded, wondering what would happen now. She wanted to make love with him, and his body was telling her he wanted that, too. But they couldn't spare the time. Not now. Maybe after they found Shelby…

Back to that again, she told herself sadly. *After you find her, you've got to become Brianna York again. A teacher. A civilian. Not a player, as Adonis would say.*

"Talk to me," Zack suggested.

She stroked his face as he'd done to hers. "I don't know what to say. You're so brave and talented. If anyone could catch Zenner, you could. But you saw him, Zack. He's… he's so sophisticated. Playing with us like we're his puppets. I don't want to hurt your feelings, but Dad was fifty-three years old when he went after Pluto. He had over twenty-five years of intelligence training and experience, and it *still* took him a year to find him. I can't take that kind of chance with Shell's safety. Going back to Sacramento is my only practical alternative."

"Sully was the best. I'm not pretending I'm that good. Or that I'll ever be that good. But he didn't have you to help him. And he didn't have Shelby. You keep telling me what a natural she is. Between three of us—"

"No!"

"Your decision, not hers? She's twenty-three years old, Sabrina." He shook his head. "Fine. We leave her out of it. We park her someplace safe."

"Like here? That was your suggestion this morning," she reminded him, shrugging out of his lap and backing two steps away. "Adonis made mincemeat out of Theo's security."

Zack's jaw tensed. "That's because Theo insisted on staying with this antiquated system. Gates and guards. And frankly, who knew he was in danger from anyone but a burglar? This system would have worked fine against that. Anyway, it changes as of today. Connor's on his way here, and so are my two best guys. There will be three men here around-the-clock until a state-of-the-art system is installed."

He stood and walked to her, taking her hands in his own. "If that's not good enough, we'll send Shelby to Dallas. The system at King Dominik's ranch is the best in the world, bar none. And they'd love her down there. The prince is a playboy with a weakness for blondes. How does that sound?"

She stared into his eyes, wanting to believe it was possible. After all these years of hiding from Adonis, the thought that she and Zack could go after him—make him pay for what he had done to her father, to Fred, maybe even to Paul Hanover—was intoxicating. Shelby would be safe in Dallas. Zack's men would see to that.

Except it was *her* job to protect Shelby. And until Johnny, she'd done a pretty good job of it by being practical. Sure it would be fun—exhilarating—to hunt Zenner down. But they could never be one hundred percent sure Shelby was safe. On the other hand, if they became the York sisters again, she was pretty sure Adonis would honor the bargain, as he'd done for five years already.

And if he decided to break the truce, she'd be ready for him.

"Am I interrupting something?" Theo asked from the doorway.

"Oh!" Sabrina pulled her hands free and hurried across the room, embracing the older man. "What are you doing out of bed?"

"I'm not an invalid," he scolded in return. "Except for a few scratches on my wrist from Sebastian's tools, I'm fine. Not like poor Marietta. Is there any news on her condition?"

"She's doing well. The doctor says she'll be home by Sunday. Sebastian's with her, so don't worry." Sabrina sighed and led Theo over to the sofa. "We're lucky he was at the store when Adonis got here. Losing Fred was bad enough. And if we had lost *you*—" she gave him a last hug before he settled down "—I never would have forgiven myself."

"Imagine how I feel," he murmured. "Dragging you down here when you should be at Donner Lake finding your sister. I swear I thought that other man was Derringer—"

"I'm glad you made that mistake," Sabrina told him. "If you hadn't, Zack and I wouldn't have come down here. You would have been at the mercy of that monster."

"She's right, boss," Zack agreed. "We can't know for sure what would have happened, but the very fact he brought that bomb cuff with him was a bad sign. I think he would have used it on you if we hadn't gotten here when we did."

"I'm so grateful," Theo assured him. "But it's strange, don't you think?"

"In what way?"

"He didn't have to give you that acronym. We had already let him go by then. Of course, you probably would have disarmed the bomb in time anyway, but it's odd, isn't it? That he helped you out?"

"That's true." Sabrina nodded. "He had already killed Fred. And he brought the cuff for a reason, like Zack said. So why did he give us the acronym?"

Zack shrugged. "He figured I'd come after him with guns blazing if that thing went off. This way, we didn't pursue him. Believe me, he wasn't doing us any favors."

Sabrina sat beside Theo and snuggled against him. "What a day. Aren't you exhausted?"

"I want to help with the search for Shelby," the older man insisted. "Isn't there something I can do? To make up for the lost time I caused?"

Sabrina was about to say 'no,' then she pursed her lips, remembering Adonis's enigmatic misstatement. "There is something, Uncle Theo. We don't know if it's important or not, but it might just be pivotal."

"How can I help?"

"We need information about the history of the company. You're the best source, right?"

"I would hope so, since I founded it and never took my eyes off it in thirty-five years."

She smiled. "In all that time, we only lost one client in the line of duty, right?"

"Right. Derringer's screwup in the Canary Islands."

"Right. But we had clients die during all those years, didn't we? I mean, from natural causes?"

When Theo just stared, clearly confused, Zack explained, "It's a hunch Sabrina has, boss. About Paul Hanover's heart attack. She thinks Zenner caused it."

"I wouldn't be surprised if he did," Theo muttered. "He almost scared *me* to death this afternoon, even before I pulled that bomb out of his pocket. If he came anywhere near San Francisco the day Paul died, then I agree with Sabrina."

"Thanks." Sabrina gave his shoulders a squeeze. "What about our clients? Any heart attacks during all those years?"

Theo frowned. "You think Adonis went to their homes and scared them to death? If he got close enough to do that, why wouldn't he just blow them up? Or shoot them?"

"Good question," Zack said, eyeing Sabrina sympathetically. "Making Perimeter look bad—and himself look good—is part of his job as an assassin. Why not get the credit?"

"Because he didn't want Dad coming after him," Sabrina reminded them, more convinced by the minute. "He said it was respect for Dad that kept him and Pluto from touching our clients, but it was really fear. So maybe somewhere along the line, they pulled a job without letting us know they'd done it. That way, they could get their fee, but there wouldn't be any repercussions."

"That makes sense," Zack admitted. "And he was right. The first time he openly hit us, Sully came after them. And Pluto ended up dead."

Theo was shaking his head. "I still don't understand. You're saying he scared one of our clients to death?"

Sabrina shrugged. "There are poisons, or overdoses, or other chemical means of simulating heart attacks, aren't there? That's what I'm really suggesting. The police in San

Francisco saw the suicide note—and had Marilyn as a witness—so they probably didn't question the validity of Paul's heart attack. Maybe Zenner did that once before as well."

Theo's eyes were beginning to glaze over. "Even if this is true, how does it help us find Michelle? I mean, Shelby."

"It doesn't," Zack agreed. "You look beat, Theo. Go to bed. When you wake up, we'll probably be gone, but Connor will be here until my crew arrives. After that, I'm sending him to Dallas—"

"Wait a minute." Theo's tone had gone from plaintive to autocratic in less than a minute. "*You're* going to Dallas. That's our agreement with King Dominik, and we're going to honor it."

Zack scowled. "We made that agreement before Shelby was kidnapped. There's no way I'm going, so just get used to it."

The older man returned the scowl. "If you use my private jet, Dallas is three short hours away. You'll be gone for less than a day. But if you don't make an appearance, Dominik will drop us. I don't have to tell you how devastating that will be for us financially. And our reputation will suffer, too. Perhaps irreparably."

For a moment Sabrina thought Zack was going to lose his temper. Then he surprised her by joining them on the couch and adopting a soothing voice. "That system we built in Dallas is so sophisticated, it could run itself. And it's so high-tech, Connor is actually the better choice. If something goes wrong, it'll be in the software. Or the hardware. Or some other gizmo." He gave his boss an encouraging smile. "The king will be so busy celebrating Nikolo's birthday, he won't even notice I'm not there. And if he does complain, I'll square it with him. I promise."

Theo cleared his throat, then turned to Sabrina. "They're

our best client. It's only because of this multimillion-dollar contract that the company survived. You know how much I love you and Michelle, but it's twenty-four hours at the most. It'll take that long for you to find the right cabin, won't it? Zack will be back in time to help with the actual rescue."

"Leave Sabrina out of it," Zack muttered.

"She deserves to know the truth," Theo retorted. "She says she would never have willingly hurt the company. So let's make sure this time she understands the facts."

The older man's voice grew terse. "Fact number one—they are our most important client. Fact number two—they only signed with Perimeter because Dominik was so impressed with Zack personally. Fact number three—these birthday parties of Nikolo's are the only time during the year when the king and prince are highly vulnerable to assassination."

"Who wants to kill them?" Sabrina asked.

"No one!" Zack jumped up and began to pace. "It's all theoretical. Like a poly-sci hypothetical, but without any real teeth." Stopping in front of Sabrina, he explained, "Dominik left Delphinia thirty years ago, driven out by the military. He has consistently made it clear he never intends to return, even though there's a rabid faction that would love to restore him to the throne."

"That's right," Theo interjected. "The problem is, Nikolo has made his intentions clear, too. The day he inherits the title, either because his father abdicates it to him, or because Dominik dies, he'll return to Delphinia and fight for his birthright."

"So?" Sabrina asked. "That's who the military wants to assassinate? Prince Nikolo?"

"They'd never dare," Zack assured her. "The day they hurt

his beloved son is the day Dominik changes sides. The militarists know that. So, even though they'd love to assassinate Nikolo, they won't. Not until he's actually the new king."

"Which the monarchists want to happen sooner or later, so *they'd* love to see Dominik die." Theo eyed Sabrina grimly. "So you see, there's a threat from each side. The militarists want the prince dead. The monarchists want to kill Dominik."

"That's ridiculous," Zack muttered. "The monarchists love their king. That's what makes them monarchists in the first place! They've sworn their allegiance to Dominik. Case closed."

As the two men continued to argue, Sabrina closed her eyes and thought about the impact this could have on her search for Shelby. As much as she could use Zack's expertise and experience, they had narrowed things down enough that she honestly believed she could handle it on her own.

And now that they had eliminated Zenner as a suspect again, the old problem had resurfaced. She didn't want Johnny to panic and do something crazy, which was exactly what might happen if he found out Perimeter was after him. She was much better off working on her own from this point forward. If Johnny caught on to her, he'd believe she was simply worried about Shelby. He'd have no reason to think she knew about the DT3, much less that he had used it on her as well as Shelby. He'd try to find a way out of his predicament short of killing anyone.

But if he caught even a glimpse of his former Perimeter colleague, he'd know he had to kill Zack *and* both Sullivan sisters.

She could try to explain that to Zack, and he might even be willing to hang back until the very end, but she knew he wouldn't let her walk into the mountain cabin alone.

He'd want to be at her side, or better still, five steps ahead of her, as he'd been when they entered the Howell mansion that afternoon.

Theo's face was turning red with anger. "I make the decisions around here. It's still my company."

"You handle the money. I handle operations."

"This *is* about money! Dominik's money, which we need to survive." Theo took a deep breath, then insisted, "Connor's crew can take over the search for Michelle temporarily. Until you get back."

"Don't make me laugh. He's the one who let Derringer grab her in the first place! He's a great guy, but he's no crew leader. We both know that. Sully knew it, too. So drop it."

"I agree with Zack," Sabrina said suddenly. "Connor can't lead a crew. But I can."

"Huh?" Zack stared at her, as did Theo.

"It's just for a few hours," she continued with a reassuring smile. "Dad raised me to be a crew leader, you know. And you could lend me a couple of your guys, right? Plus, I'd have Connor. He knows everything about using the satellite intel, which is my only weak area. By the time you get back from Dallas, we'll have the place identified and surrounded."

"Have you lost your mind?"

Theo held up his hand. "She's got a point, Zack. This is what Sully would have wanted. He trained her for it from the day she was born. He poured his blood, sweat and tears into this company just waiting for the day when she'd take over a crew."

"You're both nuts," Zack told them, his grin belying the anger in his eyes. "Drop it. Connor goes to Dallas, I stay here. That's final."

"You work for me," Theo reminded him. "I pay your salary. A very generous one, by the way. Dominik expects you by noon, Texas time, which mean I expect you on the jet tomorrow morning by 8:00 a.m. sharp. And *that's* final."

Zack stared, incredulous, then turned to Sabrina, his voice so low, it was almost a growl. "Connor can't hack it. And neither can you. If you want to save your sister's life, you'll tell Theo right this minute that you need me here."

Sabrina forced herself to look straight into his green eyes. "Give me your two best men and Connor, and I'll be fine. Be sure to station three men here to protect my uncle, too. Take everyone else to Dallas. And have a safe trip. We'll rendezvous with you in Truckee as soon as you get back. You can probably land in Reno, right? I'll have a car waiting to pick you up."

There was dead silence for so long, Sabrina actually started to twitch. Then Zack turned away from her, focusing on Theo instead. "I'll cover Dallas tomorrow night. After that, I'm out of here. I never wanted this goddamned job in the first place."

"Zack "

"Just drop it, Theo." He turned his wrath in Sabrina's direction, but she could see he was speechless. He did however manage to dig into the pocket of his jeans, pulling out the locket she had given him the afternoon they met. "Here. I won't be needing this anymore. Good luck finding your sister."

She knew she only had an instant to repair this. To plead with him to stay. To apologize for manipulating the situation so shamelessly.

But she didn't speak. She just stuck out her hand and accepted the locket, then watched in stubborn silence as he stormed out of the study.

Chapter 11

Shelby sat on the edge of the bed in the Donner Lake cabin's master bedroom, staring in wordless confusion at the folded piece of paper in her hand. It was such a simple thing, but it was scaring her to death.

She had known for days that something was wrong, but she hadn't realized *how* wrong until she found this letter tucked away—hidden, really—in the lining of her suitcase. It was a letter to Sabrina, and if the date was correct, Shelby had written it on Tuesday, the fourth day of her romantic getaway with Johnny.

The question was, why?

Unfolding the page, she warily reread its cheerful contents.

Hey, Breezie! You must be freaking out by now! Sorry I didn't call like I promised. Johnny's such a romantic fool, he snuck my cell out of my purse right before we left. And there's no phone here, so I really have been incommunicado. But there's a caretaker who prowls this place, and if you're reading this, I guess I managed to con him into mailing it for me behind Johnny's back. Please don't worry. I'm so happy, it's criminal. See ya Saturday! Love, Shell

Oh, God... Shelby wrapped her arms around herself and began to rock. *It's so much worse than I thought...*

"Hey, beautiful," a voice boomed from the doorway. "I thought you said you'd be down in five minutes. Shell?" His tone softened. "Is everything okay?"

She looked up at him, wanting to find the words to explain how miserable and confused she felt, but the effort failed her and she ran to him instead, throwing herself against his chest and bursting into the tears that had been threatening for days.

"Oh, shit!" He bundled her up and carried her to the bed, then sat with her in his lap, rocking her gently and crooning, "I'm so sorry, Shell. Can you ever forgive me?"

"You didn't do anything wrong," she said, sobbing. "It's me! There's something wrong with me, Johnny, and it's getting worse. I think I'm losing my mind."

"What are you talking about?" He pried her face from his chest and forced her to look into his clear blue eyes. "The dizziness? That's just temporary, baby. I promise."

"No, Johnny. It's not just that." She stood, then handed him the letter. "Look what I found in my suitcase."

As he scanned the page, the blank expression on his face scared her anew. She was crazy. Even he knew it now.

But to his credit, he rallied quickly. "What's the problem? I mean, besides the obvious. You actually considered talking to that psycho caretaker behind my back? Thank God you didn't do it."

"Pay attention. Look at the date. I wrote it on Tuesday. But by then I had already talked to Brie twice, remember? On Sunday, then again on Monday. But this letter—"

"Obviously you wrote this letter on Saturday. When we first got here. When we were still keeping our pledge not to contact the outside world. Which lasted exactly one day," he said, his tone gently teasing. "That's how long it took for me to learn not to come between sisters." When Shelby just stared, he explained more bluntly, "You misdated it. Mystery solved."

Shelby bit her lip. "That doesn't explain why I don't remember writing it."

"You don't?" He cleared his throat. "That's probably the dizziness again. You're light-headed. It's temporary."

"I guess."

"Come here." He pulled her back into his lap. "How do you feel now?"

She snuggled against him. "A little scared, to tell you the truth. In my family we have this…this culture. Where we trust our instincts above any of our other senses. But I—I don't trust mine anymore."

"Would it help to talk to Briana? I mean, in person? Today?"

Shelby stared up at him, allowing the suggestion to warm her. "You paid through tomorrow afternoon—"

"Yeah, but I've had it with this dump. And I kinda miss the Banshee myself. So let's hit the road, shall we?"

"Oh, Johnny." She wrapped her arms around his neck. "I don't deserve you. You're so wonderful. And I'm so brain-dead."

"Don't say that," he protested. "It's just the altitude."

She hugged him again. "Will you love me even if I stay dizzy forever?"

"Yeah." He gave her a brilliant smile. "Do you want me to pack your things while you rest?"

"No. I can do it."

"Good. Call me when you're ready and I'll carry the suitcase. Meanwhile, I'll put the finishing touches on our breakfast. It's brunch really, if that's okay. Omelets and fruit salad. And iced tea, of course. Your favorite."

"Yum."

"Our last meal here," he added softly.

She touched his cheek. "You really did pick a romantic spot. I'm sorry I ruined it."

"I'm sorry, too," he told her. "It wasn't supposed to end this way, but—" He smoothed a wisp of hair from her forehead. "It'll all be over soon. That's the best I can do."

"You make it sound so final," she scolded him.

"Right." He shook his head as though clearing away unpleasant thoughts. "Take a shower and pack. If you start feeling dizzy, call me. Otherwise, I'll meet you on the patio in ten minutes, and we'll drink one last toast to this star-crossed vacation."

Sabrina usually ran three miles every morning, rain or shine, and her body had apparently missed the workout, because she was burning up the road on Friday morning, despite the fact that she was pushing a three-wheeled baby carriage. In fact she had to remind herself to be more careful, so that onlookers would be convinced the brightly colored vehicle contained precious cargo.

And in fact it did carry some amazing possessions, including her Glock, her father's "bag of tricks" and a pair of high-powered binoculars, which she had to resist using while out in the open like this. It was very important that she appear to be vacationing, not stalking.

Would Johnny be watching for her? She suspected he would. Hopefully he wouldn't recognize her, dressed as an ultrafit new mom in her red shorts, red bikini top, expensive running shoes and stylish visor. She had considered dying her hair, but decided it might work against her if she had to convince him she was there to confront a simple fortune hunter, not a kidnapper. Anything to keep him from realizing how high the stakes had become.

The mountain air intoxicated her, as did the fact that she was so far ahead of schedule. She had set herself the goal of finding Shelby by Friday night at the latest, on the theory Johnny wouldn't do anything drastic until Saturday morning. But at this rate, she could spend a few hours surveying the area and still rescue her sister by late afternoon.

All because she had caught a break, courtesy of the satellite photos. Once she had narrowed the search to Donner Lake, she had realized quickly that only a few sectors provided what Johnny needed in a hideout—luxury and seclusion, but with a magnificent view of the lake and the ability to monitor traffic on major roads without allowing easy access to the cabin itself.

The baby carriage bounced in and out of a rut and Sabrina reminded herself again that Johnny could be watching. Plus, she didn't want the little bottle of DT3 she had "borrowed" from Theo's desk drawer to break. She couldn't wait to use *that* on John Derringer—to find out once and for all what he had been searching for in the brains of the Sullivan sisters.

She also didn't want the liquid spilling on the most precious of all items in the carriage: the image of a cabin that was tucked among the pines, commanding a sweeping view of its surroundings. She could still feel a shiver as she remembered the moment, right around midnight, when she had zeroed in on that particular property, using an image recorded by the satellite on Wednesday morning. Her eyes had detected two tiny figures—a man carrying a girl in his arms, back toward the cabin. She had zoomed, then zoomed some more, until she was almost sure she was looking at a picture of her sister.

"Time to get to work," she told herself. She estimated that she was only a few hundred yards from the cabin. All she needed was some cover, then she could use the binoculars to confirm her position. After that, she would methodically survey all possible means of ingress and egress, both for the lot and for the cabin itself.

Zack would be good at this part. Just like Dad would. So take a lesson from them and don't rush it. You've got plenty of time. Use it.

She still felt guilty about her treatment of Zack. But he was a big boy, with ego to spare, and he'd be fine. So would Connor and the others, whom she had sent on wild-goose chases before announcing that she was leaving Monterey for her house in Sacramento and would rendezvous there with them at 8:00 a.m. Friday.

By now they knew she had ditched them. They might even have called Zack in Dallas for advice. And he would have told them about the tracking sensor he had hidden in her locket under her mother's picture. It had been clever of him to plan that sort of thing in advance, just in case she took off alone at the last minute. But Sabrina had somehow known it was there and had pried it loose, attaching it instead to the bumper of a car at a gas station along the highway.

Finding the perfect spot, a dense grove of pine trees, Sabrina got to work. First she changed into jeans, boots and a dark green T-shirt, then she strapped on her shoulder holster, obscuring it as well as possible with a loose black sweatshirt. Making sure the carriage was tucked out of sight, she retrieved the binoculars and sank to one knee, careful to keep the lenses from reflecting any light as she turned them toward the cabin.

She could stay here for hours if needed. She had enough food and water. And she had patience. Because if panic was an agent's worst enemy, patience was the key to success.

Then she saw her baby sister standing all alone on the deck, her blond curls pulled into a ponytail, making her look even younger than her twenty-three years, and patience disappeared in a burst of frenzied relief.

Shelby looked so healthy. So alive! A little tired, maybe, but otherwise fine. And Sabrina was able to breathe—really breathe—for the first time in days, which made her realize she had been harboring a frightening image deep inside. An image of her baby sister with bruises and a blank expression on her face, handcuffed to a basement wall. Or worse, to a bed.

"Okay, Johnny," she murmured. "I guess I'll let you live."

Using the tall, fragrant pines as much as possible for cover, she quickly crossed to the edge of the cabin's lot, forcing herself to take it slow. Play it smart. Then John Derringer walked out onto the deck, carrying a tray of food—and drink!—and something inside the older sister snapped.

"No more," she said, her voice a low growl. Then she stepped into the clearing with her gun fixed on her target, and shouted, "Freeze!"

Johnny froze as instructed. More importantly, Shelby did the same, which didn't really surprise Sabrina. She knew now that her father had planted a suggestion in his younger daughter's brain—a suggestion that she would always follow Sabrina's instructions. It was the reason

Shelby had followed her so docilely into RAP when her heart had raged at her to go after Adonis. It was the reason Shelby had never contacted Perimeter, had barely touched the trust fund, had obeyed Sabrina in a dozen other ways, day in and day out, almost without question, despite her willful nature.

Dad really did a number on us, just like Zack said, Sabrina told her little sister, approaching the pair cautiously, her pistol pointed at Johnny's handsome face.

He leaned toward Shelby as though speaking to her under his breath and Sabrina feared he might be doing some counterprogramming, in which case, she had bigger problems than just saving Shelby's body.

"Don't talk to her!" Sabrina warned. "Shell, come over here and stand by me. Derringer, put down the tray. Then put your hands where I can see them."

Shelby practically wailed her sister's name. "Sabrina! What are you doing? Put the gun away."

"It's okay, baby," Johnny told her. "Sabrina's just confused. We'll get it all straightened out."

Edging slowly over to the picnic table, he set down the tray, then raised his hands over his head, palms forward. "Let's all just relax, okay? Are you hungry, Brie?"

Sabrina glared at him, then strode past him and swept the tray off of the table, sending it flying to the deck.

"Sabrina!" Shelby stomped her foot. "Cut it out. You're scaring us."

"Your boyfriend doesn't look scared," Sabrina countered.

"That's true." Shelby winced. "Why aren't you scared, Johnny?"

"Let's all sit down," he repeated. "You can put the gun away, Brie. I won't try anything."

"Shut up." Sabrina slipped her free arm around her sister's shoulders, hugging her warmly. Then she explained, "He's been drugging you, Shell. Hypnotizing you. Lord knows what crazy suggestions he's been planting in your brain. Which means you don't dare trust your instincts. You have to trust me instead. Do exactly what I say. Just like Dad always told you to do. Is that clear?"

Shelby opened her mouth as though she were about to argue, then her gaze fell, so that she was looking at her hands. "Johnny? Tell Sabrina she's crazy."

"I can't, baby. But I can explain."

"Explain?" she whispered. "That you've been drugging me? Planting things in my head? Making me think I'm losing my freaking mind?"

Sabrina grabbed her sister just as she began to lunge toward Johnny, her fists clenched. "Shell! Listen to me. What's an agent's worst enemy?"

"Him!" Shelby's blue eyes blazed. "He *drugged* me."

"True. But we're not going to panic. You're going to go get your gun then meet me back here. Right?"

"That's not necessary, girls," Johnny protested. "Just give me a chance to explain."

"And to drug us again?" Shelby demanded. "Do you think Sabrina's stupid?"

"She just dumped the last of my DT3 on the deck," he told her cheerfully. "And she's got a gun. So how can I hurt you? Just give me a chance to clear all this up."

Shelby turned to Sabrina and muttered, "We can do that, can't we? Just for five minutes? I really do think we can trust him."

"Shelby..." Sabrina shook her head, certain now that a posthypnotic suggestion had come into play. If that was the case, she had to proceed cautiously or she might end up facing off against her own sister. "Okay, let's go inside.

We'll listen to him, since you trust him so much. But we'll tie him to a chair first because Dad would want us to be careful. Right?"

"Right." Shelby seemed annoyed with herself for having weakened, and glared at Johnny, "Keep your hands where Brie can see them, asshole."

Sabrina bit back a smile and told Johnny, "She may trust you, but she doesn't seem to like you anymore."

He surprised her by returning the smile. "Yeah. I miscalculated a little. In my defense, it's been a real information-juggling act up here. She's too damned smart. Sneaky, too. Thank God, she's adorable enough to balance it out." His eyes warmed. "I love her, Sabrina. And I didn't hurt her. Not permanently. I swear."

"Would you two stop visiting?" Shelby interrupted impatiently. "I'll get the rope. If he moves a muscle, kill him."

"Okay." Shelby pulled the last of the bonds tight, then backed away from their prisoner and put her hands on her hips. "You've got five minutes."

"Great." He exhaled slowly. "First, let me say Sully would be proud of you both. And I hope he'd be proud of me, too. I've done all this for him. In his memory. And for you girls. And for myself. We're all in this together and we have been for years. You just never knew it."

Shelby turned to Sabrina and muttered, "Who *is* he?"

"He used to work for Perimeter. On Dad's crew."

Shelby's eyes widened. "Wow."

"He's the one who screwed up the Canary Island job—"

"I did not!" Johnny grimaced. "Sorry, I didn't mean to raise my voice. But don't say that, okay? I didn't screw it up. I was *set* up. That's why we're here. That's why things are so crazy." He cocked his head to the side. "If you know about that, and about the DT3, you must have gone to Perimeter. Where are they?"

"None of your business."

"And your five minutes are almost up," Shelby told him. "Tell us who set you up in the Canary Islands."

"Theo Howell did." Johnny gave Sabrina a sympathetic smile. "I know that's a tough one. They've been telling you just the opposite, right? That I'm some sort of criminal?"

"You mean, like a kidnapper?"

He laughed. "Okay, technically I am a criminal. But basically, I'm harmless." He leaned forward as much as the rope would allow. "Theo set me up. He was Pluto Zenner's accomplice. And after Pluto died, Theo helped Adonis get revenge. That's the truth. Or at least, as much as I can explain in five minutes."

Sabrina sat at the table, laying her Glock on the surface in front of her. "He helped Adonis get revenge? Against Dad, you mean?"

"Exactly."

"Funny. That's what *he* said about *you*. He says you were in San Francisco the day before Dad was killed. There are records to prove it, by the way, so don't bother denying it."

Shelby held up a hand in protest. "You think Johnny killed Dad? That's not possible, Brie. I know he's a kidnapper and drugger, and I hate him to death, but he's not a murderer."

"Nice work," Sabrina told Johnny, annoyed. Then she explained to her sister, "Think, Shell. He programmed you to believe him. Try to fight it, okay?"

Shelby nodded. "Okay. Johnny? Do you have any proof?"

"That's why I brought you here," he admitted. "I mean,

I've got lots of proof, but it's all circumstantial. I was hoping you might remember something that would really nail the guy. We were getting close, too." He arched an eyebrow in Sabrina's direction. "Do you want to hear what I've got so far?"

She hesitated, then nodded.

"Good." He cleared his throat. "After our client was killed in the Canaries, I was a wreck. I kept going over it and over it, and I knew I hadn't made any mistakes. Your dad was great about it, by the way. He blamed Theo and himself for sending me, and he was willing to give me a second chance. But I went to him and insisted that it must have been an inside job. Only three of us had the final code sequence for that system—Sully, Theo and me. So I wanted to accuse Theo—to have it out with him. But your dad talked me out of it. He was sure I was wrong, and told me he'd side with Theo, not me, if I persisted with such accusations. He said it was just human error and we all had to get past it. Start over. As a team."

Johnny's eyes were dark with the memory. "I couldn't just let it go. So I told Sully I was going to find proof somehow. I asked him not to interfere. To give me one year to find conclusive evidence. And he agreed. So that's what I did, financing the effort by pulling some heists—nothing fancy, and only against other crooks. Sully disapproved of that part, but he kept my secret."

"Did you find proof?" Shelby asked, clearly enthralled by her ex-lover's version of the events.

He nodded. "Theo hit it big on a real estate deal two months after the Canary Island assassination. He bought property that was grossly undervalued, then sold it at a huge profit."

"Everyone says he has a talent for that," Sabrina murmured.

"Yeah, some talent. Turns out, his talent followed a pattern. Every time the Zenners pulled a successful job, Theo made a real estate killing."

"But they hit other companies, not Perimeter."

Johnny arched an eyebrow. "And…?"

She grimaced, remembering what Theo himself had said. Perimeter provided equipment to other companies and even troubleshot their systems for them. It was possible…

"Okay," she said, half to herself. "You suspected Theo was selling information about competitors to Pluto. And Pluto was arranging these real estate deals as payment."

"And there was a pattern," Shelby added loyally. "This really does sound suspicious, Brie. Maybe Johnny's telling the truth about it. And if he is…" She paused, then suggested softly, "Maybe he's telling the truth about Dad's murder, too."

Their prisoner gave her an encouraging nod. "I know it's rough. I didn't want to present this to you guys without incontrovertible proof, but here we are."

"Here we are," Sabrina agreed. "What exactly did you hope to find in our memories?"

He hesitated, then shrugged his shoulders. "Who knows? You spent so much time at Theo's house when you were kids, I just hoped you overheard something. Maybe a phone conversation with Zenner or whatever. And after Shell told me about that setup you had in the music room…" He paused to grin proudly at them, then admitted, "It was a long shot. But I'm sick of hiding out while Theo goes unpunished for all his crimes. Especially helping Adonis get Sully."

"Do you have any proof of *that?*"

Johnny arched an eyebrow. "You tell me. Would Sully Sullivan have let Adonis Zenner catch him napping in his own home?"

"No," Shelby whispered, her eyes glistening. "That creep could never have outsmarted him. But Dad trusted Uncle Theo. Don't you see, Brie? It's like he always said— even the best security system can't keep an insider out."

"He'd be so proud of you," Johnny repeated. "Of both of you."

"Cut the crap," Sabrina warned. "As far as I'm concerned, you haven't proven anything." Turning to her sister she added softly, "We need to talk. In private. *Now.*"

"I can't believe he drugged me. And the hypno stuff is just icky. Can you just imagine the sick stuff he made me do?"

Sabrina patted her sister's arm. "It seems like he was too busy trying to get information about Uncle Theo to do much of that. Or at least, let's just assume that for the moment, or we might just have to kill him."

"I *want* to kill him," she assured Sabrina. "But he seems sincere about Dad and Uncle Theo, don't you think?"

Sabrina nodded. "Actually, yes. But he's got a reputation as a great liar. A con artist. So we have to be careful. Plus, there's stuff you don't know. Things I've learned over the past few days. For example, Adonis Zenner tried to kill Uncle Theo yesterday."

"What?"

Sabrina nodded. "Right. He rigged him with a bomb. So I don't think they're partners. But it's weird because…" She hesitated, trying to work it through as she spoke. "Adonis gave me the secret to disarming the device in time to save him. So it's possible…"

"It's possible they did that just to throw you off track?" Shelby bit her lip. "Are you saying you met Adonis Zenner? Face-to-face?"

Sabrina nodded. "It's been a strange couple of days for

me, too. Meeting Adonis. Going back to Perimeter. Kicking myself for letting Johnny steal you from under my nose using a lame routine like saving my cat."

"Saving your cat? Oh my God! *Zorro!*" Shelby's blue eyes flashed and she spun back toward the kitchen.

"Wait!" Sabrina grabbed her arm, then smiled fondly. "You can't just beat him up while we have him tied to a chair."

"Says who?"

She gave her sister a hug. "I know it sounds crazy, but I'm so grateful to him for not hurting you, I can forgive the rest."

"Except he *did* hurt me," Shelby corrected her sadly. "I thought we were in love. But he was just using me—" She shook herself and announced, "Fuck that. I'm not going to think about it. Not till we figure out what's really going on."

"Good. Now we have to—" Sabrina began.

But her sister interrupted her by muttering, "Wait," then storming back toward the kitchen again.

This time, Sabrina didn't try to stop her. Instead she followed in time to see Shelby stick her fist in Johnny's face, demanding, "What about the snakes? I suppose they were a lie, too?"

"Sorry, baby."

The angry girl glared, then explained to Sabrina, "This jerk told me the place was crawling with snakes, just so I'd stay indoors all the time."

Sabrina bit back a laugh. "Come on back to the living room, Shell. We still need to talk."

"Just a minute." The younger sister folded her arms across her chest. "What about the caretaker?"

Johnny grimaced. "Sorry, Shell."

"What caretaker?" Sabrina asked, concerned that Johnny might have an accomplice after all.

But he explained quickly. "I made him up. And said he seemed a little off, perversion-wise. To keep her from wandering around outside."

"I hate you," Shelby whispered. "You drugged me. Lied to me. Made me have sex with you. Made me think I was losing my goddamned mind."

"I never thought it would take this long," he told her sadly. "And I figured you'd understand once you found out I was trying to solve your father's murder."

"You couldn't have just asked us—asked *me*—for help?"

"I didn't want to put you in danger—"

"Right," she drawled. "So you kidnapped and drugged me. Thanks."

Johnny winced. "If Theo found out I was nosing around, he would have told Zenner. I couldn't take that chance. I figured I'd get the proof, then the three of us would contact Zack—"

"Why didn't you tell *him* right away?" Sabrina demanded. "He was your friend. He would have listened."

"I wanted to. But Sully made me promise not to bad-mouth Theo until I had real proof."

"Real proof." Sabrina exhaled slowly, then admitted, "That's what I want, too." Reaching into her pocket, she pulled out the slender black bottle she had taken from Theo's house. "And you're just the guy who can give it to me."

Johnny whistled softly. "DT3?"

She nodded.

He seemed to choose his next words carefully. "If you use it on me, you'll just confirm what I already told you. But we still won't have the proof we need to get Theo. I can't give you that last crucial piece of information because I don't have it. Only two people in the world do—Theo and Adonis. That's who you should use your DT3 on," he advised her solemnly. "And since we don't know where Adonis is, why don't we go after Theo instead?"

"He's right, Brie," Shelby said. "If that stuff makes people tell secrets, then we can clear this up with one question to Uncle Theo—did he work with the Zenners or not? If he says he didn't, then we'll know Johnny's lying. But if we use it on Johnny, and find out he's telling the truth, we still won't know more than Johnny already knows now."

"Stop being his dupe," Sabrina complained, but she had to admit they were right. And if Theo Howell was innocent—which of course he was—he would probably *want* to do this. Hadn't he already offered to let her hypnotize him back in Monterey?

"You only have one dose there," Johnny told Sabrina. "Don't waste it on me. Let's get Theo up here. I've been waiting six long years to make that murdering bastard squeal."

"He's right, Brie. Let's make the bastard squeal."

"Are you listening to yourself?" Sabrina demanded. "This is Uncle Theo we're talking about. The man who spoiled us rotten when we were kids and protected us when we were in RAP."

Shelby shrugged. "You trust Theo. I trust Johnny. There's only one way to figure out who's right."

Sabrina rolled her eyes. "Your trust of Johnny is drug-induced. Remember?"

"Call Zack," Johnny suggested. "Don't tell him what's going on. Just say Shelby's safe and he and Theo should come up here right away."

"Or we could go to Monterey and do it there," Sabrina countered. "Isn't that more logical?"

"That would be a mistake. We can control the situation here. We can't do it there."

She balked at his use of the word "we," but wasn't quite ready to disagree with him. And she knew why that was. She still had the nagging feeling she had been asking the wrong question—solving the wrong problem. Now John Derringer—a thief, a kidnapper, a con artist—had suggested a completely different one. She had to eliminate it before she could reject it.

"My father never figured this out in all his years with the company. But *you* did?"

"Sully was too close. And Howell and Zenner were smart. They targeted other companies. Rarely Perimeter."

Rarely?

The qualifier caught Sabrina by surprise and, without thinking, she murmured, "They only hit Perimeter twice on Dad's watch, right?"

"Right," Johnny agreed, then his eyes narrowed. "The Canary Islands was one. What was the other?"

Sabrina took a step back, intimidated to hear him ask the very question that had been haunting her. Did he know the answer? Was he bluffing? Did it matter?

"Call Zack," Shelby urged her. "Convince him to bring Uncle Theo up here. It's the only way we'll ever know for sure."

"Zack's in Dallas as of this morning," Sabrina confessed with a wistful smile. "Otherwise I'd be miles ahead of you."

"Let me get this straight." Johnny was shaking his head. "Zack Lansing took off for Dallas knowing Sullivan's daughters were in danger? That's not very likely, is it?"

Sabrina stared at him and saw in his vibrant blue eyes what only a best friend could know.

So she opened her cell phone and entered Zack's number.

He answered on the first ring. "Lansing."

"Zack. It's me."

"Where the hell are you! Goddamn it, Sabrina, you can't do this by yourself. Tell me where you are."

Sabrina almost laughed with relief. "Hey, Zack? Guess what?"

"What?"

"I've got her. She's safe."

There was a moment of stunned silence, then he said, "Man, that's great. What about Derringer?"

"He's not a factor. At least not for the moment. Are you in Dallas?"

"No, I'm in Truckee. In a goddamned motel, trying to figure out what the hell you've been up to. Hold on while I tell Theo the news. He's right in the next room."

"Wait!" She glanced at Johnny and was so annoyed by the cocky expression on his face, she had to turn away before insisting, "I need a favor."

"Anything."

"This is a big one," she warned. "If you can't do it for me, do it for my father. Please?"

"I'll do it for you. Name it."

Sabrina tried not to let the simple pledge distract her. Not yet, at least. "I need you to tell Uncle Theo that Shelby is physically okay, but mentally out of it. She keeps saying he's the only one she'll talk to. Alone. So he needs to get here, the sooner the better."

Zack was silent for a moment, then asked her, "You want me to tell him that? But it's not true?"

"I want you to trust me. The way I trust you. And, Zack? After you tell him, don't let him out of your sight. Or call anyone. Okay?"

She was sure she heard him grumble, but his voice was

neutral when he finally said, "Okay, Sabrina. It's your show. We'll be there in fifteen minutes tops. Give me your coordinates."

She gave him the information, then closed the phone, her heart pounding with conflicting emotions, hoping she had made the right decision. But what choice had she had? She couldn't do this alone, and while she ordinarily would have trusted Shelby to be her right hand "man," that wasn't really an option, given the girl's DT3-induced loyalty to a handsome con artist.

She wanted to trust Theo, but her statement under hypnosis to Zack was apparently accurate. She only trusted him "sometimes." And this wasn't one of them.

That left Zack, a guy who was reminding her more of Sully Sullivan by the minute. If he came through for her on this—let her drug Theo, with or without consent—that would be the final proof of his loyalty. And if he didn't. If he tried to stop her…

He won't, she decided with a rueful smile. *He wants to work with you, hang out with you, make out with you. And if he comes through for you today, he's definitely going to get his wish.*

Chapter 12

While they waited for Zack and Theo, Sabrina and Shelby retrieved the baby carriage, adding to its cargo Johnny's gun from under the seat of his truck. In the meantime, Sabrina brought her sister up to date on events. For her part, Shelby was too upset over not knowing real from planted memories to share much of her ordeal. And her sister could see that her heart, as well as her pride, were wounded.

"I'm still sure I'm missing something," Sabrina admitted. "And the last thing we need right now is a loose end."

"I'm a loose end myself, kind of," Shelby reminded her. "After you tie up Uncle Theo and Zack, you can tie me, too, if you want."

"I'm not tying you. Or Zack. It isn't necessary."

"You trust him that much? He works for Uncle Theo.

And he thinks Johnny's a traitor who might have killed Dad." Shelby bit her lip. "You guys are pretty tight?"

"We work well together. And for what it's worth, he doesn't think Johnny's capable of cold-blooded murder. They were best friends once, and there's some residual feeling there, so don't worry. Oh! Here they come. Go inside by the back door. Keep out of sight until I tell you it's okay. I don't want Uncle Theo to get suspicious."

"Okay."

"Hey, Shell?"

"Yes?"

"Don't untie him. That's a direct order."

She grimaced. "Okay. But hurry, cause we both know he's tricky. And we don't really know what other crazy things he planted in my head."

Sabrina nodded, then waited until she heard the back door slam before she approached Zack's car just as the two men were getting out. She had her Glock in her hand, but carried it at her side as though it was just an afterthought.

She walked straight up to her uncle and embraced him with her free arm. "We found her, Uncle Theo. Isn't it a miracle?"

"Yes," he admitted. "Zack said she's out of her head?"

"She's had a rough time of it," Sabrina confirmed, then she sent Zack a wistful smile. "Thanks for getting here so quickly."

"Like you could keep us away?" he asked, his tone light, his hands nowhere near his holstered gun.

"You didn't go to Dallas."

He shrugged. "I sent Connor. He's the best man for the job. Plus, I was deluded enough to think you might need my help."

"Zack didn't want to leave me at the house with Zenner in the neighborhood, so he brought me with him," Theo explained. "Now do you see why I made him head of operations? He's got everything covered, as usual."

Zack cleared his throat, then asked, "What now, Sabrina?"

"Let's go inside, shall we?" She took Theo by the hand and led him onto the porch. "Just do what I say, okay, Uncle Theo?"

"Of course."

Now that they were cooperating, her thoughts turned back to Shelby, alone in the kitchen with Johnny, and she wondered if she might not be leading these two trusting men into a trap. But to her relief, Shelby was standing right in the middle of the living room when they walked through the doorway.

"Michelle!" Theo strode up to the younger sister, embracing her heartily. "You look wonderful! I expected you to be in bed."

"Hi, Uncle Theo," Shelby murmured, returning the embrace halfheartedly while explaining to Sabrina, "I know you told me to wait in the kitchen but it got a little strange in there. Oo-oh…" She wriggled out of Theo's hug and walked over to Zack. "I've heard a lot about *you*." To Sabrina, she added, "Yum."

Zack laughed. "I've heard a lot about you, too. How's the head?"

"Filled with thoughts of giving Johnny post-hypnotic suggestions of celibacy."

"Good plan." Zack patted her arm. "Nice job staying alive. Sully would be proud."

"So I'm told." She grimaced. "Come on, Brie. Let's get this over with."

"Get what over with?" Theo asked, clearly confused by Shelby's lack of confusion.

Sabrina sighed, then leveled her pistol at the older man. "Sorry, Uncle Theo. This is just a precaution. I need you to step into the kitchen."

The older man's jaw dropped. "Huh?"

"Shelby and I have some questions for you. Some things we have to clear up. Please don't be angry. But, also, don't underestimate me. I'm determined to get the answers I need one way or the other. So just cooperate."

Theo stared for a moment, then turned to Zack. "Did you know about this?" Before his employee could respond, he added coolly, "Consider yourself fired."

"I already quit last night," Zack reminded him. "Go on now, do what she says. I for one am dying to know what's in that kitchen."

"Hey, buddy. Remember my fantasy about being tied up by two beautiful blondes? It's even better than I thought it would be," Johnny greeted Zack.

Zack scowled. Then he strode over to the bound man and methodically tested the knots binding his hands and feet. "All we need now is a gag."

"Actually," Sabrina said, "he has quite a story to tell. I don't know if a word of it is true—"

"You can't trust anything he says," Theo warned her. "Put the gun away, Sabrina. I don't know what lies he's been telling you, but—"

"Just sit down, Uncle Theo. Please?"

The older man spied a rope in Shelby's hand and shook his head frantically. "You can't be serious! He brainwashed you, Michelle. Filled your head with lies about me. Sabrina? Zack? Have you lost your minds?"

Shelby kicked an empty chair. "Sabrina said *sit*. And if Zack tries to stop us, we'll tie him up, too. Right, Brie?"

"All we want to do is ask a few questions," Sabrina said soothingly.

Zack gave her an inquiring look. "I don't get why you need to tie up Theo. He's not armed."

"If Johnny has to be tied, so does Theo," Shelby interrupted. "One of them is a liar. Until we know which one, we need to treat them equally."

Zack winced, then advised Theo, "Just go along with it. The sooner you cooperate, the sooner we can deliver John to the cops. That's the deal, right, girls?"

Sabrina nodded. "That's the deal."

Theo seemed about to protest again, then he just shrugged and settled into the chair. Shelby tied his hands behind his back, explaining to Zack and Theo as she did so, "Don't blame Sabrina. She doesn't know who to trust, and she can't cover all of us at one time. Johnny's a criminal, obviously. I'm his hypno-puppet, so she has to keep her eye on me. In fact, she should tie me up, too. And she should definitely tie you, Zack."

"I'll settle for taking his gun." Sabrina smiled. "Do you mind, Zack?"

He scowled again, but took out his weapon and handed it to her. "What's this about?"

"Let's all sit down," she murmured, adding Zack's pistol to the loot in the baby carriage. When everyone was seated, she briefly recounted Johnny's accusations, ending with, "I'm sorry, Uncle Theo, but there's an easy way to clear it all up." She held up the black bottle.

"Shit," Zack muttered. "Is that what I think it is?"

Sabrina nodded.

"Use it on John, then. I'll do the questioning. Same deal you offered Theo. He's the one who kidnapped your sister. Why treat Theo like the criminal?"

"Because Johnny admits he doesn't have all the answers," Shelby explained patiently. "He can tell us about his suspicions, but only Uncle Theo can tell us if they're true. That's what this stuff does, right? It makes you tell the truth."

"It's fine with me," Theo told them suddenly. "Give me the drug and let's get this farce over with."

Turning to a clearly startled Johnny, he said triumphantly, "That's right. I'm not afraid of your lies. You're clever—you always were. It's obvious to me that you invented these…these insults—to keep Sabrina from using the drug on you." His voice grew rich with outrage. "I'm the only one in the room who isn't blinded by you. You weren't *set* up in the Canaries. *You sold out.* You gave Pluto the codes he needed. And you've been helping Adonis ever since. I understand why Michelle believes you. You drugged her into it. But Sabrina and Zack…" He choked back a sob. "I'll never understand how you two could side with him against me. But we're going to clear it up. Right this minute. Sabrina, give me the drug."

She stared at him, humbled.

"Don't do it, Sabrina. Use it on John," Zack murmured.

She nodded slowly. "Okay."

"No," Johnny told her, his voice as soft as Zack's had been. "He's the one tricking you. Can't you see that? He knows there's just one dose there. Don't let him manipulate you, Sabrina. Give him the drug and ask him one simple question—did he help Adonis plant that bomb in Sully's house? That's the only question that counts anymore."

"No, not the only one," a new voice announced from the doorway to the living room. "But it's a good place to start."

Sabrina looked over at the speaker and for the first time in her life, she understood why people clutch their hearts when they see something fundamentally impossible.

He was larger than life, just like she remembered him, filling the doorway with his huge frame, filling the room with his warm smile. For a full thirty seconds everyone just sat and stared, then Shelby jumped out of her chair and ran to him, flinging herself into his arms. "Daddy!"

"Hey, Shellie!" He grappled her to his chest, then stared over her head in Sabrina's direction. "Hi, Breezie."

She stood, but didn't move toward him. Instead she edged closer to Zack, who quickly took her by the hand. And she knew he was feeling what she was feeling. Shock. Confusion. Disbelief. Joy.

But also betrayal, so strong and unexpected that she would have sat back down from the force of it if she had been willing to show weakness to the newcomer.

"Sully?" Theo struggled against his bonds. "My God! It's a miracle."

"Yeah, I'll bet you're thrilled to see me," Sully drawled. Then he gave Sabrina another, more encouraging smile. "I know this is a lot to take in, honey—"

"I'm fine," she told him stiffly. "I take it you're the caretaker?"

"Oh!" Shelby giggled against their father's chest. "You were here all the time? And Johnny knew? So? Johnny isn't bad? Or at least," she added with a wince, "not all bad."

"He had to lie to you, Shellie," Sully explained.

"It's okay. Everything's okay now. Right, Brie?" Shelby's smile faded. "Right?"

"Come over here and stand by me, Shelby," Sabrina told her. "Now."

Her sister's blue eyes clouded, but she dutifully pulled away from Sully and walked over to Sabrina. "Are you in shock or something?"

"Breezie…" Sully spread his hands in a gesture of apology. "I know you're confused—"

"Confused?" she demanded as tears began streaming down her cheeks. "Confused that you let Johnny drug me? And drug Shelby over and over again! That you've been alive for f-five years? You let us believe…" She choked back an outraged sob and picked up her Glock, aiming it him with a shaky hand. "Just let me think."

Zack slipped his arm around her shoulders. "Relax, Sabrina. We'll sort this out together. Remember who he is. He wouldn't have done this without a good reason." But to Sully, he added darkly, "If I were you, I'd start talking."

"You're not going to make me tie Dad up, are you, Brie?" Shelby whispered, and for some reason the question made things a little better. In fact, it seemed oddly hilarious. The thought that they might tie up Sully Sullivan. That Shelby would actually side with Sabrina against her own father, all because he made the mistake of planting suggestions in their minds so many years earlier.

Before she realized what was happening, Sabrina was laughing through her tears as she assured her sister, "No, I don't think that's necessary." Then she handed the gun to Zack, told him with a sheepish smile to, "Cover him," then she walked across the room and straight into Sully's waiting arms.

They settled back down at the table, Sully across from Sabrina, Shelby snuggled next to Sully, Zack with custody of the Glock, and Theo and Johnny still tied up.

"Tell us where you've been," Shelby insisted.

Sully exchanged glances with Johnny. "All of what John told you is true. He did come to me, after the assassination, and insist Theo must have given Pluto the codes. I defended Theo—my best friend." He shot his ex-boss a withering glare. "But I could see John was sincere in his belief. I hoped that he'd work through his feelings and eventually come back to the company. Meanwhile I went after Pluto and shot him. I expected retribution from Adonis, so I was more cautious than ever. But as Michelle—I mean, Shelby—said earlier, I didn't protect myself from insiders. In this case, Theo."

"That's insane," Theo objected. "I would have killed my*self* before I let anything happen to you! Why are you so sure I had something to do with it?"

Sully eyed him sternly. "It's time for the lies to stop. We know you planted the bomb in my house that afternoon."

Theo's eyes widened. "I did not. I visited you. I won't deny that. But we both know you were fine when I left you."

"He wasn't fine. He was unconscious," Johnny interrupted, then he began addressing the group. "Like Sabrina said, I was in town that day. It was the one-year anniversary of the Canary Islands incident, and I had gathered a lot of evidence about the timing of Theo's various real estate killings. I went to Sully's house, but I could see he had a visitor, so I waited down the street in my car. I saw Theo come out, locking the door behind him—rather furtively, I might add. Then he got into a black sedan and left. I went up to the door and knocked, but no one answered. Logic told me Sully wasn't home and Theo had a key, and had just dropped something off. But my instincts told me otherwise. So I went around back and broke in."

"And thank God he did," Sully added. "Apparently I was unconscious—"

"Apparently?" Theo arched an eyebrow. "Interesting."

Sabrina and Zack exchanged confused glances, then he said, "Go on, John. What happened next?"

"What happened was, I saw the bomb. Strapped to his chest. He was drugged. Our best guess is that Theo slipped him a mickey. The timer was set for six hours—plenty of time for Theo to get back home and go to bed. And lucky for me, it was also plenty of time for me to fake Sully's death."

"Why did you do that?" Zack demanded. "Why not just call the police?"

"Like Theo said, it was my word against Theo's. Plus, I knew Zenner had supplied the bomb. If he didn't succeed against Sully, he might have gone after the girls in Boston next." He flushed, then added, "I was out of my depth. I needed someone to bounce ideas off. I actually called you, Zack, but when I got your machine, I just wasn't comfortable leaving a message. So I got Sully out of there and hid him—dead asleep—in my motel room. Then I visited a girl I know who worked in a funeral parlor in San Jose and got some miscellaneous remains. The bomb went off as scheduled."

Sully was nodding. "The next morning I woke up with a helluva a headache. John told me what had happened. He had a plan by then—that the two of us should go after Adonis. Once we had him, we'd know the girls were safe, and we could move against Theo."

"You've been chasing Adonis all these years?" Shelby asked.

Sully grinned. "Let's hope I'm not that incompetent. No, honey, we didn't go after Adonis. I was so shaken up by…well, by Theo's betrayal. By the fact that he and Adonis were partners and might go after you girls next. I honestly didn't know what to do. I agreed with John that it was best to let Adonis think I was dead, but I took it one step further. I decided to stay dead. You girls had gone into

RAP, and I believed Adonis would respect that. Theo outlined his so-called truce at the funeral, and even though I knew it was phony, I also knew it ensured your safety. But if Adonis had caught wind of the fact that someone was after him—or worse, figured out who it was—you girls would have been in terrible jeopardy."

"Jeopardy?" Shelby frowned. "We would have helped you, Dad. He wouldn't have stood a chance against all of us."

Sully patted her cheek. "You were only eighteen then, honey. And Sabrina was twenty. You had your whole lives ahead of you. And…" He sighed. "During the year I chased Pluto, I found out something chilling—Adonis is even more clever, and more ruthless, than his old man. I couldn't take the chance."

"So?" she repeated. "Where have you been?"

"Fishing. And raising horses. John and I used his ill-gotten gains to buy some property up in Montana. I guess you could say I retired."

"Yeah," Johnny told them with a rueful smile. "He wanted me to retire, too, but I'm with you, Shell. I figured we needed to settle all our old scores. Sully made me promise not to go after Adonis, but I kept looking for evidence that Theo was working with him. I figured if I found something solid, I could take it to you, Zack. Even if Sully wouldn't let me tell the world he was still alive, I could bring down Theo for what he did to me. What he tried to do to Sully."

"But you never found the proof, did you?" Theo demanded. "Because it doesn't exist."

"I found plenty," John said with a growl. "All those deals, so conveniently following hits on our competitors. But Sully didn't think it was enough. He begged me to let it go, for the sake of the girls. And I finally did. Until four months ago."

Zack arched an eyebrow in Sabrina's direction. "Paul Hanover's heart attack?"

Johnny nodded. "I heard about it, but didn't get any details right away. If I had, I wouldn't have thought much of it, I guess. The whole suicide thing and all. But my first reaction was disbelief. Paul was one of the healthiest guys I knew. A heart attack at fifty-three seemed absurd. And it made me worried, because it happened on the fifth anniversary of Sully's death."

"There was nothing sinister about that," Theo protested. "Sure, it was the fifth anniversary. We were all very conscious of that. It's the reason Paul decided to come out of retirement. To honor Sully. That decision destroyed his marriage and led to his suicide attempt."

"Yeah, yeah, we know that now," John admitted. "But at the time, I thought maybe Adonis was having some fun. Killing Sully's right-hand man on the anniversary of the bomb."

"And even after we found out what really happened— the suicide attempt and all—John had a new obsession," Sully continued.

"Wait! Let me guess." Sabrina was tingling with excitement. "You realized Adonis might not always do his killing with a bomb, right? He could kill someone right under our noses and make it look like a heart attack or some other natural cause. He could hit a Perimeter client and we might not ever realize it."

"Jeez, it took me six years to figure it out and you did it in one week?" John's blue eyes were sparkling. "That's what you meant earlier, right? When you said he hit us twice on Sully's watch?"

She nodded. "Adonis actually said that to me a couple of days ago—"

"Adonis? You met him? Where?"

"In my kitchen."

"What the hell?" Sully's face contorted with anger. "Did he touch you? Threaten you?"

"He said he just wanted to know if I was still a civilian. He heard I was running around with Zack, asking questions and carrying a gun."

Sully shook his head. "You should have been more discreet. You shouldn't have gone to Perimeter at all. And of course, *you,* young lady," he told Shelby with a playful glare, "shouldn't have left that second message for your sister. That was the cause of all our trouble."

"But it worked out for the best," Johnny reminded him. "Sabrina had Zack to protect her. And now we've got Theo right where we want him."

Sabrina winced. She had been so busy enjoying the fact that Johnny was turning out to be one of the good guys, she had forgotten what that meant about her surrogate uncle. Turning to Theo, she said simply, "How could you?"

Theo surprised her by smiling warmly. "I don't blame you for being suspicious, Sabrina. Derringer talks a good game. He always has. I'm a little surprised at you, Sully," he told his ex-friend quietly. "But I imagine he used a little DT3 on you at some point, so I forgive you."

"Give it up," Johnny advised him. "No one believes a word you say anymore. Speaking of which, how about untying me, Sabrina?"

"Hmm?" She had barely heard the question. She was back at Theo's accusation—that Johnny might have drugged Sully that awful night. It didn't make a lot of sense, but was it possible? Absolutely. He had drugged her. And Shelby. Why not their father?

"Uh-oh, Sully, we're losing her again," Johnny murmured. "I think it's time to give them the last piece of the puzzle. When you hear this, Sabrina, you'll be so shocked…. Well, take my word for it. It's huge."

"Huge-er than Dad still being alive?" Shelby demanded. "That doesn't seem possible. What is it?"

Sabrina braced herself, then echoed Shelby's question.

Johnny arched an eyebrow. "Zenner hit us twice on Sully's watch. Once in the Canaries. When was the other one?"

"I don't know," she admitted. "But I suspect it was never detected. Right?"

"If John's suspicion is correct," Sully hedged, "then yes. I missed it completely. But in my defense…" He took a deep breath, then murmured, "This is the question we need to ask Theo, honey. The big one. Give him the DT3 and let's get it over with."

"In your defense, what?"

"I was grieving. For your mother." Sully gulped audibly. "John discovered one of those real estate deals—an extremely lucrative one—within a few months of your mother's death. Once he knew what to look for, he made the connection."

"What connection?" Theo demanded. "Perimeter wasn't hit by Zenner or anyone else that year."

"But you lost at least one client that year. That's what helped Dad focus so he wasn't swallowed up by guilt. Remember, Zack?" Sabrina whispered.

"Right." Zack was nodding. "We heard that story a million times. Sully couldn't afford to wallow in his misery because the company was having quote-unquote growing pains. Losing some clients, gaining others."

"And apparently dealing with a huge influx of cash on top of it all," Shelby added.

Zack turned to Theo, his eyes narrowed. "Sabrina asked you once if the company ever lost a client because of a heart

attack. Tell me what happened the year her mother died."
Clenching his fists, he repeated forcefully, "Tell me!"

"A client died from a heart attack," Theo admitted unhappily. "But you can't believe I had anything to do with
it, Zack. And you, Sully? Do you really think I'd exploit
Jenny's tragic accident by cooperating with Zenner while
you were grieving? Not for any amount of money!"

"So?" Shelby murmured. "That's what you wanted from
our memories, Johnny? Dad left us with Uncle Theo that
week. You hoped maybe we overheard something. Right?"

"Right."

"It all fits," Sully said. "I was so distracted that week, I
didn't pay attention to the client's heart attack the way I
should have, considering how many powerful enemies that
particular client had. I should have caught it, but I didn't."

Sabrina held up her hand. "I'm confused. If you guys
knew what you were looking for, why did you need a week
to find it?"

"Because this bastard planted a fake memory," Johnny
explained. "Whenever I asked Shell about it, she recited
the same gibberish, about coloring and tuna fish sandwiches and how much fun she had. Word for word, the
same every time. I spent all week trying to find a way to
get at the truth, but he really did a number on her."

Sabrina shot Theo a withering glare, but to her surprise,
he seemed sad, not upset or frightened. Looking directly
at Sully, he said, "Yes, I planted a memory. A sweet one,
to blot out the bad one. I should have told you about it, but
you had so much on your mind. I just couldn't bear to see
the girls crying and miserable. I had no experience with
children," he added weakly, "but it broke my heart to see
them that way. So I made them happy. That's all, Sully. I
swear."

"Give us the password then," Sully suggested, his tone neutral. "Let me recover the memory from Michelle. Then we'll know."

"There is no password! I wasn't *hiding* the memory. I didn't think I'd ever need to recover it. I just erased it. To make them happy." Tears began streaming down his face. "Did I visit your house the day you were killed? Absolutely. I have always cherished that last conversation about your trip to see the girls, when you brought them that silly kitten. You were my best friend. When I left, you were fine. I was sound asleep when the call came and it broke my heart. But I owed it to you to protect the girls, in case Zenner came after them next. So I was on a plane to Boston within an hour." His voice broke. "I almost bankrupted the company to make them safe. And somehow this...this monster perverted everything. He used DT3 on you to make you believe his twisted version of the bombing attempt—"

"*Why would I do that?*" Johnny roared. "It doesn't make any sense."

Sabrina pulled back, stunned by the intensity of the debate. This was destroying them all, she realized, scanning the miserable, angry, confused faces around her. "Okay, that's enough!" she declared, jumping to her feet. Then she twisted the lid off the DT3 bottle and demanded, "How does this stuff work?"

After a crash course in DT3 protocol from Zack, Sabrina stepped up to Theo and explained simply, "It has to be you, I think. If you've been telling the truth, I'll...well, I'll find some way to make it up to you."

"Don't be too hard on yourself, Breezie," Theo said with a halfhearted smile. "This is how Derringer operates.

Twisting the truth. Charming the unsuspecting. I don't blame you. Any of you. Only him."

She steadied her hand, then tipped the bottle, allowing the amber liquid to spill between Theo's parted lips. She almost expected him to resist at the last moment—to spill her precious supply—but he accepted the dose docilely, then began licking his lips, first as though tasting, then as though something was terribly wrong.

She turned to her father. "What if he's allergic? What should I do then?"

"He's fine. It's just numbing his mouth. Watch."

Theo's head started to list to the side and Zack prompted Sabrina, "Talk to him. Use his name."

"Okay." She took a deep breath. "Theo Howell?"

Theo cleared his throat, then murmured, "Yes?"

"I'm going to ask you some questions. I want you to answer honestly and completely. Do you understand?"

"Yes."

"Why did you drug me and my sister?"

"You were upset. I wanted to calm you down. You were miserable. I was a stranger, and you missed your parents."

"Did we see or hear something that linked you with Pluto or Adonis Zenner?"

"No."

She exhaled sharply, relieved and disappointed at the same time. "Did you help Adonis Zenner try to kill my father?"

"No."

"Ask him about the Canaries," Johnny demanded.

She nodded. "Theo Howell, did Pluto or Adonis Zenner pay you to help them with the Canary Islands assassination?"

"No."

"Oh, God…" She exchanged worried looks with Zack.

Then she asked carefully, "When you left my father's house on the day of the bombing, how was he?"

"He was angry."

Sabrina licked her lips. "Oh? Why?"

"We had an argument about Connor Boyle. I wanted to move him out of R and D, but Sully wouldn't agree."

Sabrina looked at her father, who said, "I don't remember. It could have happened. My mind's a blank."

"Maybe someone came to the house after Uncle Theo left," Shelby suggested softly.

"I would have seen them," Johnny countered, his tone showing panic. "This is crazy. Right, Sully? You know this is crazy, don't you? You don't think... *Fuck...*"

"I don't think anything," Sully assured him, "except we seem to have jumped to a conclusion or two about Theo. Breezie? Wake him up gently."

She closed her eyes, fighting tears for the third time that day. The third time in a very, very long time. Theo had done so much for her. For the Sullivans. And this was how they thanked him? It was nothing short of horrific.

"Wake him up, Sabrina," Zack echoed.

"Okay." She brushed her tears away, and as she did so, she felt something stinging her eye. Too late, she realized that a few drops of the DT3 had gotten onto her fingers, staining them a dark amber color. "Zack?" She grimaced. "I got some of the drug in my eye. Should I worry?"

When she saw the look he exchanged with her father, she demanded, "Should I wash it out? How dangerous is it? Dad? Zack?"

It was Johnny who answered her. "You should be puking all over the place right about now, beautiful. I've seen it with my own eyes, and it's disgusting. Where'd you get that bottle anyway?"

"From Uncle Theo. Oh!"

As all eyes turned to him, Theo dropped his feigned wooziness and began to squirm in his seat. "It's not like it sounds, Sully. I had to do it. You were so damned hard for him to catch off guard, he was going to go after the girls instead. So I helped him, to save them. That's the deal I made."

Sully stood and crossed to stand in front of him, his eyes blazing. "Do you want to know the truth? I never fucking believed it—not really—until right now. I always thought there must be an explanation. I figured John wanted it to be true so much, he was seeing the facts through hate-colored glasses. But you did it! You tried to kill me."

"To protect my nieces."

"Don't call them that!" He grabbed Theo by the throat. "You set John up. Admit it."

"Fine. I did! But only because Zenner was blackmailing me. And John was so young. So inexperienced. I knew you'd give him another chance. How could I have known he'd go off and start robbing banks?"

"You disgust me." Sully let go and backed away, then he walked over to Johnny's chair and began untying him. "Nice work, Sherlock."

"What about us?" Shelby asked. "Did we really overhear stuff about Pluto when we were kids?"

"I have a question, too," Sabrina interrupted. "You said Zenner was blackmailing you. With what?"

Theo winced. "After the peace summit, after Sully disarmed the bomb, Pluto came to me and admitted he planted it. He promised me he wouldn't hit our clients anymore if I would occasionally give him information from our R and D division. I should have sent him away, but we needed cash desperately. So I gave him some old manuals. That sort of thing. Then he threatened to tell Sully if I didn't continue. I just got in deeper and deeper."

"Asshole," Johnny muttered, standing and stretching. Then his expression softened. "Hey, Shelby. Are you still mad at me?"

Shelby rolled her eyes at her sister. "Is this guy for real? He thinks he can drug me into sleeping with him and I'll get over it?"

"No, sweetheart," Sully assured her. "John never touched you. Not that way. He used the DT3 to make you believe you were having an affair, but believe me, you weren't. He knows I would have killed him if he took advantage of you that way."

Uh-oh... Sabrina shook her head toward her father, but it was too late. Shelby's eyes had widened in shock and she was backing out of the room.

"Shell—" Sabrina began, hoping to soothe her.

But her sister pointed a finger at her and insisted, "Don't! Don't make excuses for him. For them! I hate you all!"

"Shelby—"

"Just leave me alone! All of you." She ran out of the room.

"Shouldn't you go after her?" Sully asked.

"No. And Johnny shouldn't, either. She needs some time. It's mortifying. What were you thinking?" she added, giving the pair a disgusted look. But she couldn't hold on to the feeling for long. Not with her father standing there, right in front of her, after all these lonely years. So she walked up to him and hugged him again, then she hugged Johnny, murmuring, "Thanks for saving my dad's life."

"Yeah, well. Return the favor and get me out of the doghouse with your sister."

"You shouldn't have pretended to sleep with her," Sabrina repeated.

"Yeah, man," Zack told him. "That's a new low even for you."

"Very funny." Johnny hesitated, then clapped his old friend on the back. "Are we okay?"

"You saved Sully," Zack replied simply. "Yeah, we're good."

Sully patted Zack's shoulder. "I couldn't have gone into hiding if I didn't know you'd be there. Running Perimeter. Keeping my girls safe. You were always my choice to succeed me. It happened pretty fast—and I know it was hard on you—but my daughters are alive and well." His tone was rich with appreciation. "I'm proud as heck of you. And your dad would be, too."

Zack grinned. "Five years of fishing and ranching? It definitely sounds like I got the short end of the stick."

Sabrina watched as the tender scene deteriorated into playful, male-bonding insults, and she smiled fondly, wondering if her father had any idea what he meant to Zack. Probably, since Johnny seemed to feel the same way, and those two had spent five long years together, almost as father and son. She couldn't wait to hear the stories.

And meanwhile Theo sat in the midst of the reunion, still tied to the chair and looking as though he had just lost his best friend again. Literally.

"Sabrina?"

She turned toward her sister's soft voice, pleased that she had returned to the room so quickly. Then she saw that Shelby wasn't alone, and her heart began to pound in her chest.

"Be smart, Sullivans," Adonis Zenner warned the group in the kitchen, forcing the barrel of a pistol against Shelby's chin for emphasis.

Everyone froze, then Adonis added grimly, "You should have died when you had the chance, Sully. Now your daughter's going to have to do it for you."

Chapter 13

Sully took a step forward, his fists balled at his sides. "Leave her alone, Zenner. This is between you and me."

"Not really." Adonis eyed the Glock resting on the table. "Sabrina, be a good sister and slide that over to me on the floor. Nothing fancy."

Once she had complied, Adonis asked Zack, "Where's your gun?"

"Out in my car. Under the front seat."

"That's unlikely," Adonis murmured, then he jammed the barrel more forcefully into Shelby's jaw.

"It's in the baby carriage," Sabrina said quickly. "So is Johnny's."

"Quaint. Push that over here, too. But first, Sully? Add yours to it, won't you?"

Sully grimaced but complied, pulling a Tomcat from the waistband of his pants, under his shirt, and tossing it into the carriage, which Sabrina sent across the room to Adonis.

Adonis grinned, surveying Theo's bound condition. "Not your best day, I see, partner. It's a good thing I put that sensor in your pocketwatch way back when. I was sure you'd try to disappear one day, to get out of our alliance. Who knew it would lead me to a Sullivan reunion?"

"I'm ready to disappear now," Theo assured him. "Help me and I'll pay you whatever you want."

Adonis laughed. "I'm not here to rescue you. I went back to your place to finish what I started the other day—getting information about that birthday party in Dallas—but you weren't there. And from the looks of things, your friends finally figured out you've been double dealing them. Works for me. It always seemed like a shame Sully didn't know the truth—that Pluto killed that pretty wife of his."

Sabrina gasped, while Sully muttered, "God*damn* it. I should have known."

Zack stepped forward and Sabrina thought he was going for Adonis's throat, but he surprised her by speaking in a reasonable tone. "That was twenty years ago, Adonis. Let's deal with today, shall we? You want access to the party in Dallas, and I can give you that. Just let Shelby go and I'm all yours."

"Interesting," Adonis admitted. "But I don't just need access. I need a date. *And* an insurance policy. So here's what we're going to do. You'll give me the information I need and make sure your crew doesn't stop me. Little Shelby here will do the rest. Reach into my pocket now, Shelby, and I'll show you the toy I brought for you."

"No!" Sabrina shook her head at her sister, then told Adonis, "Stop playing games. You know this isn't about Shelby. It isn't even about Dad anymore. Like you said, he and Pluto were the past. We're the future. You and me." She locked gazes with him and challenged softly, "Remember? You predicted our alliance. Let my sister go and you've got it."

His ebony eyes twinkled. "It's true. You're the one. I have so many uses for you, I've lost count. Come here then. And no tricks or you've killed your sister."

"Sabrina, don't," Sully said with a growl, but she ignored him and walked over to Adonis, still looking straight into his eyes, trying not to notice the miserable expression on Shelby's face.

"Sabrina," Shelby whispered. "Don't do this."

"Do what I say," Sabrina answered firmly. "Reach into Adonis's pocket. There's a cuff. Take it out and put it on my wrist."

She knew the men were watching, helpless and furious, and her heart went out to them. She had the easiest role here, she decided. She only hoped they understood that she couldn't live with herself if this went down any other way. They needed to stay out of it. She had the best shot at saving Shelby and maybe, just maybe, handling Adonis until an opportunity presented itself for her to do more.

The cuff looked a lot like the one he had used on Theo, and she knew as she heard the click that secured it to her wrist that a timer had begun to count down. "How many minutes?" she asked Adonis.

"Two. So tell your family to back off." He held the detonator where Sully and Zack could see it, keeping the pistol in his other hand trained on Shelby, instructing her, "Walk over to your father."

"Do it, Shell," Sabrina insisted.

"Sabrina…." She bit back a sob, then gave her sister a quick hug and ran to her father's waiting arms.

"Now listen," Adonis said, his voice cold and commanding. "You have just about ninety seconds. I'll stop the timer as soon as we get to my car. But the remote will still be operational, so be smart. *Don't* follow us. If I see one of you in the next twenty-four hours, Sabrina will pay the price. Lansing?"

"Yeah, I'll pave the way. No one will interfere with you in Dallas. But after that—"

"Of course I'll let her go. With this last big score, I'll be able to retire. I won't care what the community thinks of me." To Sully he added, "Give me your word you won't follow us and you'll have mine that I'll let her go when it's done."

Sully nodded. "I swear on my dead wife's grave I won't follow you. But if you hurt her, I'll hunt you down and rip your guts out."

Adonis laughed, then pulled Sabrina flush against himself with his detonator hand while training the pistol on the group. "Come on, beautiful. We don't want to miss the first dance."

Shelby watched in helpless despair as her sister and Adonis disappeared from the cabin. Then she buried her face in her father's shirtfront. "He'll kill her."

"I don't understand why Sabrina did that," Sully murmured. "It should have been me."

"She *had* to do it. It's her mission, remember?" Zack retorted, his eyes spitting green bullets.

"Her mission?" Sully winced.

"She'll be okay in the short run," Zack added, patting Shelby on the head. "But we've got to mobilize quickly."

"Oh, thank God!" She turned to smile up at him. "We *are* going after them then?"

"Absolutely."

"Zack's right," Sully said. "But we need to be smart about it. If Adonis even senses we're around, he'll take it out on Sabrina. So... Zack? You stay here with Shelby. I won't be able to concentrate unless I know she's safe. Keep Theo under wraps until we've got Sabrina back, then we can turn him over to the authorities. John, you'll back me up in Dallas."

Zack shook his head. "Like you said, we need to be smart about this. The party starts in seven hours, and you've been out of the game for a while. I know that system inside and out. I've got recent experience with Adonis's work. And I know how Sabrina thinks."

"So?" Sully pursed his lips. "You're saying John should stay and *you* should back me up?"

"I'm saying, I should run the operation. But I'd like you for backup because you've got more experience with explosives than John does."

Shelby grimaced, expecting her father to erupt at such insubordination, and in fact he did scowl for a second. Then he muttered, "Fine. Let's just get going."

She watched as they fished weapons and other paraphernalia out of the baby carriage, then her father gave her a bear hug and strode out the back door on Zack's heels.

"Wow," she murmured. "Dad's alive. And Sabrina has a hunky boyfriend who's not afraid of him. Meanwhile, I'm stuck here with a liar and a traitor."

"Hey." Johnny rested his hands on her hips. "Just for the record, I actually did sleep with you."

"What?" She glared. "My God, it just keeps getting worse!"

His eyes twinkled. "Sully and I agreed I wouldn't, and it made sense at first. Then we started falling in love— don't argue with me, because you know it's true. But I knew he'd kick my ass if I touched you, and yeah, I'm afraid of him." He grinned. "But you kept coming at me, remember?"

"Maybe you just planted that memory, too," she retorted, although she had to admit it did sound like her.

His gaze warmed. "Remember the day you came out in the yard in your nightie? I freaked out, because I figured if Sully saw you like that, he'd see red. And blame me. So I yelled at you. Hurt your feelings. And you said you thought I didn't love you, and something snapped. I couldn't let you believe that, when just the opposite was true. So…" He brushed his lips across hers. "I don't regret it."

"So? You defied him once? Do you think you can manage it again?"

"With pleasure," he said, moving in for another kiss.

"Not that way!" She gave him a challenging smile. "Let's go to Dallas."

Johnny arched an eyebrow. "You heard what Adonis said—"

"We won't let him see us." She touched his cheek and explained, "I can't just stay behind, Johnny."

"Yeah, neither can I," he admitted. "What should we do with Theo?"

"Interesting question," the prisoner said, his tone surprisingly confident. "My prediction is you'll let me go. And we'll never speak of this again. If you don't—if you turn me over to the authorities—I'll tell them about DT3. I guarantee you they'll want to study it."

When Shelby and Johnny just stared, Theo laughed. "That's right. It has always been my insurance policy, as Adonis would say. Sully doesn't want DT3 falling into any hands—not even the good guys. You're proof of how wrong it can go, Michelle. So you can't turn me in. But you can't kill me in cold blood, either. So untie me, then go save your sister. I promise I'll disappear from the face of the earth with my money and never bother any of you again."

"That's one way to deal with it," Johnny admitted. "Or we could just erase the secret from your memory, then leave you here, drugged and happy, while we go save Sabrina." With a wink toward Shelby, he went to the spice rack, pulled out a jar, and spilled its contents—three tiny vials—onto the counter. "Voilà."

"You said you didn't have any more DT3." Shelby shook her head. "You're such a liar."

"Sorry, Shell."

"More apologies?" She folded her arms across her chest. "Just drug him so we can get going. There'll be plenty of time for groveling on the plane."

"Do you think they'll try to save you?"

Sabrina looked at the assassin, who was sitting at a desk in their posh Dallas hotel room, working on an intricate maze of wires protruding from a flat metal box. She was still wearing the cuff, and Adonis had its palm-size detonator within easy reach, as well as his shiny silver pistol, which had been fitted with a silencer.

And for the hundredth time that afternoon, she thought about just rushing him, on the theory he wouldn't dare explode the cuff without a safe distance between them, so all she had to do was wrestle his gun from him. Or try to knock him out. Anything but just sitting here cross-legged on the bed, watching him build a new and better bomb with which to assassinate an exiled king.

But the moment didn't seem right, so she opted for pretending to truthfully answer his question instead. "I think they'll want to come after me. But Dad gave his word. And Zack's pretty practical. He'll play the odds—sacrifice the client for my sake, and just pray you'll keep your promise to let me go. Shelby's the only one who'll try, and Dad'll stop her. So…" Sabrina shrugged. "No. I don't think they'll follow us."

"Interesting."

"I also don't think you'll let me go when it's over. So you can drop the new-best-friends routine."

"What about our alliance?" he said, his tone mocking.

She pretended to ignore him, but actually watched with great care as he twisted a red wire into place. For the last five hours, she had tried her best to memorize his every move, hoping that the information could be of use to Zack and her father when they arrived. She wasn't foolish enough to believe she could actually disarm a bomb herself, even if she could manage to get away from Adonis. But she could help Zack by telling him what was hooked to what, or in what order Adonis had installed them. She was also hoping to solve any potential anagram associated with the device.

The bomb in Monterey had had wires of green, red, orange and white. G-R-O-W. With any luck, Adonis would do the same here, so she noted the wire colors—in this case, brown, yellow, red, orange and purple. B-Y-R-O-P. Proby? Byrop? Proby?

It was going to take some work.

Meanwhile, she was safe. Adonis needed her to get at his target, which he had admitted to her was King Dominik. As long as she was by Adonis's side, no one from Perimeter would question him. Connor and the others would believe her claim that her escort was an old friend of Sully's. And even if someone got suspicious, Zack would make sure no one made a move on them.

She knew in her gut that Sully and Zack would be somewhere in the crowd. Watching. Waiting. Willing to sacrifice Dominik for Sabrina, but determined to save them both. They wouldn't dare come too close or move too soon. They'd rely on Sabrina to create an opportunity, and she wasn't about to let them down.

She already knew the combination Adonis had punched into the detonator outside the cabin to turn off the timer for her cuff bomb. He hadn't even tried to shield it from her, which told her he didn't plan on activating the bomb that way. Definitely good news, bad news. He wasn't going to use the timer. Instead he'd rely on the button, instantly detonating the cuff from a safe distance once the job was completed.

Don't think about that, she warned herself. *Just be alert. Some sort of opening is bound to present itself.*

In the meantime, it was clear that Adonis was enjoying having someone to talk to while he built his bomb, and she was doing her best to foster the "relationship," especially since it hadn't taken a sexual turn. She wasn't kidding herself, though. He hated her—she knew that from the emptiness in his black eyes. Even when he spoke of Pluto, it was with a fierce combination of respect and fear, without a trace of real love. And as for the fury directed at Sully Sullivan whenever his name came up....

No, there was no chance Adonis would decide to spare Sully's daughter. But in the meantime, she could and would use their chats to get information.

"So the monarchists decided they just couldn't wait for King Dominik to die naturally. Do you think they'll succeed in restoring the monarchy in Delphinia? It's been almost twenty years, hasn't it? Will the people really go backward like that?"

Adonis seemed intrigued by the question. "Is there such a difference between a monarchy and a dictatorship? That's what they have now, you know. Either way, the people are powerless. But they have short memories. They believe a king will be more benevolent. So yes, I think a monarchy would succeed there now."

"Do you care?"

"Why should I? As long as I get my fee, I'm happy."

"It must be a lot of money if you're serious about retiring after this job."

"Without Howell to feed information to me, I'd have to work too hard. I'm spoiled. *This* is the part I enjoy," he confessed, motioning to the bomb in front of him. "I'm an artist, not a criminal."

"Interesting distinction."

He laughed. "I'm ready for retirement. Howell wasn't, though. That day you and Lansing interrupted me in Monterey, he was resisting my request to help me infiltrate the birthday party. Even with the distraction of your sister's kidnapping, he was sure Lansing would sense that it was an inside job."

"But you were going to force him to tell you?"

Adonis nodded. "I would have succeeded, too. He's basically a coward. Then you and Lansing arrived. It was inconvenient—especially when Lansing left so many people guarding him. I wasn't sure I'd ever get a second chance."

"You cut it pretty close," she agreed.

Adonis laughed. "Never fear. I had a backup plan. Someone else on the inside that even Howell didn't know about."

"Really? Who?"

"Never mind." He flashed a provocative smile. "I knew it would work out. I'm a lucky man. And a patient one. The right opportunity always seems to present itself."

He stood and crossed to stand in front of her, the detonator in the palm of his hand. "I see you've learned to be patient, too. You think I'll make a mistake. But I won't. Fortunately, I do intend to let you go. Who knows? Maybe you'll even agree to retire with me to some secluded Shangri-la."

Sabrina forced herself not to pull back in revulsion. Instead she decided to play along, within limits. And if it went beyond that, and she resisted, he probably wouldn't physically abuse her. He'd want her to look presentable for the party. "If you leave my family alone—and take this stupid thing off my wrist as soon as the job is done—I'll think about it. But not before. So back off."

His eyes narrowed and she was afraid for a moment that she had made a mistake. That he was going to attack her after all. But then maybe she could wrestle the detonator from him—

A knock at the door ruined both their fantasies and Adonis turned away from her, calling, "Just a moment!" as he strode to the duffel bag sitting on a nearby luggage stand. Rummaging, he pulled out a pair of traditional handcuffs and told Sabrina, "Your dress has arrived. Be a good girl and don't make a sound. Is that clear?"

She nodded, allowing him to cuff her to a bedpost. She had to admit she was glad to have some distance from him. He was one scary guy, and all the judo training in the world didn't seem to matter once C-4 entered the equation, and she just wasn't ready to die yet.

Adonis threw open the door to the hall and exclaimed, "Darling! Either you've grown more beautiful or I'm just incredibly turned on by my house guest. Come in."

Confused, Sabrina held her breath, then gasped when Marilyn Hanover stepped into the room, a garment bag in her hand. Adonis swept it onto a nearby chair, then closed the door and shoved Marilyn up against the wall, nuzzling her neck greedily while unfastening his pants with his free hand.

Yuck… Sabrina turned away and cringed, and while she could shield herself from the sight, the sounds were a little too graphic to mistake for anything but carnal pillaging. But at least it was mutual.

And over quickly.

"That's better," Adonis murmured.

Almost immediately Marilyn yelped, "Sully's daughter!"

"Yes, as I mentioned, we have a guest."

Sabrina turned back to face them, trying not to notice Marilyn's rumpled red sundress, smeared red lipstick or the high heels that matched both. "Hi, Marilyn. I see you've met Adonis."

The assassin burst into laughter. "Do you see why I was so needy, darling? Sabrina is irresistible, but I resisted. To keep myself fresh for you. Let's see the dress."

Marilyn's gaze roved from the handcuffs to the bomb on the desk. Then she complained, "I thought we were going to a fancy party. I spent all day shopping! And getting my hair done—"

"And you look beautiful. But my plans changed. Sabrina's going with me instead of you. Help her get dressed, won't you?" He pulled a stunning, waltz-length white dress from the garment bag. "Perfect. Just what I had in mind."

"*She's* going to wear it? That's not fair. You never take me anyplace anymore."

Adonis shot her a reproachful look and immediately Marilyn's demeanor changed to one of apology. And fear. "I'm sure you have a good reason. But…" She smiled weakly. "I can't dress her if you don't take her handcuffs off first."

"Excellent point. That's why I keep you around. For

your brain." He walked over to Sabrina and freed her hands, cautioning, "Be good. I wouldn't want you to blow up and take part of my precious Marilyn with you."

Crossing to his seat at the desk, he picked up the detonator again. "Darling, if Sabrina gives you any trouble, let me know." Then he turned his attention back to his work.

"How long has this been going on, Marilyn?" Sabrina whispered.

"We're in love," she retorted. "After tonight, he's retiring and we're going away together. Hopefully without *you*."

Sabrina inhaled sharply, wondering if this wasn't the chance she had been waiting for. And even if it wasn't, Adonis didn't make many mistakes. This might be her only chance at all.

So she exhaled, then grabbed Marilyn, making sure that the incendiary cuff was visible, pressed right into the widow's stomach. "I might lose a hand, but she'll die," Sabrina warned the assassin. "Put down the detonator and back away from it."

Adonis sighed. Then he seemed to follow her instruction, placing the device on the desktop.

Only too late did Sabrina see that he was picking something up in its place, and before she could react, he had calmly fired a bullet into Marilyn's forehead, the sound being little more than a *swush* thanks to the silencer.

"Oh, God!" Sabrina jumped back, allowing the body to slip to the ground.

"Don't get any blood on you. I want you to look beautiful. Put the dress on now," Adonis instructed her calmly. "Right here where I can see you."

"Oh, God," she repeated, trying not to tremble. "How could you—"

"I believe it was your fault, not mine. Haven't you ever

seen a person shot before?" His eyes sparkled. "Go and sit on the bed for a moment. I want to show you something."

She did what he said, too numb to protest.

"I have a gift for you, Sabrina." He gestured toward his duffel bag again. "It will look lovely on your new dress."

As she watched, still half in a trance of guilt—not to mention disgust over the casual killing of a human being— he picked up the flat box filled with wires that had been preoccupying him for hours. Then he brought it, along with his duffel bag, to the bed, and pulled out a beautiful silver belt that buckled in the back. In front was an elaborate starburst six inches in diameter encrusted with rhinestones.

Adonis detached the sunburst, then fitted the bomb neatly into place. Then he snapped the jeweled disk over it, and as he did so, she was sure she heard two distinct clicks—clicks that had nothing to do with fastening and everything to do with arming.

The sounds were clearly music to Adonis's ears.

"Beautiful, isn't it?" he murmured. Then he gave Sabrina a wink. "You didn't think I was going to make you wear that ugly cuff to the party, did you?"

Chapter 14

Κing Dominik's ranch house—a sprawling white stucco structure ranging from one to three stories, with a center courtyard large enough to accommodate dining tables for a hundred guests—would have been breathtaking even without the thousands upon thousands of tiny white lights strung all around it, inside and out. It was quite simply the ideal venue for the social event of the year. Even the weather—warm with just a hint of a breeze—was perfect for a party under the stars, real or incandescent.

As Sabrina stepped from the long black limousine and allowed Adonis Zenner to take her by the arm, she imagined that they must make a provocative couple. The low-cut, sleeveless dress fit her perfectly, hugging curves she had never really bothered to accentuate before. It contrasted richly with Adonis's traditional black tuxedo, and while she despised him with every fiber of her being, she had to admit he was born for this particular attire. It accentuated his commanding posture and made his ebony eyes seem almost otherworldly, even through a pair of copper wire-rimmed glasses. He would have been even more stunning had he not dyed his platinum curls black and shaved himself the equivalent of a receding hairline, a technique that actually made him appear more distinguished and infinitely more trustworthy.

But the pièce de résistance was Sabrina's belt. Everyone who saw the jeweled wonder gave it second and third glances, and Sabrina prayed that Zack and her father, hiding somewhere in that elegant crowd, would notice it, too, and see it for what it was. If they didn't—if they saw only that the cuff had been removed from her wrist, and assumed it was safe to move in—she wouldn't just lose an arm. They would all die, and die horribly.

At first she had believed that this was the bomb Adonis would use on King Dominik, but he had explained in the limousine that he had built the ex-monarch's device days earlier. It was now strapped to Adonis's chest under his shirt, but would be transferred to Dominik in due course.

How she wished she could wrestle the madman to the ground, grab a detonator out of his pocket and blow *him* to bits. She would gladly jeopardize her own safety for that. But he had guessed at her fantasy and had cheerfully informed her that Dominik's bomb was not yet armed. And there was no remote detonator for it in any event. Just a built-in timer.

For Sabrina's belt, of course, there *was* a remote device, one he could trigger anytime she tried to escape his clutches. Her only safe course if she wanted to stay alive long enough to save the client was to stay so close to Adonis that triggering the device might injure him, as well.

"Come along, darling," he murmured, ushering her toward the receiving line where an assortment of handsomely dressed men and women were waiting. She exchanged pleasantries with them automatically, not really bothering to engage.

Then a soft voice chided her, "I did my best to provide a breathtaking environment for my guests, but your beauty puts all else to shame."

"What?" Sabrina stared into a pair of stunning hazel eyes and smiled sheepishly. There was simply no doubt as to this man's identity. "Your Highness?"

"Welcome to my home away from home." Dominik, the fifty-one-year-old exiled king, made a sweeping bow. "Perhaps you'll grace me with a dance before the night is done?"

"Wow." She felt her cheeks warm and quickly reminded herself that she was no fan of royalty. But there was something about this particular monarch that could convert her if she wasn't careful.

She wanted to warn him to run, but of course that would be counterproductive, given the device in Adonis's pocket a few feet away.

"You are a friend of Zack Lansing's?" he asked her.

"What?"

"That's how you are described on the list," Dominik explained. "I myself would have described you as a goddess."

She sighed, then pulled herself together and said simply, "Zack's the best."

"He deserted me."

She wanted to reassure him. To tell him Zack was there somewhere, waiting for the right moment. But she settled for murmuring, "I look forward to our dance, Your Highness."

She glanced at her escort, who was right behind her in the receiving line, curious to see if he would be uncomfortable trading pleasantries with the man he intended to kill.

But he shocked her when he stepped up to the king, bowing with a grandiose show of humility, then grasping the ex-monarch's hand and gushing with praise.

Sickened, Sabrina moved to the last person in the line, an adorable young man who didn't look old enough to shave. His hazel eyes, coupled with the stature he had inherited from his father, touched her. "Prince Nikolo?"

"Call me Nick."

She had to smile. She had seen this face on the cover of Shelby's gossip magazines. Absolutely gorgeous. And so young, it made Sabrina's twenty-five years seem like forever. "Hi."

"I'm honored. You're a friend of Zack's?"

"Yes."

"Why isn't he here?"

Sabrina knew she couldn't look the prince in the eye for fear of revealing too much, so she pulled her hand from his and said simply, "Don't worry." Then she walked briskly toward a magnificent ice sculpture as she gestured for Adonis to skip his pleasantries with Nikolo and accompany her immediately.

Adonis's claim that he had an informant other than Theo inside Perimeter stuck in Sabrina's mind. Who could it be? Someone on Zack's team? Or someone in the IT division? Zack had said that the computer system was the heart of Dominik's security. He had even suggested that Connor would be a better fit than Zack if something went wrong during the party.

And luckily, Connor Boyle was the one who had actually drawn the duty. It should have comforted Sabrina, but instead her insides were in turmoil.

Connor—the one who had provided her and Shelby with lackadaisical security. Connor—the one who hadn't scored a spot on Sully Sullivan's crew. Connor—the one who was either too lazy or too unmotivated or too something else…

"Dance with me," Adonis suggested, taking her by the arm. "And stay close. I have the strangest feeling there's a rifle pointed at my head."

"I bet you get that feeling a lot," she replied lightly.

"What did you think of Dominik?"

Sabrina shrugged. "He's so regal. You looked like a peasant next to him."

"You know what they say," Adonis quipped, undaunted. "The only good king is a dead king. Or is it, the only good Sullivan is a dead Sullivan?" He flashed a cruel smile. "They say so many things, don't they? I hear your father is a great one for the platitudes. What's that shrewd one?"

She looked straight into his bottomless eyes. "Do you mean, 'Sometimes the problem is the problem'?"

Adonis cocked his head to the side. "I never heard that one. What does it mean?"

"It means, you have to be careful to ask the right questions or you'll get off track. I made that mistake with you. More than once."

He nodded. "If it's any comfort, I made the same mistake with you." When she didn't react, he explained anyway. "I came to your house that day to find out if you knew enough to be dangerous. But the truth is, you were born dangerous, weren't you?" He licked his lips. "That's why I can't trust myself where you're concerned. That alliance I joked about? You can't imagine how much I want it."

He seemed sincere in his own way and a part of her wanted to encourage it. But he repulsed her so completely, she couldn't stop herself from reminding him, "Your father killed my mother."

"True. I can see how that might bother you on a theoretical level. But in actuality, he did you a favor."

"Pardon?"

Adonis leaned into her, his voice eerily earnest. "Think about it. Had she lived, Sully wouldn't have trained you in his image and likeness. She wasn't a fan of that, I'm told. You would have gone into teaching, like her. You never would have had your ridiculous affair with Lansing. Most important, you never would have had the skills—the drive—to protect your little sister. To expose the truth about Theo Howell. Your whole life would have been meaningless."

"Is this where I'm supposed to thank you?"

"No. Just respect me. The way I respect you."

Hoping she was reading him correctly, Sabrina murmured, "If I decided to respect you, would you leave my sister and father alone? And Zack?"

"Lansing?" Adonis arched an eyebrow. "He didn't come to your rescue. Are you sure you still want to save him?"

"Yes."

"Fine. They will all be spared."

"And we'll leave right now? No more killing?"

Adonis stared deep into her eyes for a long, long moment, then burst into laughter. "And you called *me* a peasant?"

Sabrina glared.

"There's no future for us, Sabrina. We both knew that from the start. But I have enough respect for our past to let you live." He stroked her jaw. "I'll kill Sully eventually—that's a given. But I'll leave you and your sister alone. You've earned that."

She didn't believe him, but she nodded as if she did. Thanks to him, she was learning how to negotiate, liar-style. "That seems fair."

"So?" He flashed a confident smile. "Shall we get this over with?"

He led her up to an elevator marked Private, taking care to use the other partygoers for cover. Then he showed her a translucent piece of material before he fitted it onto his thumb, then ran it by a scanner on the control panel. Immediately the elevator opened.

"You really do have an inside man?"

"Of course."

They had reached the third floor, which was little more than a pair of private residences joined by a common sitting room that sported a magnificent balcony.

Adonis took a slim rod out of his pocket, then telescoped it and jammed it between the elevator doors. Without pausing to admire his handiwork, he moved to the adjacent stairwell and closed a heavy fire door, then secured its dead bolt.

Then he led Sabrina to one of the suites. "Dominik's in there," he said, motioning toward a closed door. "Be smart. Stay alive."

Sabrina didn't have to ask how Adonis knew where the king was. His "inside man" had told him, and she made up her mind on the spot to wring Connor's thick neck if she survived.

When Adonis threw open the door, the king and his son were standing in the luxurious, multipillowed bedroom as though waiting for the new arrivals.

Nikolo stepped forward as soon as Adonis had shut the door. "There's a change in plans. You'll get your fee, but only as long as you don't harm a hair on my father's head."

Sabrina gasped. "You know about the plot?"

"Know about it?" Adonis sneered, shedding his jacket and ripping open his shirt. "He *is* the plot."

Sabrina gasped again. Then Dominik spoke up, his hazel eyes shadowed with pain. "My son told me everything. He's a true prince who loves his country. So do I. I will never judge him for choosing Delphinia over me." The ex-monarch turned to Adonis. "Your fee has been transferred to your account. Go now, and never speak of this to anyone."

Adonis arched an eyebrow. "Enlighten me, please."

Prince Nikolo's face was flushed. "I acted in haste. For my countrymen. For my ancestors. Father had promised to relinquish the throne to me on my twenty-first birthday. Last week he withdrew that promise, offering me five million dollars instead. I was so furious, I hired you. But shame followed quickly. I tried to reach you, but you did not respond. To my everlasting relief, my father has forgiven me. Accept our payment and go away. Never speak of this, and another two million will be placed in your account in one year. You can't ask for more."

"True." Adonis gave Sabrina a wink. "It seems we caught a break, as you Americans say. No one needs to die, assuming our young friend here is telling the truth. If not—" his voice grew dark "—you will regret it."

"You have my word," Dominik told him.

"Fine." Pulling a set of handcuffs from his pocket, Adonis quickly chained Sabrina to the brass bedframe. Then he took out a second, more substantial pair of cuffs and told Nikolo, "Secure your father and yourself to the bed while I verify the transfer."

Before Sabrina could react, Nikolo snatched the handcuffs from Adonis's hand and eagerly snapped one section around his father's wrist. Then he twined the chain around a bedpost and closed the other cuff over his own arm. "Call your people, assassin. They will tell you that the money is there."

"Let's hope so." Adonis stripped off his C-4-laden vest and snapped one end to the cuff on Dominik's wrist, then did the same with Nikolo's. Pulling out his handheld computer, he studied the screen, then grinned.

"Is the money there, Adonis?" Sabrina demanded, her heart pounding.

"An unexpected bonus," he admitted. Reaching over, he pulled a cord on the vest bomb, warning cheerfully, "Ten minutes, folks. The most foolproof device I've ever designed. Sabrina?" He held up the detonator that could blow her into bits, then he unlocked her handcuff and growled at her with a determination that chilled her. "Let's get out of here."

She let him drag her out of Dominik's suite, not because she wanted to abandon the king, but because ten minutes was better than three minutes, which she suspected was the amount of time Adonis had programmed into her belt. But once they were in the anteroom, she insisted, "You got your payment! Why are you still going to kill them? Dominik won't breathe a word of it. And Nick won't, either, obviously."

Adonis grinned. "Nikolo's millions were never an issue. The Delphinian military is paying me three times that to kill them both. I just needed the prince's help to get inside. Still, ten million is a nice bonus."

"You're destroying the royal lineage forever?"

Adonis laughed. "That's why I love you, Sabrina. You can't quite take a position, can you? You want to save everyone, but it can't be done. If it could," he added with a wistful smile, "I'd consider doing it for you."

"Adonis, don't kill them," she begged him, looking at his thumb on the trigger of the remote detonator that controlled her existence. "Let them go, and I'll do whatever you want. Go wherever you want. I promise."

"Actually," he admitted, "you're too high-maintenance for me. And you're Sully's daughter. It would never work." Holding the detonator in full view, he triggered the timer. "Three minutes, my love."

He started to move toward the staircase leading to the roof, but Sabrina stopped him by murmuring, "Hey, Adonis?"

"Yes?"

"When we were dancing, you said you liked one of Dad's platitudes. Which one was it?"

"The one about the liars." He paused, then recited, " 'Sometimes the truth stings a little. But it's the lies that will kill you.' I always took that one to heart."

Sabrina hadn't heard that one before and she balked at the sincerity—almost devotion—in Adonis's tone. "That's crazy. You lie to me all the time."

"Do I?" He seemed honestly confused. Then he said with unexpected force, "Here's the truth. You're going to die tonight. But you don't deserve it, so I'm giving you a fighting chance."

"How?"

He walked out onto the balcony and tossed the remote detonator into the air. "Use your time wisely. You can run down three flights of stairs and retrieve it—I *know* you memorized the combination—or you can start disarming the bomb, which we both know you're not qualified to do. Choose wisely," he admonished as he headed for the roof, adding over his shoulder, "Sabrina?"

"Yes?"

"Be sure to ask the right questions."

Three minutes or less. That's how much time she had. So? Should she run down three flights of stairs, hoping the combination for the remote still worked? Or should she get to work on the bomb itself?

Peering over the balcony, she could barely see the detonator. Hardly a wise choice. And the option of screaming for help—as Dominik and Nikolo were doing—wasn't practical, since the partygoers were all clustered on the dance floor, three stories down, enjoying a rousing mamba. So she sat and tried to pry the rhinestone cover off the bomb.

"Hey! Sabrina! Is that you up there?"

She shot to her feet and looked down to see Connor Boyle staring up at her, the detonator in his hand. She was about to declare her undying love for him when a new burst of ear-splitting music assaulted them, and while she shouted to Connor, "The combination is two, period, zero, pound," she knew he couldn't hear her, even before he grimaced and pointed to his ears, shaking his head.

"Two, period, zero, pound!" she tried again, but the cymbals were crashing, the horns were blaring and time was running out.

She tried to signal with her fingers, but Connor just shook his head, obviously confused. Then she remembered what Zack had told her. Connor was a sports geek. A pitcher from birth, who would have made the big leagues if not for an injury.

So she cupped her hands over the edge of the balcony in the universal symbol of "Just throw it to me, for freaking sake!"

And Connor amazed her. First by tossing her the world's

most dazzling smile, then by lobbing the remote to her in an arc so gorgeous, it would have made Ty Cobb weep.

Needless to say, it landed right in her hands.

"I *love* you!" she mouthed to him, then because of her wobbly legs she sank to the ground before entering the code into the detonator.

It worked. She knew that in an instant because of the loud reassuring beep, but still she forced the rhinestone-encrusted cap off the bomb and studied the mass of wires warily.

Because it just wasn't like Adonis to let a Sullivan live.

The timer display was blank, apparently dormant. Then as she stared, not daring to relax, it lit up again, counting down from three minutes, second by second.

"Perfect," she muttered. "Where the hell are my experts?"

A yellow wire. And a red one. And brown, yellow and purple ones. And to top it all off, *two* orange ones.

What the hell does this mean? Sabrina demanded of the universe. *Two oranges. So—what? Two O's, like the bomb at Theo's house? Or is it a trick?*

"Don't panic," she reminded herself aloud. "Think about Zack and Dad. This is what they get up for in the morning, right? And Zack said ninety seconds is plenty of time, which means you've got a cushion. So think."

She had to go the acronym route. After all, Adonis had admitted to her that this was a new kind of bomb for him, and in Monterey he had said that he always used a mnemonic for new bombs. So…

R for red. B for brown. Y for yellow. P for purple. O for orange. Was she really going to settle for PROBY?

No. There were two O's. Which meant the O was at the beginning of the word, or at the end of it. Right?

Think! she commanded herself. *The last one was reversed, so maybe this one isn't. Ugh...*

She concentrated on the orange wires to see if one of them was attached to a tiny receiver as Zack had shown her in the picture of the Monterey bomb.

With relief, she confirmed that it was. Inspired, she dashed into Dominik's bedroom and demanded, "Do you have scissors?"

"In the top drawer of my desk," he told her, his swollen, bloodshot eyes fixed on the bomb around her waist, his voice hoarse from yelling.

"Thanks. Don't worry. I'm going to go back in the foyer in case I—well, in case I go off. But don't worry! You've still got eight whole minutes. That's a lifetime in the world of explosives."

She ran back out the door, then crouched and cut the orange wire connected to the receiver, cringing as she did so. When nothing happened, she felt another surge of confidence and cut the second orange one. And again, she didn't blow up.

"You're getting the hang of this," she congratulated herself.

Someone was banging on the door to the stairs and she figured it was Zack, but she couldn't really spare another second. Then she heard him fire a series of shots and she smiled proudly. Hot blood—her favorite kind.

"Sabrina, thank God," he began as soon as he reached her, then he saw the contraption around her waist. "Oh, shit."

"It's not as bad as it looks. I'm working on the acronym. It either starts with O or ends with it. Oh!" She squealed with delight, remembering Adonis's nonstop tribute to his father on the plane ride from Reno. "It's got to be Pluto."

"Don't move," Zack commanded her. "Let me look at

it. Hey, Sully, she's up here!" he called, and in an instant her father was striding through the door, a long-range rifle in his hand.

"Where's Adonis?"

"Shh! Go help the king and prince. Let me concentrate," Sabrina pleaded. "I've almost got it worked out. P-L-U-T-O. O for orange. P for purple. But these other three...."

"You pried the cap off?" Sully murmured. "How did you know it wasn't booby-trapped?"

"Booby-trapped?"

When Zack sent her father a worried look, she glared. "You're making me nervous. If you want to help, figure out what red, brown and yellow have to do with U, T and L."

"Maybe L stands for light yellow?" Zack asked. "That's more accurate than just yellow."

"Light yellow." She nodded. "Or maybe *lemon* yellow. That's good. In fact, it's great. Orange and lemon. And the purple is really plum. It's all fruit, Zack!" She laughed in frenzied relief. "So, what's a red fruit? Apple. Strawberry. No. Tomato. The red one is the T. And since we're going backward, T is next."

"Wait!" her father protested.

"There isn't time." Sabrina cut the red wire, then smiled. "Okay, we know P is plum and L is lemon. So the brown one is the U, I guess. It has to be. Right?" She snipped the brown wire, then lemon-yellow for L, then plum for P in rapid succession.

And only then, when she still had lungs with which to breathe, did she finally exhale. "Wow."

"My God, Sabrina, what if you had been wrong?" Sully asked, using his knife to slice through the belt, which he laid carefully on the floor.

She looked up at his ashen face and smiled happily. "Don't worry, Dad. This is what I get up for in the morning. Now—" She jumped to her feet. "You two rescue the royal guys. I'm going after Adonis. Do you hear that helicopter in the distance? He must have signaled it. Right?"

Sully nodded. "Zack, you go with her."

But Zack shook his head and handed Sabrina the rifle, instructing her briskly, "Be careful. We'll defuse the other bomb then meet you on the roof. Good hunting."

She took the steps to the roof two at a time, reaching the top just as the helicopter was beginning to set down about one hundred yards from the building. Adonis was waiting for it, waving his arms at the pilot. Two Perimeter men were rushing from the house toward the scene, but clearly wouldn't reach it in time, so Sabrina aimed and fired, hitting the hovering vehicle three times. Upon impact, the third shot ignited the fuel supply and the copter burst into flames.

The explosion was so intense, it sent her flying backward and she could only imagine what it had done to Adonis. The Perimeter men were staggering back toward the ranch house, but didn't appear to be seriously injured.

Through it all, Sabrina kept the rifle trained on the smoky debris. Logic told her Adonis had to be dead, but she was unwilling to take the slightest chance that he might escape.

"Are you okay?" Zack demanded, joining her. "That was a hell of an explosion."

"I'm fine. Can I use those?" She gestured to the compact binoculars hanging around his neck and he handed them over.

"See anything?"

"No. I'm sure he's dead, but…" She kept scanning the surroundings. "How's Dominik?"

"All in one piece. Connor's with them." Zack arched an eyebrow. "I heard what Nick did. Unbelievable."

"He and his father have a lot to talk about," she agreed softly. "I know the feeling."

The smoke was finally clearing and she could just make out a figure, stumbling in the distance. He had something shiny in his hand that appeared to be a pistol. "My God, he's getting away. Oh, *no!*" she added as two other figures appeared, running at the armed man from the parking lot area. "It's Shell and Johnny! Those idiots are going to get themselves killed!"

She let the binoculars fall onto her chest and raised the rifle again, but Sully grabbed it from her hand. "Let your sister take care of it."

"What?" Sabrina demanded, horrified at the bizarre suggestion.

"Your mission is over, Breezie," he explained, his voice thick with emotion. "I know I've put you through hell, but it's over. She's grown up now."

"Dad, no," Sabrina murmured, staring up at him in dismay.

"That settles it. You're the world's most dysfunctional family," Zack said with a growl. Then he grabbed the rifle from Sully's hand, aimed and fired off a shot without a moment's hesitation.

She raised her binoculars just in time to see Adonis Zenner's head snap backward as he fell to the ground, motionless.

Running right up to the body, Shelby gave it a kick, then she looked over toward the roof and began waving her hands, wild with delight. Spinning toward Johnny, she jumped into his arms, wrapping herself around his neck and his torso, kissing him greedily.

It seemed like a pretty good idea to Sabrina, and she turned to Zack, sliding her hands behind his neck. "Nice shot."

"Thanks." He gave her a proud grin. "I always wanted to kill that guy."

"I know. It's so perfect that it was you."

"Yeah? Well get used to it, because it's going to be me—a *lot* of the time—from now on."

"As Shell would say, yum." Sabrina pulled his head down and savored a long, slow kiss.

Finally, Sully muttered from behind them, "In case you didn't get the memo, I'm not dead. And I have rules about my employees manhandling my daughters."

"Better go talk to Johnny then," Sabrina told him, pulling the binoculars over her head and handing them to him without shifting her gaze from Zack's mesmerizing green eyes.

Sully took one look into the distance and roared in disbelief, then stormed toward the stairwell, muttering Johnny's name and a few well-chosen threats.

"I'm glad he's back," Zack told Sabrina, "but I can't work with him anymore."

"Shell and Johnny can be his new crew. With Connor, of course. You were right about him. He's got a big heart. And a great arm." She stroked Zack's face. "Obviously the CIA will take you in a heartbeat. Can you use your connections to get *me* an interview?"

"Yeah. I'm determined to work under the covers with you," he said, teasing. Then he cleared his throat. "At the risk of asking the wrong question—"

Sabrina put her finger to his lips. "There are no wrong

questions where you're concerned. Not anymore. So," she advised with throaty anticipation, "ask me anything. I'm pretty sure the answer's going to be yes."

* * * * *

Chapter 1

The morning started off bad the instant Paige Carmichael woke in her hotel suite, flipped on the TV and heard the date. Just the reminder that it was February tenth shifted her mood from half asleep to sulky to totally ticked.

Offended and resentful soon jumped into the mix as things went downhill fast.

She burned her tongue on the coffee she brewed in the unit atop the minibar. While dressing, she snagged her only pair of panty hose. Dropped and lost the tiny back of her earring. Made two wrong turns in Oklahoma City's unfamiliar rush-hour traffic.

When she finally nosed her rental car into a slot marked Guest Instructor at the police training center, it was fifteen minutes after the scheduled start of her workshop.

Her spiky red-suede heels sounded like gunshots as she rushed along the building's tiled hallway. She pulled open the door to her classroom, dashed inside and stumbled over the outstretched legs of a lanky cop with a gold badge clipped to his belt.

"Careful," he said. The only thing that kept her upright was the hand he'd locked on her elbow.

"Sorry," she managed when she got her balance back.

"I'm not," he murmured. Easing his feet out of her way, he hooked a dark brow and let his gaze do a slow slide starting at the top of her head, on down over her cherry-red jacket and slim skirt. Then he hitched up one corner of his mouth while he scoped out her legs as if memorizing them for some lurid identity lineup.

Eyes narrowed, Paige wrenched her elbow from his grip. He leaned back in his chair, rested an ankle over one knee and flashed a grin. He wore a dark suit, starched white dress shirt and a crimson tie. His hair was jet-black and his Mediterranean complexion gave him an air of mystery that only added to his looks.

Mysterious or not, he was an arrogant jerk, she thought as she strode past rows of tables toward the front of the classroom.

She settled her briefcase, purse and coat on the table beside the speaker's podium. She'd called ahead when she'd realized she was running late and had asked the training center's secretary to have the mix of twenty-five cop and civilian investigator attendees fill out a seating chart with their name and agency. Paige noted the chart was now on the podium. Her gaze focused on the list of names on the back row. Sergeant Nate McCall, Oklahoma City P.D. Homicide.

"I apologize for being late," she said, scanning the attendees. There were about three-quarters more men than women enrolled in the workshop; more commissioned law enforcement officers than civilians employed by local security firms.

As usual for the first day of a workshop, they were all currently sizing her up.

A few regarded her with outward skepticism. The majority studied her through unreadable, hooded eyes. Having worn a badge for eight years, Paige knew that everyone—especially cynical, seen-it-all cops—would take tons of convincing before they bought into the idea that forensic statement analysis was a viable investigative technique.

Not a problem.

She stepped to the closest table and handed the pad to an attractive female cop with a heavy black braid looped over one shoulder. "Tear off one page and pass the pad along. I want each of you to write down everything you did yesterday, from the time you woke up to the time you went to bed."

Most of the hooded expressions clicked down another notch. The previous day had been Sunday, so it was logical to think the majority of the workshop attendees had been off duty. Cops were inherently tight-lipped, so she didn't expect anyone to be forthcoming enough to tell all they did on their personal time. Nor would a suspect. That didn't impede Paige from getting to the truth.

"Don't put your name on the page. You'll turn it in anonymously." She glanced at her watch, then retrieved a pen that had been left on the podium. "I have to check in at the commander's office, so you've got half an hour to complete your assignment."

She retraced her steps along the center aisle. When she reached the back row of tables, she dropped the pen behind Nate McCall's chair. Leaning, she swept up the pen, pausing long enough to zero in on his paper. It took only seconds for her to commit his handwriting to memory.

* * *

A half hour later, Paige was back at the podium, the twenty-five assignment sheets stacked on the nearby table.

"Over the next few days you'll learn to view statements by suspects, victims and witnesses in an entirely different way. This technique is hard for a lot of investigators to accept at first because you're conditioned to believe a person with something to hide is going to lie."

"Get a clue, lady," the man sitting next to McCall said. "They *do* lie."

The comment garnered a slew of laughs. Paige checked the seating chart for the name of the man who looked something akin to an Italian playboy. Hugh Hunter, O.C.P.D. Homicide. The jerk quotient for that particular division just rose.

Paige knew from experience she had to dish up solid proof if she hoped to start making converts.

"Let's take a look at one of these." She fanned through the pages, spotted McCall's handwriting, plucked out the sheet and began to read.

"I woke up, showered, shaved, got dressed, then drove across town and picked up a friend. We went to Nick's for champagne brunch. We left Nick's and drove to a movie. After the movie we stopped and had a drink. Then she and I went to a mall, did some shopping. Later I took her back to her condo. She unlocked the door, I turned on the lights. I went home not long after that. I worked on my car, watched TV, then read for a while."

Paige glanced up.

"I'm guessing this statement was written by a male since the author mentioned shaving and working on a car."

She met McCall's gaze for an instant before looking back at the paper. "The author didn't introduce his lady friend by name. The norm for healthy relationships is a proper, clear introduction. For example, 'My friend, Sally.' But in tumultuous relationships, introductions often are missing. Still, there's a sense of togetherness in that the author uses the word *we* in his initial description of his and his friend's activities."

"Hey, McCall," Hunter said, sending his co-worker a leering look. "Just how much *togetherness* went on?"

Muted chuckles sounded while McCall shrugged, said nothing.

"A problem," Paige continued, "or perhaps a disagreement occurred between the time the author and his friend stopped to have a drink and went to the mall. I know that because he shifted his language from *we* to *she and I*. That change shows a distancing. This relational difficulty continued when he got to his friend's condo. He was hoping to…" Paige paused. "Well, let's just say hope is all he did."

"Holy…" The female detective flipped her braid over her shoulder and flicked a slightly amused look at McCall before turning back to Paige. "How do you know that? How the heck can you tell when someone doesn't score?"

Paige glanced at the seating chart. The woman's name was Tia Alvarado, a sergeant in O.C.P.D.'s vice detail. "The author mentioned that when he and his friend arrived at her condo, he turned on the lights."

"So?" Tia asked. "It must have been dark out."

"And turning on the lights was incidental information that would be taken for granted. So, mentioning the activity indicates it has meaning for the author." Despite her best intention not to, Paige looked at McCall. Even from a distance she could tell his jaw was locked tight and his eyes were smoldering. "A reference to turning on the lights is very prevalent in statements where a person wanted sex, but didn't get it."

"Why is that?" a man from a security consulting firm asked.

"No one knows for sure. It just is." Paige held up a hand to ward off the inevitable protests. "I realize that's a long way from a scientific explanation. So is a cop's following some off-the-wall hunch that winds up solving a crime. You can't explain it. It just is."

"Hey, Teach, can I get my assignment back before you read it?" a man's voice spiked with humor asked.

"No can do." Smiling, Paige opened her briefcase, slid the stack of assignments inside.

Hours later, Paige rose from behind the desk in the office used by the training center's guest instructors. Grateful she had the first day of the workshop behind her, she set the locks on her briefcase, then retrieved her coat from the small closet tucked into one corner. A headache hammered behind her eyes, tension knotted her shoulders and she hoped she could find her hotel without repeating the wrong turns she'd made that morning.

Paige grabbed her briefcase, then headed out of her temporary office. The clip of her heels echoed against the now deserted main hallway.

To acknowledge the three-year anniversary of her life getting blasted to smithereens, her evening plans included cracking open the minibar, room service and a long soak in the tub. With her headache drumming, she revised those plans to include a couple of aspirin.

Car keys clenched in one hand, briefcase in the other,

she shoved open the door, stepped into the cold afternoon gloom and headed around the side of the building.

The instant she came abreast of a thick, bushy shrub she sensed a presence. Motion. The hair rose on the back of her neck. Her right hand instinctively went for the holstered Glock she hadn't carried in three years.

At the edge of her vision she glimpsed a towering black-clad figure wearing a leather mask charge from the shadows. Adrenaline blew through her system and she had a crazy half second to think that her day was about to get worse.

PRESENTS

Peggy Nicholson's

THE BONE HUNTERS

FEATURING THE ASHAWAYS

Ruthless killers, steamy jungles and treacherous rivals won't stop this family of adventurous archaeologists from hunting down the rarest, most precious dinosaur bones.

AN ANGEL IN STONE
June 2005

What wouldn't savvy archaeologist Raine Ashaway do to get her hands on a rare T. rex fossil? Find out in this exhilarating tale!

And watch for more Ashaway stories. Coming soon, only from Silhouette Bombshell!

Available at your favorite retail outlet.

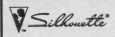

COMING NEXT MONTH

#45 DOUBLE VISION—Vicki Hinze
War Games

U.S. Air Force captain Katherine Kane had been sent to the Middle East to look for a suspected terrorist weapons cache, but stumbled upon much more than she had bargained for— American hostages, biological weapons and the most feared terrorist in the world, a man Kate could have sworn was locked away for good. But seeing was believing, and Kate suspected the criminal mastermind was no double vision after all....

#46 CHECKMATE—Doranna Durgin
Athena Force

Her marriage on the rocks, FBI legal attaché Serena Jones took refuge in an assignment to a foreign land only to be caught when rebels took over the capitol. Trapped in the building but free to move inside, Serena would take on the crafty rebel leader and lay a trap using the weapons at hand—her dying cell phone, her wits and an unexpected ally, her estranged husband....

#47 TRIGGER EFFECT—Maggie Price
Line of Duty

Hours after arriving in Oklahoma City, Paige Carmichael had clashed with a tough homicide detective, had her briefcase stolen and wound up in the E.R. And when she was asked to consult on a murder case, things didn't get any better. Because the killer knew Paige held the key to solving the mystery, and was determined to keep her from revealing the truth—by any means necessary.

#48 AN ANGEL IN STONE—Peggy Nicholson
The Bone Hunters

Archaeologist Raine Ashaway was determined to beat her rival, Kincade, and buy a precious rare fossil. But when the fossil's owner was murdered, Raine was plunged into a mystery that led her to the other side of the world. She had to join forces with Kincade. And with a killer on their heels, they'd have to learn to get along....